MURDER MOST OWL

MURDER MOST OWL

Sarah Fox

**SEVERN
HOUSE**

First world edition published in Great Britain and the USA in 2024
by Severn House, an imprint of Canongate Books Ltd,
14 High Street, Edinburgh EH1 1TE.

severnhouse.com

British Library Cataloguing-in-Publication Data
A CIP catalogue record for this title is available from the British Library.

ISBN-13: 978-1-4483-1229-0 (cased)
ISBN-13: 978-1-4483-1230-6 (e-book)

All Severn House titles are printed on acid-free paper.

Typeset by Palimpsest Book Production Ltd.,
Falkirk, Stirlingshire, Scotland.
Printed and bound in Great Britain by
TJ Books, Padstow, Cornwall.

Praise for Sarah Fox

"A prototypical shopkeeper cozy, right down to the pun-filled recipes at the end"
Kirkus Reviews on *Claret and Present Danger*

"The Inkwell's charming atmosphere, solid plotting, and several enticing recipes are sure to please cozy fans. Readers will look forward to Sadie's further adventures"
Publishers Weekly on *The Malt in Our Stars*

"Fox offers plenty of plausible suspects and a thrilling confrontation with the killer, along with a dash of decorous romance."
Publishers Weekly on *An Ale of Two Cities*

"Readers will cheer this brisk, literate addition to the world of small-town cozies"
Kirkus Reviews on *Wine and Punishment*

"Fox capably combines a smart, relatable heroine; plenty of clever red herrings; and the well-realized orchestra setting. Multiple kinds of appeal for cozy lovers"
Booklist on *Dead Ringer*

About the author

Sarah Fox was born and raised in Vancouver, British Columbia, where she developed a love for mysteries at a young age. When not writing novels, she is often reading her way through a stack of books or spending time outdoors with her English springer spaniel.

www.authorsarahfox.com

In loving memory of Fergus

ONE

By the time the sun rose over the town of Twilight Cove, Oregon, I'd already eaten breakfast. I hadn't meant to get up quite so early, but I never slept well the first night in a new place. My aunt's Victorian farmhouse wasn't exactly new to me, but I hadn't slept there in years, so it was apparently going to take me time to adjust. Plus, there was the rooster, who'd decided to start crowing a good half-hour before the break of dawn.

Tossing and turning for much of the night had left me with plenty of time to think. For my brain, that usually meant an endless loop of worrying about something or coming up with new scenes for whatever screenplay I was working on at the time. Fortunately, last night had been the latter. When I'd finally given up on getting any more sleep, I'd opened my laptop, pounded out the scene running through my head, and then grabbed a quick breakfast of toast and homemade strawberry jam in the farmhouse kitchen.

Now, dressed in jeans, a T-shirt and sturdy boots, I made my way out onto the back porch of the yellow and white house. From there, I could see across the fields and over the treetops to the ocean beyond.

My aunt Olivia – Auntie O to me – owned several acres of land. Some of it was wooded, but most of it consisted of fields and pastures, along with a barn, a couple of smaller outbuildings, the main farmhouse, a converted carriage house, and a small cabin. Normally, Auntie O lived in the farmhouse, but she'd broken her ankle a week ago and, with the help of friends, had moved into the carriage house, where she had a living area, bathroom and bedroom, all on the ground floor. Her broken ankle was the reason I'd come to Twilight Cove for the first time in years. While my aunt was out of commission, she needed help caring for all her animals, so I'd packed up some of my belongings and made the drive from Los Angeles to the small seaside town on the coast of Oregon.

I'd arrived after dark the evening before, so I was only now getting my first good look at the farm since I'd been back. The yellow barn, which matched the house, appeared to have received a fresh coat of paint in recent times, but the buildings otherwise looked much the same as I remembered. The land also hadn't changed much, as far as I could tell. I knew from my phone conversations with Auntie O that something was different, though.

Back when I'd lived with my aunt for a year in my teens, she'd had a few chickens, a couple of ducks, and two ponies on the farm. A few years ago, she'd transformed the place from a hobby farm to an animal sanctuary. I knew she still had chickens, ducks, and a couple of horses, but she also had goats, donkeys and alpacas. Whenever an animal in the area needed a safe haven, Auntie O welcomed it with open arms. Sometimes she rehomed the animals, but others stayed here to live out the rest of their lives in peace.

Now, with her ankle broken, Auntie O needed me to help out. She had a farmhand – a recent replacement for the farm manager who'd retired back in April – and he lived in the old cabin on the property, but my aunt still put in a lot of work each day herself, so I was here to pick up the slack while she recovered.

From my vantage point on the back porch, I caught a glimpse of a man clad in jeans, a plaid shirt and a cowboy hat. He entered the barn and disappeared from sight. The new farmhand, I figured. He was probably getting ready to move the animals outdoors for the day. I'd planned to drop in on Auntie O at the carriage house before heading for the barn, but I decided to help out with the farm chores first. My aunt was typically an early riser, but if she was sleeping in while she recuperated, I didn't want to disturb her.

The barn door was open, leaving a dark, shadowy rectangle that contrasted sharply with the bright yellow of the exterior walls, currently highlighted by the slanting rays of the rising sun. I trekked across the spacious lawn that separated the house from the barn, breathing in the fresh air. The official start of summer was fast approaching, but the gentle morning breeze felt cool against my skin.

When I stepped over the barn's threshold, I paused and waited for my eyes to adjust to the dimmer light inside. The smell of manure and straw met my nose. I didn't find the scent unpleasant. It brought back fond memories of hanging out with Auntie O's ponies when I was a teenager. I wished I'd had more of those days, but there was no changing the past.

The man I'd seen entering the barn now stood in front of one of the animal stalls, fastening a halter on an alpaca. He'd rolled up the sleeves of his red plaid shirt to reveal muscled and tanned forearms and, despite his cowboy hat, I could see that he had blond hair that matched the stubble on his jaw. I could also tell that he stood several inches taller than my height of five feet nine inches. Auntie O hadn't mentioned that the farmhand looked like a cowboy from the cover of a romance novel. Then again, she hadn't told me anything about him. Not even his name.

I was about to call out a greeting when he turned his head my way. My eyes had adjusted well enough to see that his expression was far from welcoming. I hesitated a split second before approaching him.

He watched my every move with wary green eyes. 'Who are you?' he asked as I drew closer. His voice held the same wariness and frostiness as his eyes.

I stopped several feet away from him. 'Georgie Johansen.'

His tense stance relaxed a fraction. 'Olivia's niece?'

I nodded. 'I'm guessing you're the farmhand.'

'Callum,' he offered, albeit somewhat grudgingly.

OK, so he wasn't the friendliest guy. Or maybe he just wasn't good with people.

'My aunt probably told you that I'm here to help with the animals.'

He returned his attention to the alpaca in the stall. 'You know how to feed the chickens?'

I figured he was addressing me, rather than the alpaca.

'Yes,' I replied. 'That was my job when I lived here years ago.'

'You'll find the food in the storage room.'

With that, he opened the stall door and led the alpaca past me and out of the barn.

I stood in the same spot, watching him go.

It didn't seem like we'd be friends any time soon, but that didn't really matter. I was here for a few weeks and then I'd be heading back to my screenwriting career in Los Angeles.

With Callum and the alpaca now out of sight, I headed for the feed storage room and got to work.

After I'd fed the chickens, Callum got me to muck out the stalls in the barn. By the time I'd finished that job, my muscles ached and I longed for a cold drink. I dusted off my sore hands and inspected my palms. A couple of blisters were taking shape. I needed to get myself some work gloves.

I headed out into the sunshine to see if Callum wanted me to do anything else. I didn't spot him right away, so I leaned against the wooden fence and watched the alpacas grazing. It felt good to be back on the farm. I'd stayed away too long. I'd told myself it was because I'd been so busy building my screenwriting career since I'd finished college, but I knew that wasn't the whole truth.

When I'd left the farm at age seventeen, after living with Auntie O for a year, I'd gone against my will. Moving away had been more difficult than any of the previous moves I'd endured before that. Twilight Cove got under my skin, made me want to stay. Leaving had felt like having some part of me torn away. That wasn't something I wanted to go through again, but when Auntie O called and said she needed my help, I couldn't turn her down.

The sunlight flickered off to my left in the split second before a majestic great horned owl landed on the fence, about ten feet from where my forearms rested against the top rail.

My breath caught in my throat and I froze, staring at the beautiful creature with its characteristic feather tufts on its head. The owl had mostly dark brown plumage, with speckles of reddish brown and white throughout. It also had a white patch on its upper chest, which puffed outward as it let out a gentle hoo-hoo. All the while, the owl's yellow eyes regarded me closely.

'Hello, gorgeous,' I whispered, afraid that speaking any louder would scare the bird away.

After staring at me for another moment, the beautiful owl swiveled its head to one side.

A blur of movement off to my right distracted me. I whirled around in time to see someone vault over the fence of the western-most paddock.

'Hey!' I called out as alarm shot through me.

I glanced back toward the owl to find it gone.

The person who'd vaulted over the fence darted into the woods.

I didn't know why someone would be sneaking around the farm, but if they were on the property for a legitimate purpose, they'd have no reason to run.

Without taking time to think about my actions, I charged toward the tree line. Although I moved as fast as I could, the fences slowed me down. I had to clamber over two of them before reaching the woods. By then I couldn't see or hear my quarry. I kept running anyway.

With Auntie O dealing with her broken ankle, the last thing she needed was to worry about trespassers. What if they'd intended to steal or harm the animals?

That thought lit a fire inside of me. I picked up my pace, but soon I had to slow down again as the trees and underbrush grew thicker. I leapt over a clump of ferns, but then the toe of my boot caught on a tree root and I fell forward. I landed on my hands and knees, winded from my run.

'You should respect the plants.'

I jumped to my feet, alarmed by the voice. Where no one had been moments before, a woman now stood, clutching a gnarled wooden walking stick with one hand. I knew right away that she wasn't the person I'd chased from the farm. That person had worn a baseball cap and jeans. This woman wore a gray cloak over loose, moss-green pants and a matching top. Her long gray hair hung halfway down her back in scraggly waves, and she watched me with dark blue eyes.

As I stared at her, she nodded toward my feet. I looked down to see a sword fern crushed beneath my left boot. I lifted my foot and stepped forward to stand on a patch of dirt and dried pine needles.

'Sorry,' I said. 'Did you see someone running through the woods a moment ago?'

The woman regarded me silently, and something about her gaze reminded me of the owl I'd just met.

'Too many have passed through these woods of late,' she said eventually.

'But did you see somebody running just now?' I pressed. 'Aside from me.'

The woman continued to stare at me and said nothing.

I caught sight of a brown blur a split second before an owl landed on the woman's shoulder. It looked exactly like the owl I'd seen back by the paddock.

The woman didn't even bat an eye when the owl came to rest on her shoulder, despite its massive talons. The bird raised its wings slightly and then ruffled its feathers before bobbing its head and settling in, its wings now resting close to its body.

The woman smiled serenely. 'It's all right, my friends.'

For a second, I didn't know who she was talking to. Then the undergrowth rustled behind her and two English springer spaniels appeared and sat down, one on either side of the woman. The one on her left was brown and white while the other was black and white.

The woman spoke to me again. 'You're Olivia van Oosten's niece.'

It was a statement rather than a question, but I confirmed it anyway. 'Yes. Georgie Johansen.'

'I've been expecting you.'

'You have?' I said with surprise.

Auntie O hadn't mentioned this woman to me, let alone that she expected to see me while I was in town.

'Our paths will cross again.' She turned her back on me and walked deeper into the woods, the dogs sticking close to her.

When the woman had taken a few steps, the owl took to the air and flew silently up toward the sky with majestic beats of its wings. I followed its flight with my eyes until it disappeared above the tree canopy. When I lowered my gaze, the woman and her dogs had vanished. I couldn't even hear them moving through the woods.

The whole encounter left me feeling off-kilter, though I didn't know exactly why. I turned in a slow circle, scanning the woods around me for any sign of the person I'd chased from the farm. Aside from the occasional twittering of a bird, all remained quiet.

A sense of eeriness crept over me. I felt like I was being watched. I scanned the area around me again, but I still saw nothing but trees and undergrowth. I told myself that my overactive imagination was getting the best of me, but that didn't make me feel any less spooked.

Suddenly longing for the familiarity of my aunt's farm, I turned back the way I'd come and hurried toward the tree line, all the while taking care not to crush any plants beneath my feet.

TWO

'It looks like you've already been hard at work,' my aunt remarked when I arrived at the carriage house.

I'd knocked on the door and she'd called out that it was unlocked. Upon entering, I found her on the loveseat in the cozy living area, her boot-encased foot propped up on an ottoman. She wore her gray hair cut short and she had deep blue eyes like my dad and so many others on his side of the family, which was mostly Scandinavian in origin. I, however, got my hazel eyes and brown hair – sometimes wavy and sometimes curly – from my mom. Her family had roots in Spain, Italy, Scotland and Ireland. I kept my hair short, but not as short as Olivia's. I'd grown out what had once been a pixie cut so my hair was now just long enough to tuck behind my ears when I wanted it out of my face.

Auntie O set aside a magazine and took off her reading glasses as I shut the door behind me. I glanced down at my dusty clothes and bent over to untie and remove my dirty boots.

When I straightened up, I sniffed the air. 'I could say the same about you.' Across the room in the open-plan kitchen, I spied a pie in the oven. 'I thought you were supposed to be taking it easy.'

'Taking it easy, yes. Dying from boredom, no.'

I smiled at that. Auntie O always liked to keep busy. Lazing about watching television all day would probably drive her mad in no time.

'I hope you didn't overdo it,' I said as I crossed the room to kiss her on the cheek.

'Not quite. I sat on a stool most of the time I was in the kitchen. My ankle was starting to hurt by the time I finished, so that's why I've got it propped up now.'

I sank down into the armchair across from her. 'I'm sure your doctor would be proud that you're being such a good patient.'

She smiled, her blue eyes bright. 'Doc Adams is just glad I agreed to give up salsa dancing until this ankle has healed.'

'The boot would make dancing a bit awkward.'

'I can still shimmy as well as anyone,' she said.

It was my turn to smile. 'I don't doubt that.'

Olivia studied me from her spot on the loveseat. 'It's nice to finally get a good look at you, Georgie.'

I'd arrived so late the night before that we'd visited for only a few short minutes before I'd headed over to the main house to fall into bed.

A familiar sense of guilt welled up inside of me. 'I'm sorry it's taken me so long to come and visit.'

Auntie O waved off my apology. 'You've been busy with your career, and I understand why you haven't been back.'

'You do?' I asked with surprise.

'I think so.' The thoughtful way she looked at me made me believe she was right.

Back in my teens, my dad had sent me to live with Auntie O while he traveled overseas for work. He'd returned a year later, with a new wife in tow, and insisted that I move to Michigan with him and my stepmother, who was a complete stranger to me at that time. I'd begged my dad to let me finish high school in Twilight Cove, but he refused. His job had taken us to many different towns and cities, and I'd changed schools and left friends behind many times while growing up, but that move had been the hardest of them all. I didn't want to suffer through that same heartbreak again, so I'd stayed away. Even now, at age thirty-two, I feared how I'd feel when it came time to return to my life in LA.

'Besides,' Auntie O continued, 'you've given me an excuse to travel at least once every year so I can see you. As much as I love it here, it does me good to get away now and then.' She grabbed her crutches and carefully pushed herself up to stand on her good leg. 'The timer is about to go off.'

As if she'd commanded it to do so, the oven timer began beeping.

I jumped up and hurried over to the kitchen to shut it off.

'I'm sure you've got writing to do now that you've finished the morning chores, but do you have any time to drive me across town?'

'Of course.' I grabbed a set of oven mitts and removed the pie – pecan, as I'd suspected from the smell – from the oven, setting it on the range. My mouth watered at the sight and smell of it.

'I'd like to deliver that basket.' Olivia nodded at a basket on the kitchen table that held a couple of jars of homemade jam and jelly, along with some scones and croissants that had probably come from the local bakery. 'Do you remember the old mansion up on the hill?'

'I always thought it looked like the home of a vampire,' I said.

Built from dark gray stone and with a battlement and turrets, the mansion looked more like a castle than a house.

'With your imagination, that doesn't surprise me.' Olivia hobbled into the kitchen on her crutches. 'At the moment, it's owned by a man named Victor Clyde. I don't think he's a vampire, especially considering his ill-health. He suffered a stroke recently and is going downhill. He's not expected to last much longer.'

'I'm sorry to hear that. Is he a friend of yours?'

My aunt inspected the pecan pie and seemed satisfied. 'Not really. He moved here about two years ago and many of us around town tried to welcome him into the community, but he's kept himself to himself. He's not eating croissants and scones these days, of course, but his stepdaughter is staying with him, and I wanted to pay her a neighborly visit and see how she's doing.'

That was so like my aunt, always looking out for others.

'When would you like to go?' I asked.

'Any time you're free.'

'How about right now?' I offered.

'Perfect.'

We decided to take my car instead of Auntie O's aging farm truck. With her broken ankle, climbing into the truck would have been more difficult than sliding into my red Honda Civic. After safely stowing the basket of goods in the back seat, we got on our way. I followed Larkspur Lane – a quiet country road – toward the heart of town and soon turned onto Ocean Drive, which hugged the coastline and curved around the cove. A few boats bobbed out on the water and the sun shone brightly in the cloudless blue sky, making the ocean sparkle.

Although the influx of summer tourists hadn't yet started in earnest, pedestrians strolled along the beach, a few with coffee or ice-cream cones in hand, enjoying the view of the water.

I turned up Main Street, which ran perpendicular to the coast, and followed its cobblestone roadway past the cute shops in their colorful buildings, on through a residential neighborhood with many Victorian houses and neat lawns, and farther up the hill to the solitary spot where Victor Clyde's mansion perched, overlooking the town and the Pacific Ocean.

The long driveway curved around a fountain with a mermaid

sculpture at its center. I drove around the fountain and brought the car to a stop by the wide front steps that led to arched double doors.

Auntie O didn't make a move to get out of the car. 'I think I'll stay here until we know if Avery has time for a visit. Avery is Victor's stepdaughter.'

'Good idea,' I agreed.

There was no sense in Olivia going through the trouble of getting out of the car on her broken ankle if we wouldn't be going inside the mansion. Several seconds after I rang the doorbell, the imposing double doors opened. A woman in a gray dress and white apron – the housekeeper, I assumed – informed me that Avery wasn't at home. I ended up leaving the basket with her and returned to the car, letting my aunt know what the housekeeper had said.

'Not to worry,' Olivia said. 'I'll check in on Avery another time.'

'Where to now?' I asked as I started the car's engine.

'Home, I think,' my aunt said. 'I'd love to get you reacquainted with Twilight Cove, but I'd better have a rest. A couple of ladies from my needlework group are going to stop by for a visit this afternoon.'

I smiled at that. The needlework group was called Gins and Needles, and my aunt had confessed to me in the past that once the cocktails started flowing, there was typically as much gossiping as needlework, sometimes more so.

'I'll have plenty of time to get to know the town again,' I assured my aunt.

I did, however, take note of a few spots I wanted to visit. A bookstore caught my eye, as did a coffee shop. When I turned on-to Ocean Drive, I took in the sight of three food trucks parked by the beach. One sold Lebanese food, another Mexican food, and the third sold fish and chips. A little farther along, a seafood restaurant faced the ocean.

Seeing the restaurant and the trucks reminded me that it was nearly lunchtime. My stomach grumbled at the thought. I'd need to grab something to eat before getting back to my writing, otherwise I'd have trouble concentrating.

'You must have met Callum this morning,' my aunt said, inter-rupting my thoughts.

'He seems to know what he's doing,' I said by way of response.

'He's great with the animals, but I still have to keep searching for a permanent farm manager.'

'Callum's not staying?' I didn't know why I found that disappointing. I wouldn't be here long myself.

'He'll be here for a while yet, but he was clear up front that he was looking for temporary work.'

'How temporary?'

'A few weeks, maybe. That gives me time to find a replacement.'

'Where's Callum from?' I asked, unable to repress a sense of curiosity about the handsome cowboy.

'Colorado, originally, I think,' my aunt said.

'He never told me his last name.'

'It's McQuade,' Olivia supplied. Then she quickly changed the subject. 'Tell me about your latest screenplay.'

After I helped get Auntie O settled in the carriage house, I ate a quick lunch and spent a couple of hours at my laptop, getting more scenes down on the page, and enjoying every minute of it. Stories had always provided me with a safe haven. Reading books and writing screenplays brought me a sense of calm and equilibrium, even when those screenplays were thrillers involving murders and plot twists. I could lose myself in reading or writing for hours, sometimes forgetting to eat until a headache finally signaled to me that it was time to take a break.

There were probably days when I worked far too much. That was mostly because of how much I loved being a screenwriter, but I suspected my tendency to bury myself in my work also gave me an excuse to keep the rest of the world at arm's length. I had friends in LA, and I wasn't a complete hermit, but I definitely wasn't a social butterfly. Getting close to people wasn't always easy for me. Maybe the fact that I'd lost my mom at a young age contributed to that, but frequent moves for my dad's job during my school-age years had also had a lasting impact on me.

As was so often the case, I kept writing until a headache demanded I give myself a break. I was due to help out with more farm chores in the late afternoon, but I decided to get out for some fresh air before then. Maybe some relaxation would alleviate the dull pounding behind my eyes.

As I headed out the back door of the farmhouse, I realized I'd forgotten to tell Auntie O about the mysterious person I'd seen running from the farm that morning. Maybe she'd have some idea who it could have been and what they might have been doing. I made a mental note to mention it to her later.

Tucking my wavy, side-swept bangs behind my ear, I jogged down the porch steps. I crossed the lawn and stopped by the nearest paddock to pet one of the donkeys, a cute spotted male named Hamish. Soon, he wandered off to join the other donkeys and I continued on my way, passing the barn and two more paddocks before reaching an open field. I didn't see Callum anywhere, but maybe he was working in the barn. I struck across the grass and entered the woods at the back of the property. The shade came as a relief after the hot afternoon sunshine and I felt myself relax as I followed a narrow dirt path through the trees.

I recalled from my time in Twilight Cove years ago that a path through the woods led all the way to a secluded stretch of beach. I wasn't entirely sure if that was the path I was on at the moment, but this one was taking me in the general direction of the ocean, and I figured I'd find out eventually if it was the one I'd traveled so many times in the past.

As I walked, my mind drifted to the story I was writing. It was a TV movie, a thriller. That was what I wrote the most, although I occasionally wrote seasonal romance movies for TV, and I'd recently had my first feature film produced. I was mulling over the upcoming scene in the story, my eyes on the narrow path ahead of me, when a dog materialized in front of me.

There was no better way to put it. One second, there was nothing there, and the next the dog stood on the path, wagging its tail at me. I blinked, wondering how I could have missed it coming through the underbrush and emerging onto the path. My mind must have wandered more than I'd realized.

'Hey, there,' I said, noting that the brown and white springer spaniel looked like one of the two dogs that had been with the old woman in the woods that morning.

I was about to take a step closer to the dog when it gave a woof and dashed off the pathway into the trees.

Did the dog know where it was going, or would it get lost in the woods?

I figured it probably knew its way home but, just in case, I plunged off the path and followed the dog as it bounded along ahead of me. I struggled to keep up. Bushes and spindly branches grabbed at my clothes and scratched my bare arms. I was also trying to take care not to crush any plants, remembering my encounter with the gray-haired woman that morning.

Within seconds, I lost sight of the dog. I slowed my steps, realizing that I was more likely to get lost than the dog. I was about to turn back and retrace my steps when I heard a murmur of angry voices up ahead.

Moving more slowly and carefully now, I continued forward. When I rounded a large pine tree, I discovered another path winding its way through the forest. I stepped out onto it and followed it through the trees, picking up my pace again.

I slowed down as the voices grew louder.

'Everyone's got a price,' a man said, his voice loud and aggressive. 'Everyone. Just name yours.'

'This land is priceless to me,' a woman said in response. 'You think money can buy you anything you want, but it won't buy you this land. It's mine, and it's staying that way.'

I spotted two people through the trees, standing in a clearing. The woman was the same one I'd met in the woods earlier that day, without her cloak now, but still gripping her walking stick. The man appeared to be in his fifties, with a balding head and a generous girth. His cheeks were flushed red, but he otherwise had a pale complexion.

'Stubborn old bat,' he hurled at the woman. 'I always get what I want. You'll see. My oceanfront condos will get built. And they'll get built right here on this land.'

The woman narrowed her eyes and tightened her grip on her walking stick.

A shiver ran down my spine at her next words.

'Over my dead body.'

THREE

'Everything OK here?' I asked.

The man whipped around to face me, startled, but the woman didn't seem surprised by my presence.

'Who are you?' the man demanded.

'That's not relevant,' the woman answered before I had a chance.

The man glowered at her for a second before turning his stormy gray eyes on me again. 'Whoever you are, you should convince her to sell me this land. What does an old woman need with all these trees, anyway?'

He didn't wait for a response, instead stomping off down a pathway with the stealth of an angry elephant.

I stared after him, stunned by his behavior. When I returned my gaze to the woman, she smiled at me, apparently unfazed by her visitor.

'Come have tea with me,' she said.

Without waiting to see if I'd agree, she crossed the clearing and entered an old cabin that looked as though it had become part of the woods. Moss grew on the roof and on some of the logs making up the walls. The door and the trim around the windows had been painted dark green, and the entire structure almost blended in with the forest around it.

The two springer spaniels emerged from the trees and followed the woman into the cabin. After a brief hesitation, I brought up the rear, stopping once I stepped over the threshold. As my eyes adjusted to the dim interior, I saw that the cabin had only one room. A narrow bed stood along one wall, covered with a blue and white quilt. Much of the opposite wall was taken up by a woodstove and an old cabinet with glass doors. I could see that its shelves held an assortment of camp dishes as well as two dainty teacups decorated with a pattern of pink roses. A rocking chair sat near the woodstove and an old wooden table dominated the middle of the room.

'I'm Dorothy,' the woman said as she lifted a kettle off the woodstove and poured hot water into a teapot that sat on the table. 'Dorothy Shale. That's Flossie on your left.' She indicated the black-and-white dog. 'And Fancy on your right.'

I rested a hand on the head of each dog and smiled down at them. 'Hello, girls.'

They wagged their tails and Fancy let out a 'woo-ooo' as she looked up at me with happy brown eyes.

'Fancy's a real talker.' Dorothy gestured at one of the chairs tucked beneath the table. 'Have a seat. No need to be warming the welcome mat.'

I glanced down to see that I was indeed standing on a coco coir mat. I tugged the cabin door shut and pulled the chair out from the table. 'Who was that man?' I asked as I sat down.

'Ed Grimshaw.' Dorothy fetched the two dainty teacups from the cabinet and set them on the table. 'A real estate developer. He blew into town about a year ago and he's been hounding me for several months now.' She fetched a sugar bowl and set it on the table as well. 'I think he might have been in my cabin a couple of weeks ago when I wasn't home. Somebody was, anyway, but I always leave the place unlocked so it could have been anyone. Nothing was taken, so I assumed he was just waiting for another chance to threaten me.'

'Have you told the police?' I asked with concern.

'I don't think there's any need to bring the police into it.'

Based on what I'd witnessed, I wasn't sure I agreed. Grimshaw clearly had a temper and wanted to get his way. I hoped he wouldn't escalate his tactics.

'How's your aunt doing?' Dorothy asked as she poured tea into the two cups.

'Very well, considering her broken ankle. She's not letting it keep her from having fun.'

'I'm glad to hear it.' Dorothy nudged one of the cups toward me.

'Do you know my aunt well?'

'Enough to know she's a good woman.' Dorothy settled into the chair across from me and the dogs lay down on either side of her. 'She cares for animals, and that's a sign of good character.'

'She has a heart of gold,' I said in agreement. My thoughts circled back to earlier in the day. 'This morning you said you were expecting me. Did Aunt Olivia tell you I was coming?'

Auntie O certainly hadn't mentioned Dorothy to me, but we hadn't yet had a whole lot of time to chat.

Dorothy smiled and took a sip of her tea. 'The universe told me.'

I wasn't sure what to say to that.

I was about to take a drink of my tea when a blur of movement startled me half out of my chair. The great horned owl swooped in through the open window to land on Dorothy's shoulder. She didn't even blink at the bird's arrival.

'Euclid didn't mean to startle you,' Dorothy said to me as she smiled at the owl.

I sank back down into my seat. Fortunately, I hadn't spilled any of my tea.

'Was he a rescue?' I asked. 'Did you raise him?'

'Oh, no. We met in the woods one day and became fast friends.'

Euclid bobbed his head, as if agreeing with what Dorothy had said.

I kept an eye on the owl as I busied myself with drinking my tea, unsure what to say next. I didn't know what to make of Dorothy. She was different from anyone else I'd ever known, and I'd met some unique characters while living in Los Angeles.

'You get headaches,' Dorothy said as I set down my empty teacup. It was a statement rather than a question.

'Um, yes,' I said, wondering how she could possibly know that. Maybe Auntie O had talked to her about me after all, but I didn't know why my aunt would have mentioned that I got headaches. 'They run in my family and I spend a lot of time staring at my computer screen.'

'You have one now.' Again, it wasn't a question.

An eerie, tingling sensation tickled the back of my neck.

I tried to provide myself with an explanation as to how she could know what I was feeling. Maybe I'd winced without realizing it and that's how she knew that my head was hurting. The dull pain from earlier had grown stronger, threatening to turn into a full-blown migraine.

'I have something for you.' Dorothy got up from the table and fetched a small item from the windowsill.

As she did so, Euclid took off from her shoulder, hopped to the sill, and then flew up into the sky.

Dorothy handed me a smooth, purple crystal.

'Amethyst with a little something extra added,' she said. 'It'll help with headaches and stress.'

I had no idea what she meant by 'a little something extra added', but I also wasn't sure if I should ask her to explain. I settled on a simple, 'Thank you.' I got up from the table. 'And thank you for the tea. I should get back to the farm.'

Dorothy nodded. 'We are so blessed to have animals in our lives.'

Fancy and Flossie trotted over to me and nudged my legs with their noses. I crouched down and gave them each a good pat before straightening up.

'It was nice to meet you, Dorothy,' I said.

'You as well,' she returned.

I left the cabin and found a path that I hoped would lead me back to the farm. As I walked, I fingered the smooth surface of the amethyst and then tucked it in my pocket. Dorothy was certainly unique, but she seemed like a nice woman. The thought of Ed Grimshaw bothering her further troubled me, so I decided to bring up the subject with Auntie O. Maybe she'd have some idea of how to protect Dorothy from the developer's harassment.

A rustling sound jolted me out of my thoughts and I halted on the narrow path. I heard the sound again, coming from my right. I peered through the trees in that direction, but couldn't see any movement. I waited, watching and listening, but didn't hear the noise again. After a few more seconds, I resumed walking, hoping that I wouldn't run into a bear.

Thankfully, I made it back to the farm without getting lost, running into ornery developers, or coming across large animals. It wasn't until I'd almost reached the barn that I realized something had changed. My head no longer hurt. Not even a trace of my earlier headache remained.

Perhaps it was the power of suggestion, I thought as I pulled the smooth, purple stone from my pocket and ran my thumb over it. I tucked the amethyst away again as I entered the barn.

In the tack room, I found a pair of work gloves that would hopefully protect my hands from further blisters. With few words, Callum directed me to the chores he wanted me to complete, and by the time I had them finished, my muscles ached and my stomach rumbled, but my headache hadn't returned. I checked my phone on my way back to the farmhouse. Auntie O had texted me to let me know that two of her friends had taken her out for dinner, but she hoped that she and I could spend more time together the following day.

After a shower and some food, I spent another few hours working on my screenplay. By the time I shut my laptop, night had fallen and my body was crying out for sleep. It would take time for me to get used to doing physical work every day. In Los Angeles I tried to go for a walk or a jog most days, but that wasn't the same as shoveling manure or hefting bales of straw.

Up in the guest bedroom at the back of the house – the same bedroom I'd slept in as a teenager – I crossed to the window and opened it a crack. Cool, fresh air seeped into the room and tickled my skin.

I was about to close the curtains when a strange light caught my attention. I leaned closer to the window, almost touching my nose to the glass, trying to see better. A faint blue glow moved off in the distance, near the tree line beyond the barn. It didn't look like the beam of a flashlight, or light from a phone. I couldn't figure out what it might be.

I blinked, and the light was gone.

I reached for the curtains, but stopped again. A shadow moved near the barn. Then a figure melted out of the deepest darkness and moved across the grass, heading for the line of trees at the southern side of the property, off to my left, beyond which was the neighboring asparagus farm. The scattered clouds drifted away from the nearly full moon, giving me a chance to recognize Callum, just before he disappeared from sight.

Strange, I thought as I finally closed the curtains.

Then I fell into bed and forgot about everything as sleep pulled me firmly into its grasp.

I slept soundly through the night and woke to the sound of Herald the rooster crowing. I had some stiff muscles but I nevertheless felt ready to face another day of farm work. After breakfast, I stepped out onto the back porch and breathed in the fresh air. I closed my eyes, enjoying a moment of peace and quiet unlike any I could experience in Los Angeles or any other big city. There was something about Twilight Cove that soothed me and fed my creativity. I'd woken up with a slew of new ideas for my screenplay, and I'd jotted them down with pen and paper while eating breakfast so I wouldn't forget anything.

As I walked across the lawn toward the barn, I heard a dog bark nearby. Then Flossie and Fancy came running from the field behind the barn, heading straight for me.

'Morning, girls,' I greeted, surprised to see them on the farm.

I looked for Dorothy, but couldn't see her. The dogs circled behind me and started nudging the back of my legs.

'What are you doing?' I asked, taking a few steps forward so they wouldn't knock me off balance.

Fancy, the brown and white dog, trotted a few paces past the barn then stopped and looked back at me with an urgent 'a-wooo'. Meanwhile, Flossie kept nudging the back of my knees. I took another step forward and Fancy trotted ahead before stopping and looking back at me again. Flossie gave me another persistent nudge.

'What's going on?' I asked.

'A-wooo,' Fancy said again, bounding ahead another few feet before stopping and looking back.

'You want me to come with you?' I guessed.

Flossie gave a loud woof and ran ahead to join Fancy. Then they both stopped and stared at me.

I figured they'd answered my question.

'All right,' I said. 'I'll come with you.'

Apparently satisfied, they both took off across the field toward the woods at the back of the property.

'Wait up!' I called as I broke into a jog.

Momentarily, I wondered if I was crazy for thinking that the dogs wanted me to follow them. I decided it didn't matter. There was no one around to see me, as far as I could tell. And crazy or not, I truly believed I was doing exactly as the dogs wanted.

We entered the woods and the two spaniels led me along a narrow path, pausing occasionally with a woof of encouragement as they waited for me to catch up. It didn't take long to reach the clearing where Dorothy's cabin stood. As I broke free of the trees, a blur of black and gray streaked out the door and around the back of the cabin.

'Hey!' I chased after the figure.

By the time I rounded the cabin, my quarry was running full tilt through the trees. A second later, the woods seemed to swallow her up. I hadn't seen the girl's face clearly, but I'd caught enough of a glimpse to guess that she was in her early to mid-teens. She had long, dark hair tied back in a ponytail and she wore black cargo pants and a gray hoodie. I wasn't positive, but I thought she might have been the same person I'd seen running from Auntie O's farm the day before.

'What was she up to?' I asked the dogs as I returned to the front of the cabin to find them sitting on either side of the door.

Whoever the girl was, the dogs didn't seem bothered by her flight from Dorothy's home. They were fully focused on the cabin door.

Fancy tipped her head back and bayed, the sound eerie and full of sorrow.

Flossie nudged the unlatched door and it swung open with a creak.

Fancy circled around and touched the back of my legs with her nose.

Apprehension skittered up my spine.

Suddenly the woods seemed too quiet.

I stepped closer to the door and knocked on its frame.

'Dorothy? Are you home?'

Heavy silence greeted me.

Dread settled in my chest, although I wasn't sure why.

I pushed the door open farther and it creaked again. The sound struck me as ominous.

I stepped into the dim interior of the cabin and my gaze immediately skipped to the bed. Dorothy lay on top of the quilt, on her back, completely still.

'Dorothy?' I said again.

She didn't stir.

I realized then that she was *too* still. Her chest wasn't rising and falling.

'Oh no,' I whispered.

One of the dogs whined behind me.

I approached the bed and looked down at Dorothy. Her eyes were closed, her head turned slightly to one side.

'Dorothy?' I said for a third time, even though I knew I wouldn't receive a response.

I swallowed hard and touched my fingers to her neck.

No pulse.

Dorothy was dead.

FOUR

I stared at Dorothy while my brain tried to process the fact that she would never open her eyes again. She was fully clothed in loose jeans, a white T-shirt and a light cardigan, so she'd likely passed away after getting dressed for the day. Blue bruises stood out against the pale skin near her collarbone, but I didn't notice any other obvious signs of injury. Maybe she'd decided to lie down because she was tired or didn't feel well, and then she died from a heart attack or stroke.

One of the dogs nudged my leg, as if trying to spur me into action, but I wasn't sure what to do. I wasn't keen to stay in the cabin with Dorothy's lifeless body, but it also didn't seem right to leave her all alone. The two dogs whined softly and then hopped up onto the bed and lay down, resting their chins on Dorothy's stomach. The sight brought tears to my eyes and sent a sharp stab of sorrow through my heart. I didn't think I could look at the broken-hearted dogs and manage to speak coherently, so I stepped outside. Dorothy wouldn't be alone as long as Flossie and Fancy watched over her.

I'd never seen a dead body before and as soon as I stepped out of the cabin, I realized that my legs were shaking beneath me. I found a large tree stump and sank down onto it after fishing my phone out of my pocket. I placed a call to 9-1-1 and explained the situation. The emergency operator had a kind voice and the sense of calm she exuded over the line helped to ease some of my stress.

Sooner than I expected, I heard the low rumble of an approaching vehicle. A police SUV slowly made its way along the rutted dirt track that provided access to Dorothy's cabin from the main road. The man who climbed out of the driver's seat had deep brown skin, graying hair, and carried some extra weight around his middle. He shut the door of his vehicle and headed my way.

'Isaac Stratton,' he introduced himself. 'Chief of the Twilight Cove PD.'

I got to my feet, relieved to find that my legs had ceased trembling. 'Georgie Johansen.'

Recognition flashed in his dark brown eyes. 'Olivia van Oosten's niece?' When I nodded, he continued, 'I heard you were in town.' He looked toward the cabin. 'Is Dorothy inside?'

'Yes. Her dogs too.'

'I never saw her without them.'

An ambulance made its way toward us and parked behind the police chief's vehicle. Stratton raised a hand in greeting and then made his way into the cabin. A moment later, he gently herded Flossie and Fancy out the door.

I clicked my tongue and the two dogs trotted over and pressed against my legs. I crouched down and put an arm around each one. A flicker of movement overhead caught my attention. Euclid perched on a branch in a nearby tree. The four of us watched as the paramedics unloaded their gear and joined the police chief in Dorothy's cabin.

It didn't take long for the paramedics to emerge and return to their ambulance. My legs started to cramp from staying crouched by the dogs, so I returned to the tree stump. Flossie and Fancy followed and sat on either side of me. Fancy let out a quiet, mournful whine and then lay down, resting her chin on her paws. I stroked her fur, and Flossie's too.

The paramedics drove off in the ambulance as Stratton came out of the cabin. He had his phone to his ear and walked off across the clearing so he could have his conversation in private. After he ended the call, he came over my way.

'What will happen to Dorothy's dogs?' I asked as I continued stroking the spaniels' glossy coats.

'Maybe Ms Shale left instructions in her will.'

'And in the meantime?'

Stratton rubbed the stubble on his jaw. 'Ms Shale liked to keep to herself. I don't know that she had any family around these parts. I can call the local shelter.'

'No,' I said quickly. 'I'll take them. I mean, just until we know what Dorothy wanted to happen.'

I hated the thought of them staying in a shelter. It was bad enough that they were mourning the loss of their favorite human. I wasn't much more than a stranger to them, but they seemed to like me, and I didn't doubt that they'd be happier on the farm than at a shelter.

'I suppose that would be all right,' Stratton said, much to my relief.

A police cruiser arrived on the scene, parking in the spot where the ambulance had been minutes earlier. Stratton glanced at the cruiser before returning his attention to me.

'I'm afraid I have to ask you to stick around for a few minutes. One of my officers will take your statement.'

'Is it all right if I text my aunt?' I asked. 'She'll be wondering where I am.'

That wasn't quite true. Aunt Olivia wouldn't have noticed my absence yet, especially since a friend was picking her up to take her to a dental appointment that morning, so we hadn't expected to see each other before lunchtime. Callum might be wondering why I wasn't helping out with the morning chores, though. I didn't have Callum's phone number, so I hoped Olivia could pass on a message to him. He might not care if I showed up or not, but I'd told him the evening before that I'd help out each day and I didn't want him to think I was unreliable.

'That's fine.' Stratton's gaze landed on Flossie and Fancy and I saw kindness in his eyes. 'Thanks for looking after the dogs.'

Before I had a chance to say anything in response, he turned and strode across the clearing to meet the two male officers who'd climbed out of the cruiser. The three men had a short discussion that I couldn't hear, though I noticed Stratton tilt his head in my direction at one point. Then they split up. Stratton pulled out his phone again and one of his officers wandered back to the cruiser while talking into his radio. The other officer, the taller of the two, approached me. He was a Native American man with short dark hair, high cheekbones and a lean, athletic build.

'I'm Officer Williams,' he said when he reached me. 'I understand you found the deceased.'

'Yes,' I said as I continued to stroke the dogs' fur, as much for my own comfort as theirs.

Williams asked me to walk him through how I'd discovered Dorothy's body. If he thought it was strange or unbelievable that I'd sensed that Flossie and Fancy had wanted me to follow them from the farm to Dorothy's cabin, he didn't let on. I felt a bit silly telling him that part, but all the officer did was glance at the dogs and then continue filling out the witness statement form.

I also told him about seeing the teenage girl running from the cabin when I arrived.

'She was probably the first to find Dorothy,' I said, feeling sorry for the girl. 'It must have freaked her out.'

'Do you know who she is?' Williams asked.

'Sorry, no.' I described the girl as best I could, but I didn't have many details to share.

Whoever the girl was, I hoped she was OK. Finding Dorothy's body had left me shaken. The teenager might have been even more affected, especially if she'd known Dorothy well.

Williams had me read and sign the witness statement and then left to confer with his colleagues. Eventually, Chief Stratton told me I could leave. By then the medical examiner's van had arrived on the scene.

I took a few steps into the woods and then looked back at the dogs.

'Come on, girls,' I coaxed. 'You're staying with me for now.'

Flossie and Fancy glanced back toward the cabin. Fancy let out a whine and Flossie hung her head. Then they both fell into step behind me. Overhead, Euclid glided from tree to tree, his yellow eyes always watching our progress on the ground below. I wondered if, like the dogs, the owl somehow knew that Dorothy was no longer in this world with us.

When I reached the farm, I found Callum in one of the paddocks close to the barn, shoveling manure into a wheelbarrow. He leaned the shovel against the wheelbarrow and came to meet me as I climbed the fence.

Flossie and Fancy scooted beneath the lowest fence rail and sniffed at Callum's jean-clad legs. He gave them both a pat on the head and then focused on me.

'Are you OK?' he asked as I hopped down to the ground.

The concern in his green eyes took me by surprise. Up until this moment, he hadn't shown me much – if any – warmth.

I brushed away the dirt that got on my hands when I climbed the fence. 'Did Olivia tell you what happened?'

'She sent me a text. You don't need to help out with the chores today if you don't feel up to it.'

His kindness caused tears to prickle at my eyes. I quickly blinked them away and reached down to rest my hands on the dogs' heads.

'Thanks, but I'm OK. The dogs will be staying on the farm until someone figures out what Dorothy wanted to happen with them.' I looked down at the dogs and noticed how they completely ignored the alpacas in the next paddock. 'I don't think they'll bother the animals.'

'I don't think so either,' Callum agreed. 'I've seen them around now and then and they've never caused any trouble. They were here at dawn this morning, chasing rabbits in the back field. I've never seen them harm the rabbits, and they've never chased the farm animals.'

That was good to know. Maybe the dogs had found Dorothy dead when they returned home from their early morning rabbit chasing.

I immersed myself in the physical work of cleaning out stalls and grooming donkeys for the next couple of hours. Flossie and Fancy kept me company the whole time, occasionally exploring the surroundings with their noses to the ground, but mostly lying nearby where I could keep an eye on them. I hadn't seen Euclid since leaving the woods, but that wasn't surprising. He was a nocturnal animal and was probably catching some shuteye. How he'd known that something was wrong with Dorothy, I had no idea, but I had an eerie feeling that he did know.

Shortly before noon, I received a text from Aunt Olivia, letting me know that she was home and asking me to join her for lunch. After cleaning myself up at the farmhouse, I crossed the lawn to the carriage house, with Flossie and Fancy on my heels. When I stepped inside, the two dogs hesitated on the threshold.

Aunt Olivia was sitting on the loveseat, with her foot propped up on the ottoman. When she saw the dogs, she patted her legs.

'Come on in, girls,' she called.

Flossie and Fancy perked up and brushed past me as they trotted over to my aunt. I'd texted her earlier about looking after the dogs for a while, so it didn't come as a surprise to her that they were with me.

'There's pasta salad and some of yesterday's pecan pie in the fridge,' my aunt said to me as she fussed over the dogs.

'You've been busy again.'

Sadness weighed down the brief smile she sent me. 'Cooking always helps me when I'm feeling sad.'

'I'm so sorry you lost your neighbor,' I said, a wave of sorrow washing over me. 'Did you also consider her a friend?'

'I did, yes,' Auntie O replied. 'She mostly kept to herself, but we visited each other on occasion and I enjoyed our chats.'

She grabbed her crutches and eased herself to her feet. She carefully made her way into the kitchen as I took plates down from one of the cupboards.

'Now, tell me how you're doing,' she said with her blue eyes watching me closely.

I let out a deep sigh. 'I'm all right.'

A knock on the front door kept me from saying anything else. The two dogs ran ahead of me and pressed their noses to the door.

'A-wooooo!' Fancy sounded impatient to see who waited on the other side.

I smiled despite my lingering sadness, and opened the door to find Chief Stratton standing on the other side.

He removed his hat. 'Georgie.' He nodded at my aunt as she came up behind me on her crutches. 'Olivia.'

Apprehension settled heavily in my chest, though I couldn't have said exactly why. I stepped back and held the door open wider. 'Chief Stratton. Come on in.'

'How's the ankle, Olivia?' he asked as he stepped inside.

'On the mend,' she replied. 'How are you doing, Isaac?'

He tucked his hat under his arm. 'I've had better days.'

I shut the door and rubbed my arms, as if that would somehow ease my sense of foreboding. The dogs sat, one on either side of me, and leaned against my legs.

Stratton directed his gaze at me. 'I've got more questions for you, Georgie.' He paused for a brief moment before saying his next words. 'I'm afraid we're treating Ms Shale's death as suspicious.'

FIVE

'Are you saying she was murdered?' I asked, shocked by the thought.

'Surely not!' Aunt Olivia exclaimed in dismay.

Chief Stratton held up a pacifying hand. 'We haven't declared it a murder as of yet. We'll know more once the postmortem is complete.'

'But what makes you think Dorothy's death was suspicious?' I recalled the marks I'd seen near her collarbone. 'The bruises?'

'You noticed those?'

'I didn't think much of them at the time,' I admitted. I wondered what else I might have missed.

'There were more bruises hidden beneath her shirt,' Stratton said. 'Roughly in the shape of a handprint.'

'Why would anyone want to hurt Dorothy?' My aunt appeared as shocked and horrified as I felt. Maybe more so.

Her face had gone pale, and I worried she might not be able to hold herself up much longer.

'Come and sit down.' I guided her back to the loveseat.

Once she was settled, she invited Chief Stratton to sit down as well.

'Would you like any lunch while you're here?' she asked him. 'Georgie and I were just about to eat.'

'Thank you, but I won't stay long.' He took a seat in an armchair. 'I'll speak to Georgie for a minute and then be on my way.'

I perched next to Olivia. The dogs lay down on the rug and rested their chins on their paws, but they kept their eyes trained on the police chief.

'Had you ever been to Ms Shales's cabin before this morning?' Stratton asked me.

'Once,' I replied. 'Yesterday afternoon. She invited me in for tea. I met her for the first time yesterday morning, when we ran into each other in the woods.'

Stratton produced a notebook from his pocket and jotted down a few words. 'I understand that you wouldn't be too familiar with the cabin, but when you arrived this morning, did you notice anything unusual or out of place?'

I took time to think back carefully. Nothing about the cabin itself stood out to me, but there was something I needed to mention.

'There was someone there when I arrived. A teenage girl.'

Stratton nodded. 'You mentioned that to Officer Williams. He said you couldn't identify her.'

'No, but I just arrived in town a couple of days ago. I don't know many people here. I think I did see her once before, here on the farm. I can't be sure she was the same person though. Whoever I saw on the farm jumped the fence and ran into the woods as soon as I saw them.'

'That must be Roxy Russo,' Aunt Olivia said. 'I've seen her visiting the animals here a few times. She always takes off as soon as she's spotted. I'm sure she couldn't have harmed Dorothy. She's just a child!'

'I'm familiar with Roxy.' Stratton wrote another note in his book.

I wondered if his familiarity arose simply from Twilight Cove being a small town, or if the girl had been in trouble with the police. I hoped it was the former. If she was a troublemaker, I didn't like the idea of her hanging around the animal sanctuary.

'There's something else you should know,' I said to Chief Stratton.

I told him about the argument I'd overheard between Dorothy and Ed Grimshaw the day before. 'He sounded really angry.'

Olivia shook her head with disgust. 'That man is ruthless. He wants to cut down all the trees and build oceanfront condos.'

'That would be terrible,' I said. 'The forest is beautiful, and putting up condos would ruin the view from here, and from a lot of other homes.'

Olivia frowned. 'All Ed Grimshaw cares about is money.'

'I'll be sure to talk to him,' Stratton said. 'Is there anything else you can tell me?'

I thought for another moment and then shook my head. 'Sorry. That's all I can think of.'

'How about you, Olivia?' Stratton asked. 'You knew Dorothy, didn't you?'

'Of course,' my aunt replied. 'We had tea together now and then. She was a bit eccentric, perhaps, considering how she lived, but she was a nice woman and we shared a love of animals. I certainly didn't believe the ridiculous rumors about her being a witch.'

'A witch?' I echoed, incredulous.

Chief Stratton heaved himself to his feet. 'Small towns do like their rumors.' He tucked his notebook away. 'I won't keep you ladies any longer.'

'I hope it turns out that Dorothy died a natural and peaceful death,' my aunt said.

'As do I, Olivia.' The chief settled his hat on his head.

I walked him to the door, and he handed me a business card.

'If you think of anything else you want to tell me, give me a call.'

I assured him I would.

He tipped his hat and walked off to the SUV he'd left parked at the edge of the road.

I shut the door and leaned against it, my gaze landing on the two dogs. They were now sitting in the middle of the living room, watching me.

If someone had attempted to harm Dorothy in their presence, would they have tried to protect her?

Probably, but I knew there was a good chance that the killer had struck while the dogs were here on the farm, chasing wild rabbits.

'Let's have lunch,' Olivia said, pulling me out of my thoughts. 'You look like you could use some food.'

My stomach rumbled, and a rush of guilt followed the sensation. How could I have an appetite after finding Dorothy dead just hours before?

I knew the answer. Upset or not, the physical work I'd put in had left me hungry. The dogs would get hungry too, eventually.

'I'd better go buy some dog food this afternoon,' I said as I took the pasta salad out of the fridge. 'I should have brought their kibble and beds from the cabin.'

'The police might not have let you remove anything, especially once they decided Dorothy's death might not be natural,' Olivia pointed out.

'That's probably true,' I agreed.

I poured us each a tall glass of lemonade and joined my aunt at the kitchen table.

'Why do people say Dorothy was a witch?' I asked as I dished out the pasta salad. 'I get that it's unusual around here for a woman to live in the woods without modern conveniences. And to have an owl as a friend. Still . . . it's a bit of a leap to label her as a witch, isn't it?'

Aunt Olivia thanked me for the plate of salad I passed her before she replied. 'People like to stick labels on others, especially when they're different. Add to that the fact that she was known for her natural remedies, and that's probably how the rumor started.'

I remembered the amethyst Dorothy had given me. I'd left it in my bedroom, on the nightstand.

'Did her natural remedies work?' My headache had disappeared after Dorothy had given me the stone, but I figured that had to be a coincidence.

'People swear by them.' Aunt Olivia paused to take a sip of lemonade. 'It even caused some animosity.'

I speared a piece of pasta with my fork. 'Why would helping people cause animosity?'

'There's a woman who lives in town, Marlene Hooper. She owns a cosmetics and skincare shop. Some of the townsfolk who used to buy her skincare products had started buying all-natural equivalents from Dorothy instead.'

'Did that really have a major effect on Marlene's sales?' I asked.

'I don't think so,' Olivia replied. 'But Marlene has always bristled at anyone she viewed as competition in any aspect of life. She saw those customers as hers, and even though most of them probably still bought cosmetics and other products from her, she didn't like sharing them with Dorothy.'

'Do you think she might have wanted to hurt Dorothy?'

That question gave Olivia pause, but then she shook her head. 'I can't imagine Marlene would do something so drastic.'

'It was probably Ed Grimshaw,' I said.

My aunt frowned. 'I'm still holding out hope that Dorothy's death was completely natural and peaceful.'

I sighed. 'Me too.' I thought back to the last time I was in Twilight Cove. 'I don't remember anyone living in the woods when I was here before.'

'I think it was a year or two after you left that Dorothy bought that parcel of land.'

I looked down at the dogs lying on either side of my chair and my heart ached for them.

'Do you know if Dorothy had any family?' I asked my aunt, wondering what was going to happen to my new canine friends.

'When we had our chats over tea, she never outright said that she didn't have any family, but I got the feeling that she was alone in the world, aside from her animals.'

'That's sad.'

'Perhaps,' Olivia said, 'but I don't think Dorothy minded. She was happiest in the woods with her dogs and all the wild creatures.'

I could understand that. When I'd lived on the farm as a teenager, I'd often gone walking in the woods. Spending time among the trees with the birds and the squirrels had always relaxed me and made me feel calmer, no matter what was going on in my life. The same was true of the time I'd spent hanging out at the local beaches, whether alone or with company.

After we'd finished eating, I washed the dishes while Aunt Olivia fussed over Flossie and Fancy.

'I'd take them into town with me, but I don't have leashes for them,' I said as Olivia stroked their fur.

'You can leave them here with me, but I'm sure you could take them if you wanted to. They always accompanied Dorothy into town, off leash. I never saw them stray from her side and they were always perfectly behaved.'

I set the last dish in the draining rack. 'I'll give it a try then.'

After drying my hands, I left the carriage house with the dogs and took them over to my car. They hopped into the back seat without hesitation when I opened the door for them. As I drove toward town, I glanced at the spaniels in the rearview mirror and my heart clenched.

Wherever they ended up, I desperately hoped they would have a good, loving home. I dreaded the thought of saying goodbye to them. They'd been in my care for only a few hours, but I couldn't deny that I was already getting attached. I told myself that wasn't wise. Too many times in my life I'd become attached to places or people, only to have to move on and leave them behind, or to have them disappear out of my life in some other way.

Sometimes my heart felt battered and bruised from those experiences, and I had a tendency to keep myself closed off, not wanting to get too close to anyone. With Flossie and Fancy, however, I wasn't sure I'd have any success with that. If the ache in my chest was any indication, it was far too late to keep them out of my heart.

SIX

I found a free parking spot on Main Street outside the Pet Palace. When I climbed out of the car, I took a moment to gaze down the cobblestone street toward the ocean. Seagulls cried out in the distance and I caught a hint of salt on the breeze. My trip to the beach had been interrupted the day before, and I still hadn't made it down to the water. I would soon, I promised myself. For me, the ocean was as soothing as the peaceful forest, if not even more so.

I made sure there was no traffic coming when I let the dogs out of the back seat onto the sidewalk, just in case they decided to take off. Fortunately, they simply sat down on the pavement and waited for me to make the next move. When I opened the door to the Pet Palace, the spaniels squeezed past me and trotted into the store ahead of me.

A petite woman around the age of thirty was in the midst of stocking shelves. She had glossy black hair that fell below her shoulders and she wore a white T-shirt with jeans and bright yellow high-top sneakers with adorable cartoon cats on them.

She glanced up as the bell above the door announced our arrival.

'Sorry, all dogs need to be leashed . . .' She cut herself off and set down the cans of cat food she'd been holding. 'Aren't those—'

'Dorothy Shale's dogs,' I finished for her.

She studied me with a mixture of curiosity and sadness. 'I heard about Dorothy's passing.'

News traveled fast in Twilight Cove.

'You must be Olivia van Oosten's niece,' she continued. 'I heard you found Dorothy. I'm sorry you went through that.'

'Thank you,' I said. 'And, yes, I'm Olivia's niece, Georgie Johansen.'

She knelt down on the floor and held out her arms to Flossie and Fancy. They rushed toward her for attention, their tails wagging. 'And I'm so sorry that you two lost your human. I know you loved her dearly.' She gave them each a hug and a kiss on the head before standing up and offering me a hand. 'Cindy Yoon. I own the shop. Dorothy came in here regularly with Flossie and Fancy.'

I shook her hand. 'I'm sorry about not having leashes,' I apologized.

'That's partly why I'm here. I'm looking after Flossie and Fancy temporarily, but I don't have any of their belongings. I need to get them leashes and some food.'

'That's no problem.' She smiled at the dogs. 'These two are always perfectly behaved. And I can show you which food Dorothy fed them.'

'That would be great,' I said with relief and gratitude.

Flossie and Fancy trotted off down the dog food aisle.

Cindy watched them and laughed. 'I don't think you need me to help you. They know exactly what they want.'

We followed the dogs down the aisle. Sure enough, they'd stopped to sit in front of a particular brand of dog food.

'If you're just feeding them temporarily, would you like to go with a small bag of the kibble?' Cindy asked.

'That's probably a good idea,' I said. 'Do they eat wet food as well?'

'Same brand. The chicken flavor is their favorite.'

I grabbed four cans of the wet food while Cindy picked up a bag of the kibble.

'Leashes are down the aisle next to the door,' Cindy said with a nod in that direction. 'You can leave all this food on the counter while you look.'

I thanked her and set the cans near the cash register before heading for the display of leashes, collars and harnesses. Flossie and Fancy accompanied me. I picked out a couple of leashes, one pink and one purple. I held them out to the dogs, and they sniffed them before sitting down, looking satisfied. Maybe I imagined that expression, but I liked to think that they'd approved of my choices.

On our way back toward the sales counter, Fancy stopped by a display of individually wrapped specialty dog cookies. Some were shaped like bones, in large and small sizes, and others were circular and decorated as soccer balls. Still others were cut in the shape of dog paws. Some said things like spaw day, happy birthday, or pawsitive vibes written on with icing.

Fancy stood on her hind legs and rested her front paws on the shelf so she could touch her nose to a bone-shaped cookie that said pawsitive vibes. She gave me a pointed look before staring at the cookie again.

'OK, message received,' I said with a smile. 'I think a cookie is the least you deserve today.'

Fancy dropped back down to the floor and sat with a swish of her tail.

'What about you, Flossie?' I asked the black-and-white dog.

She went up on her hind legs and sniffed at the same cookie that had caught Fancy's attention.

'All right. Two of those.' I picked up two of the cookies and took them over to the sales counter.

'Do you know what will happen to the girls?' Cindy asked me as she rang up my purchases.

I tapped my credit card to pay. 'Not yet. I'm hoping Dorothy left a will with instructions regarding the dogs, or family members will come forward to look after them.'

Cindy handed me my receipt. 'I'll miss seeing them if they end up moving out of town.'

She came around the counter to crouch down and shower Flossie and Fancy with attention again. Then she rose to greet a customer who'd just come in the door.

Before leaving the Pet Palace, I hooked a new leash to each dog's collar and instantly felt better, knowing it would be easier to keep them safe. Once outside, I stashed the dog food in the trunk of my car and considered my options. The coffee shop, Déjà Brew, was just across the street. Maybe I could grab a latte to go and walk the dogs down to the beach before returning to the farm.

We crossed Main Street during a break in the light traffic and I caught a whiff of the smell of coffee as the shop door opened and a customer came out onto the sidewalk. I paused outside the shop, wondering what to do. The dogs probably weren't allowed inside, but I didn't like the thought of leaving them tied up on their own. I peered in through the window. The counter wasn't far from the door, so I'd likely be able to see the dogs while I was inside.

'Georgie?'

I turned at the sound of my name and braced myself in the nick of time.

A woman with long brown hair let out a squeal of happiness and threw her arms around me.

'I *cannot* believe it's you!' Tessa Ortiz said in a rush as she stepped back and beamed at me. 'OK, I can, because I knew you were in town, but at the same time . . .' She stopped to take a breath.

The brightness of my smile probably matched that of Tessa's. 'I was hoping I'd get to see you,' I said.

Tessa had been my closest friend when I lived in Twilight Cove in my teens. We lost touch after I moved away – my fault, mostly – but I'd forever missed her friendship. I knew from chatting with Aunt Olivia that Tessa still lived in Twilight Cove and I'd wanted to see her again, but I'd also hesitated to get in touch with her in case she didn't feel the same way. Now that I could see her reaction to my presence, any such worries disappeared in a flash.

'Do you have time for a coffee and a chat?' Tessa clasped her hands together. 'Please tell me you have time.'

'I have time,' I said, still smiling at her enthusiasm. 'I was going to grab a latte and walk the dogs down to the beach. Do you want to join us?'

'Definitely.' She crouched down to greet the dogs. 'Aren't you both so cute?' she crooned at them. Then she stood up again. 'How about I pop inside and get our drinks so you can stay with the dogs?'

I readily agreed to that plan and told her what I wanted. I tried to give her some money, but she wouldn't let me.

'My treat,' she said. She waved off my further attempt to protest. 'You can pay next time.'

I smiled again at the thought of there being a next time.

Tessa disappeared into the coffee shop. While the dogs and I waited, I sat down in one of two wrought-iron chairs placed next to a small bistro table beneath the shop's awning. Fancy and Flossie sat by my feet, tongues lolling out as they watched the world. About a minute or so after I sat down, a stocky man with light brown hair and gray eyes came out of Déjà Brew and stopped on the sidewalk in front of me.

He thrust a hand out toward me. 'Byron Szabo of the *Twilight Cove Gazette*. I understand you found Dorothy Shale's body this morning. What can you tell me about that?'

'I'm sorry,' I hedged, taken aback. 'How do you even know who I am?'

He hooked a thumb toward the coffee shop's door. 'I overheard Tessa Ortiz telling the barista that you were waiting outside.' He held up his cell phone. 'You don't mind if I record our conversation, do you?'

Without waiting for an answer, he started a recording app.

'There's really nothing I can tell you,' I said, feeling distinctly uncomfortable. I glanced from right to left, wishing I could escape the conversation.

Both dogs sat up at attention, as if sensing my unease.

'Just walk me through what you saw,' Byron said, holding his phone out toward me, the screen facing up.

'I'd rather not.' I got to my feet.

The dogs jumped up too, their stances tense and wary.

The door to Déjà Brew opened and Tessa emerged with two takeout cups in hand. She narrowed her eyes as soon as she saw the reporter.

'Byron, are you harassing Georgie?' she asked.

'I'm not harassing anyone,' he replied. 'I'm doing my job.'

'You'll have to do it somewhere else. Georgie and I are busy.' She handed me one of the cups and put a hand on my elbow to steer me down the street.

Byron followed us. 'I need some quotes for my article.'

Tessa shot him an icy glare over her shoulder. 'Tough. Now get lost before I call the cops.'

Byron muttered something under his breath, but he stopped following us.

'Thank you,' I said quietly to Tessa.

'My pleasure. I can't stand the guy.'

Holding the dogs' leashes in one hand and my latte in the other, I took in a deep breath as we walked. Ocean air filled my lungs and the tension brought on by my encounter with Byron eased away. The dogs were walking with their tails down, almost tucked between their hind legs, but I hoped they'd relax soon now that we'd left Byron behind.

I was about to ask Tessa to catch me up on her life when a blonde woman came out of a shop two doors ahead of us. Tessa waved to get her attention.

'It's Avery, isn't it?' Tessa asked when we reached the woman.

'That's right. Avery Hembridge,' the woman confirmed.

She appeared to be close to my age of thirty-two, with shoulder-length hair. She wore what looked like designer jeans with ankle boots and a white leather jacket.

'I'm sorry about your stepfather,' Tessa said. 'I heard he's not doing well.'

Mental puzzle pieces clicked together in my head and I realized that Avery was the recipient of the gift basket Auntie O had put together, the one we'd left at Victor's mansion the day before.

'Thank you,' Avery said. 'I'm glad I'm able to be here with him.

I never did understand why he chose to move away from Chicago, but now that I've spent some time in this town, I can see its charm.'

'Twilight Cove definitely has plenty of charm.' Tessa tucked her arm through mine. 'Avery, this is my friend Georgie Johansen.'

I held the leashes and my latte in one hand and offered Avery the other. 'Nice to meet you.'

'You and your aunt dropped off the gift basket for me yesterday,' Avery said as she shook my hand.

'That's right.'

'Thank you. It was such a kind gesture. Will you please pass on my thanks to your aunt as well?'

'Of course,' I said.

I transferred my latte back to my free hand, just in time. The dogs tugged on their leashes, eager to keep going. They nearly pulled me off balance but I steadied myself and stayed put.

'I'll stop by to thank her in person,' Avery said, 'or at the very least I'll send a note when I get a chance, but I'd like her to know right away that I appreciate the gift.'

'I'll definitely let her know,' I assured her.

'I'm afraid I need to get back to the house,' Avery said, 'but it was nice to run into both of you.'

We shared some parting words, and then Avery climbed into a white Mercedes-Benz parked at the curb.

The spaniels tugged at their leashes again. I laughed. 'Eager to get to the beach?' I asked as Tessa and I followed them down the street.

By the time we'd crossed Ocean Drive, the dogs had their tails up in the air, wagging. Like the day before, food trucks were parked along the road and were doing business with passersby. The delicious smells wafting toward us from the trucks made my stomach rumble. I would make do with my latte for now, but I was tempted to pick up some food before heading back to the farm.

'I can take one of the leashes,' Tessa offered as we started walking across the sand.

Now that we'd reached the beach, the dogs had stopped pulling and trotted happily at my side. I could easily sip at my latte while holding both leashes in one hand, but I passed one over to Tessa anyway.

'Now,' she said as we made our way down toward the water, 'tell me everything I've missed over the past fifteen years.'

SEVEN

We didn't manage to fill each other in on everything that had transpired in our lives, of course, but we did catch up on the basics while we enjoyed our drinks and a stroll along the shoreline. Back in high school, Tessa had loved drama and fashion. Now she worked as a teacher at the local high school, teaching drama and English. She sewed costumes for the school's theater productions and also made some of her own outfits. Like me, she was single, never married, with no children.

'But I've got two cats,' she added. 'And I see you've got two dogs.'

I explained to her how the dogs had come into my care temporarily.

'You poor thing,' she said when I told her that I'd found Dorothy that morning. 'And the poor dogs.'

As if they understood her, Flossie and Fancy glanced up at her. Fancy let out a quiet whine, but then they returned their focus to watching the seagulls bobbing on the waves near the shore.

'I guess that's why Byron was hassling you,' Tessa said.

'Unfortunately.' We sat down on a sun-bleached log to enjoy the view.

Fancy and Flossie tugged gently on their leashes, wanting to go to the water's edge. Since we were well away from the road and I doubted they would stray too far, I unhooked their leashes. They trotted down to the water and splashed about in the shallows.

'Do you know everyone in Twilight Cove?' I asked Tessa.

She laughed. 'Anyone who's been here a while. I recognized Avery because she's been in town for a few weeks now. I don't really know her though. I believe she lives in Chicago, which is where Victor is originally from. She's probably around our age, and I'd invite her out to meet some of my friends, but with her stepfather dying, I thought maybe I should wait.'

'That can't be easy, caring for him.'

'She's got nurses helping around the clock,' Tessa said, 'but still, it must be difficult to watch a loved one slip away.'

We lapsed into silence for a moment, but then Tessa brightened again.

'Speaking of meeting my friends, that's exactly what you should do.'

'I'm here temporarily,' I reminded her. 'And I've got my writing and the farm chores.'

Tessa waved off my excuses. 'You should still have time for fun and relaxation. And don't worry. I remember that you're an introvert. I won't force you to attend any crazy, wild parties. That's not my sort of thing either. A few of us have a games night twice a month. We just had one so the next won't be for a couple of weeks, but I'd really like you to come with me.'

'That sounds fun,' I said.

Tessa had errands to run, and I didn't want to stay away from the farm too long, so we parted ways a short time later. Before returning to my car, I made a stop at a truck selling Mexican food and brought lunch for myself and Aunt Olivia. I would have asked Callum if he wanted something, but I still didn't have his phone number. I made a mental note to ask him for it. If he ever needed my help with something on the farm, or vice versa, it would be better if we could get in touch with each other without having to go through my aunt.

Auntie O and I ate together on the carriage house's patio and then I spent a few hours working on my latest script before helping Callum with the animals again. As I changed into my pajamas that night, I realized I should have bought beds for the dogs. They, however, didn't seem to think there was a problem. They followed me into my bedroom and hopped up on the queen bed without hesitation.

'All right,' I said as I climbed under the covers. 'I guess that will work for tonight. If you're going to be with me for a while, I'll get you beds of your own.'

The spaniels looked at one another, and I could have sworn that a silent message passed between them. I suspected they thought they had no need for any other beds when mine was so comfy.

I switched off the lamp and snuggled deeper into bed. I'd left the window open a crack and, as I drifted off to sleep, I heard the call of a great horned owl. Maybe I was reading too much into it, but the call sounded mournful to me.

*   *   *

Two days later, on Monday, Aunt Olivia received word from one of her many friends that Victor Clyde had passed away the day before. Olivia wanted to send a sympathy card to Avery but didn't have any on hand, so I told her I'd go out and buy one for her. She suggested I look for one at Cursive, the local stationery shop. I left Flossie and Fancy with her, so I wouldn't have to leave them in the car or out on the sidewalk while I browsed the card selection in the store.

When I arrived on Main Street, I easily found a parking spot. I climbed out of my car and saw that I'd parked in front of a shop called Siren Beauty. The lettering on the large front window proclaimed that the store sold cosmetics and other beauty products. I figured it had to be Marlene Hooper's store. There probably weren't many cosmetic shops in Twilight Cove.

On a whim, I decided to go inside, curious to know if the store carried any natural cosmetics. I was allergic to many brands of makeup – they tended to make my eyes burn and water – so I leaned toward all natural, mineral products.

When I stepped inside the shop, I almost backed out the door, but it had shut behind me and I didn't want to set off the bell again and draw attention to myself. Byron Szabo stood by the sales counter near the back of the store, pestering the woman stationed behind it. At least, I figured by her annoyed expression that he was pestering her.

Unfortunately, there weren't any aisles formed by high shelves for me to hide in, so I edged my way to the left and turned my back on the sales counter. I tried to focus on the display of eyeshadows and eyeliners, but I couldn't help but overhear Byron's conversation.

'The dispute between you and Dorothy has been documented in the *Gazette*,' Byron was saying.

'So what if it was?' the woman said.

'Come on, Marlene,' Byron wheedled. 'You're the best source for this angle of the story. Give me something to work with.'

I glanced over my shoulder to see Marlene cross her arms over her chest.

She let out an irritated huff. 'Even after her death, that woman is getting all the attention.'

'You thought she got too much attention when she was alive?' Byron prodded.

'Of course she did!' Marlene groused. 'I've had this store for fifteen years. I built this business from the ground up. Then one day Jeanine Duckworth gets some sort of funky tea from Dorothy that helps her arthritis pain and suddenly everyone's running to that witch for potions and spells.'

'Potions and spells?' Byron echoed. 'I never heard about any of those. Just poultices and teas.'

'I'm sure there were potions and spells too,' Marlene grumbled. 'That woman was up to no good. She was probably a devil worshipper.'

I thought that was quite a leap, but Byron didn't seem to have the same concern.

'What makes you say that?' he asked with undisguised eagerness.

'She was a witch, wasn't she?' Marlene said. 'Isn't that what witches do?'

I rolled my eyes and pretended to study a golden shade of eyeliner.

'I was hoping you'd have some evidence,' Byron said, sounding disappointed now.

'She lured my customers away with all her woo-woo stuff,' Marlene said. 'Isn't that evidence enough? And don't forget that curse she put on me.'

I thought Marlene was being ridiculous.

Maybe Byron did too, judging by the hint of exasperation in his voice when he said, 'There's no such thing as curses.'

'You'd be singing a different tune if she'd put one on you,' Marlene argued. 'Ever since she put the curse on me, I've had a whole string of bad luck.'

'So, you're saying the feud between you two was escalating?' Byron asked.

Marlene sniffed. 'It wasn't a feud. I merely told her what was on my mind a time or two and she decided to curse me.'

'And now that she's dead,' Byron said, 'I assume the customers Dorothy stole will come back to you.'

'I'm sure they would have seen the error of their ways eventually, whether Dorothy lived or died,' Marlene said.

'But it's convenient that you didn't have to wait for them to come to their senses,' Byron pressed.

I angled myself so I'd have a view of Marlene and the reporter out of the corner of my eye.

Marlene put her hands on her hips. 'What's that supposed to mean?'

Byron shrugged. 'Just that it's a good thing for you that she died.'

'I would never wish for anyone to die,' Marlene said. 'But I certainly won't miss her. I doubt anyone will.'

My jaw almost dropped. What a terrible thing to say. I barely knew Dorothy, but she seemed nice enough to me, and the spaniels and Euclid clearly loved her. I figured they were probably better judges of character than Marlene Hooper.

'Now, perhaps you can get out of my store and let me get back to work,' she said. 'I have a customer to serve.'

I held back a wince as Byron turned and spotted me. I didn't like the way his eyes lit up when he recognized me.

'Georgie Johansen.' He headed my way.

I shifted to the right so a table displaying bottles of hand cream stood between us.

'No comment,' I said, wondering if I could flee from the store without him following me. Probably not.

'Come on,' Byron pressed. 'You were first on the scene. Give me a few lines to run with.'

'No comment,' I repeated.

'Of course,' he said, as if I hadn't spoken, 'the person to find the body is often a suspect.' He scrutinized my face. 'What was your history with the victim?'

'Suspect? Victim?' I echoed. 'So Dorothy's death really was suspicious?'

He gave me a disapproving frown. 'Clearly you didn't read the online version of the *Gazette* this morning.'

Marlene came over to join us and crossed her arms again, letting out a heavy sigh. 'Some people have better things to do, Byron.'

'There's nothing better than staying on top of current events,' he countered. Then he returned his attention to me and smiled with glee. 'The police released a statement first thing this morning. It's now official. Dorothy was murdered.'

EIGHT

I mumbled something about needing to leave and then dashed out of the store. I ran up the street and ducked into the stationery shop before Byron emerged from Siren Beauty. Afraid that he might track me down, I didn't want to linger. When I couldn't make an immediate decision between the various sympathy cards on offer, I grabbed two and quickly paid for them at the front counter.

I peeked out the door of Cursive before stepping out onto the sidewalk. The coast appeared to be clear, with no sign of Byron. I made a beeline for my car and made a quick getaway from the town center.

When I parked my car next to the farmhouse, I stayed in the driver's seat while I looked up the *Twilight Cove Gazette* on my phone. Sure enough, the top story announced that the police had in fact declared that Dorothy Shale had been murdered. The postmortem must have confirmed Chief Stratton's suspicions about Dorothy's death.

I tried to picture Dorothy's bruises. They were located near her collarbone, not around her throat, and I didn't recall any marks on her neck. So, she probably hadn't been strangled. The online article didn't reveal how Dorothy had been killed. Maybe the police were keeping that to themselves. Perhaps the bruises had been caused by some sort of struggle. I tried again to picture the purplish marks. Dorothy could have sustained them when somebody held her up against a wall, or down on her bed.

I shuddered at the thought. I didn't want to imagine her being killed.

I registered a flicker of movement out of the corner of my eye a split second before someone tapped on the driver's side window. I nearly jumped out of my skin.

Relief eased the tension in my shoulders when I saw that it was Callum standing outside the car, although my heart took longer to settle down. He stepped back as I opened the door and climbed out of the vehicle.

'I saw you sitting there and wanted to make sure everything was OK,' he said, his green eyes studying me.

Tears flooded my eyes and a couple of them spilled over onto my cheeks. I wiped them away quickly, embarrassed. 'I'm fine.'

Thoughts of Flossie and Fancy had brought on the tears, but I wished I'd been able to hold them at bay while Callum was around.

A small crease appeared between his eyebrows. Clearly, he didn't buy my claim of being fine.

'If there's anything I can do . . .' He let the offer hang.

Part of me wanted to push him away, but another part of me also wanted someone to talk with.

'I was thinking about the dogs,' I said before I had a chance to think better of sharing my thoughts with him. 'The police have officially declared Dorothy's death a murder.'

Shock registered on Callum's face, quickly followed by understanding. 'You think the dogs might have witnessed the crime?'

'I hope not,' I said. 'It's bad enough that they lost her.'

'They may have found her after it happened,' Callum said, his voice kind. 'Like I said before, they were here on the farm that morning.'

I nodded, hoping that was what had happened. At the same time, they were smart dogs. If they'd been present during the murder, maybe they could identify the killer. I couldn't imagine them standing by while someone harmed Dorothy in front of them. Perhaps they tried to stop the killer, leaving bite marks as incriminating evidence. I hoped Chief Stratton and his officers had considered that possibility.

'I should check in on Aunt Olivia,' I said, averting my gaze from Callum's. My embarrassment about shedding tears in front of him still burned inside my chest. 'I'll help you with the chores later today.'

I hurried to the carriage house, not looking back. I hoped Callum didn't think I was rude, or overly emotional. His opinion of me shouldn't matter, especially since we'd be out of each other's lives in a few short weeks, but I hated crying in front of anyone.

I made sure I had control of my emotions before I entered the carriage house. While I was gone, Aunt Olivia had read the online version of the *Twilight Cove Gazette* and already knew that Dorothy had been murdered. I filled her in on the conversation I'd overheard between Byron and Marlene.

She rolled her eyes when I mentioned the purported curse. 'I heard about that. It happened about a month ago. Dorothy did pretend to put a curse on Marlene and her shop, but only after Marlene drove her up the wall squawking at her about stealing customers.'

'Marlene seems to think the curse is real,' I said.

'Marlene will believe whatever creates the most drama.'

After spending a few minutes in Marlene's shop with her, I didn't have much trouble believing that.

I left the sympathy cards with my aunt and returned to the farm- house with Flossie and Fancy on my heels, intending to work on my script. I managed to add about half a page before I got up from the kitchen table and paced around. After two more attempts to get myself to sit in front of my computer and get some work done, I gave up. My thoughts kept returning to Dorothy and her murder, making it impossible for me to concentrate on the plot of my latest thriller.

Closing the screenwriting program, I answered a couple of emails and then shut my laptop and wandered out onto the back porch. The dogs trotted down to lie on the grass while I sat on the steps. My gaze traveled across the farmyard to the woods in the distance. Cutting through the trees to take a walk on the beach might help clear my mind and allow me to focus on writing, but Dorothy's murder had left me spooked. What if her killer was still wandering through the woods? Maybe that wasn't likely, but I couldn't rule out the possibility.

I was thinking about going back inside to pour myself a glass of lemonade when I noticed Callum walking past the barn, heading in my direction. He carried what looked like a plate in one hand.

The dogs bounced up from the grass and ran to meet Callum. He gave them each a pat on the head and continued toward me, the dogs trotting along happily on either side of him.

As he drew closer, I moved to stand up, but he waved me back down.

'Don't get up,' he said. 'Do you mind if I join you?'

'Of course not.' I managed not to show my surprise at the fact that he wanted to sit with me. Aside from when I'd returned from town earlier, he'd spoken to me as little as possible.

He settled next to me on the steps and removed his cowboy hat. He smelled faintly of hay and chocolate. Or maybe it was the brownies on the plate that were giving off the heavenly scent of chocolate.

'I baked these this morning and wanted to share.' He handed me the plate.

'You bake?' I asked with surprise.

He laughed, and the low rumble sent a pleasant tingling sensation through me. I tried not to think about how close we were sitting, with only a couple of inches between our arms, but it was hard when he took up so much space. Not just physical space. His presence seemed to permeate the air around me in a way I wasn't used to. My cheeks warmed up, and I hoped they weren't too flushed.

His amusement lit up his green eyes. 'My skills do extend beyond farm work.'

My cheeks still warm, I focused on the plate now resting on my lap. 'These look delicious.' My mouth watered at the sight of the chocolate-glazed brownies. 'What's the occasion?'

Callum ran a hand through his wavy golden hair. 'I guess you could say it's a peace offering. I haven't been very friendly since you arrived, and I'm sorry about that.'

'Did I do something to put you on edge?' I asked.

'Not at all. Having someone new around just made me . . . cautious.'

'I guess I can understand that.' I could be that way around new people sometimes too.

'You didn't deserve it, though. I hope I can make it up to you.'

I nodded at the brownies. 'I think you already have.'

He laughed again and I wondered if I should worry about how my stomach warmed at the sound.

'You probably shouldn't say that until you've tasted them,' he advised.

'Do your baked goods usually look better than they taste?' I asked, eyeing the brownies.

'Generally, it's the other way around, to be honest, but a taste test is always wise.'

'Sometimes two or three,' I said.

He grinned. 'That's my philosophy too.'

I picked up one of the brownies and bit into it. I closed my eyes as the fudgy deliciousness hit my tongue.

'Wow,' I said after the first bite.

'Good?' he asked.

Instead of answering, I devoured the rest of the brownie in one big but well-savored bite.

'Amazing,' I finally managed to say. 'I think that might be the best brownie I've ever tasted. You didn't really have anything to be sorry about, but I'll take the apology anyway.'

Smiling, he leaned back and rested his elbows on the step behind us.

I offered him the plate. 'Are you going to have one?'

'I'm good,' he assured me. 'Trust me, I've already indulged.'

'Quality control?' I said with a smile.

'Wouldn't want to share before I know they're safe for consumption,' he agreed. The happy light in his green eyes dimmed and his entire demeanor became more serious. 'Are you doing better?'

'I am, thanks.' I realized that was the truth. Enjoying the past few minutes with him had taken my mind off Dorothy, if only for a short time, and my head felt clearer for it. I decided to make an attempt to get to know the man beside me better. 'Aunt Olivia mentioned that you're from Colorado.'

He sat up straighter, no longer quite so relaxed. 'That's right. What else did she say about me?'

'Only that you're working here temporarily.'

He nodded, his gaze fixed on something off in the distance. 'She told me you're a screenwriter.'

'She's been talking about me?' I hoped my aunt hadn't bored him with stories about me.

The tension eased out of him. 'She's only had good things to say. She's proud of you and your career.'

'I'm no Oscar winner, but I love what I do.'

'That's the most important thing.' After a brief pause, he tugged his phone out of his pocket. 'Before I forget, we should exchange numbers.'

'Good idea.' I had to warn my heart not to get too happy as I pulled out my own phone. He wanted my number so we could keep each other up to date on farm business, not for any more personal reason.

We'd just finished exchanging numbers when I heard a vehicle turn into the driveway. Seconds later a police SUV pulled up next to my car and stopped. Flossie and Fancy jumped to their feet as Chief Stratton climbed out of the driver's seat.

Callum and I stood up at the same time. I set the plate of brownies on the small table near the porch swing and descended the steps to greet the police chief. The dogs had already beat me to it.

'Do you have a few minutes, Georgie?' Chief Stratton asked after he'd said hello to all of us, including the spaniels.

'Sure.'

'I'll be in the barn if you need me, Georgie.' Callum eyed Stratton and then me as he turned to go, as if he wasn't entirely sure if he should leave me alone with the police chief.

'I heard that Dorothy's death has been declared a murder,' I said as Callum strode away from us.

'Dorothy is why I'm here.'

I glanced at the spaniels where they had once again settled down on the grass. A sinking sensation unsettled my stomach. 'Has somebody claimed the dogs?'

'No, but that's something I want to talk to Olivia about.'

'Should we go over to the carriage house?' I asked.

'In a minute. I have a few questions for you first.'

Something about the way he said that added to my apprehension.

'I'll do my best to answer them,' I said.

'How much time did you spend with Dorothy after you arrived here in Twilight Cove?'

'In total?' I considered the question for a second or two. 'Maybe half an hour.'

'But you met with her on multiple occasions?'

'Twice. The first time we exchanged a few words when we ran into each other in the woods. The second time I had tea with her at her cabin.'

'And what did you talk about?' Stratton asked.

I didn't see why that mattered, but I answered anyway. 'The dogs. My aunt. Then Dorothy's argument with Ed Grimshaw. She mentioned that he'd been bothering her for several months.'

'Did you talk about Dorothy's land?'

I wondered where he was going with his questions. 'Only in relation to Ed Grimshaw and the fact that he wants it. Do you think the land has something to do with Dorothy's murder?'

Instead of answering my question, Stratton asked another of his own. 'You didn't speak to her about her will or what she wanted to happen with her land after her death?'

'No, of course not.'

Chief Stratton removed his hat and ran his hand over his graying hair. 'If that plot of land were to come up for sale, would you or Olivia consider purchasing it?'

'I wouldn't. I can't speak for my aunt.'

'She'll have the chance to do that for herself.'

Anxiety and dread weighed heavily in the middle of my chest. I had a terrible feeling I knew why he had so many questions for us.

Somehow, I managed to ask another question without my voice shaking. 'Do we need a lawyer?'

The police chief replaced his hat on his head and levelled his gaze at me. 'That's entirely up to you.'

NINE

'I'd better speak to Olivia now,' Stratton said.

He strode toward the carriage house.

I gave myself a mental shake and hurried after him. 'Aunt Olivia doesn't know anything about Dorothy's murder.'

'I still have questions I need to ask her.' He rapped on the front door.

'I'm around back!' Aunt Olivia called out.

We circled around to the rear of the carriage house. My aunt sat in a cushioned wicker chair on the patio, her injured ankle elevated on a footrest. She closed the book she held and took off her reading glasses as we came around the corner.

'Isaac,' she greeted the police chief. 'It's good to see you again, although perhaps the circumstances aren't what we would hope.'

'I'm afraid that's the case.' Stratton removed his hat and kept it off this time. 'I have a few questions for you about Dorothy Shale.'

'I hope I can help you,' Aunt Olivia said.

Stratton looked my way. 'Georgie, would you mind giving us a few minutes?'

'Auntie O, do you want me to stay? Should I call a lawyer?' I didn't know any lawyers around these parts, but I figured I could probably look one up online.

My aunt laughed. 'There's no need for that, Georgie. I'll be fine. You go ahead and get on with your day.'

I didn't want to leave her alone with the police chief, but I didn't see that I had much choice. Stratton's questions had left me worried for myself, but even more so for my aunt. Olivia probably thought he was simply going to ask her if she'd seen or heard anything unusual around the time of the murder. I was willing to bet he was going to ask her far more than that.

As I walked away, I tried to reassure myself. Aunt Olivia had nothing to do with Dorothy's murder. If Stratton didn't know that already, he soon would. I had no reason to worry.

My mind didn't seem to want to listen to those words.

I returned to the porch and stress-ate two more brownies while

I waited for Chief Stratton to reappear from behind the carriage house. When he did, he came over my way again, so I met him halfway. I wanted to ask him what questions he'd put to my aunt, but he didn't give me a chance.

'We found a copy of Dorothy's will in her cabin,' he informed me. 'As I just told Olivia, Dorothy wanted her dogs to go into your aunt's care. Whether Olivia wants to adopt them or find them a good home is up to her. We're keeping everything from the cabin as evidence for the time being, so I'm afraid we can't release the dog food or beds yet.'

'I already bought them some things in town,' I said. 'We'll get them whatever they need.'

Stratton nodded and set his hat on his head before climbing into his SUV without another word. I stood there and watched as he turned the vehicle around and drove off down the road. Then I grabbed the plate of brownies and jogged over to the carriage house. Flossie and Fancy woke up from their naps to bound along at my side.

I found Auntie O sitting in the same chair as before. She'd set her book and reading glasses on the patio table and now stared off into the distance, her face somber and thoughtful.

'What was that all about?' I dropped into a free wicker chair, not sure if I really wanted to hear the answer.

Aunt Olivia reeled in her gaze and focused on me. 'I'm afraid you and I might be murder suspects.'

That was exactly what I'd feared. 'But that's crazy!'

The dogs pressed their noses against my legs and looked up at me, as if worried about my agitated voice. I stroked their fur to reassure them.

'I wouldn't worry about it too much,' Aunt Olivia said. 'At this point, we're probably two suspects among many. Isaac is just doing his job.'

I still couldn't believe he suspected my aunt to any degree. 'How could he think there's even the slightest chance that you had anything to do with Dorothy's murder? You have a broken ankle and it's not like you want to build oceanfront condos.'

'I don't want to build condos,' Olivia agreed, 'but word gets around this town, and Isaac knows that I offered to buy the land from Dorothy in the past.'

'You did?' That was news to me, but it wasn't as if my aunt and

I had kept up-to-date on every detail of each other's lives over the years.

'Not all of it,' she said. 'But I was hoping to get a tract of land that led from the farm to the ocean. That way I could have made sure that at least part of the woodland would be preserved, and I would have had access to the water. Dorothy never minded me walking through the woods, and I knew she'd never let anyone develop the land in her lifetime, but I was concerned about the future.'

'Because someone like Ed Grimshaw could end up with the land?' I guessed.

'Sadly, yes.'

'So Chief Stratton thinks that you hobbled over there on your broken ankle and killed Dorothy because you were angry that she didn't sell you any of her land?' That theory struck me as preposterous.

'That would be a stretch, not just because of my ankle but because I made the offer several years ago. Dorothy turned me down and told me that I didn't need to worry about the future of the woodland. I never brought up the subject again, and we've always been on friendly terms, before and since that conversation.'

'Did she tell you why there was no need to worry about the woodland?' I asked.

'No, and I didn't ask,' Aunt Olivia replied. 'I don't think she would have told me even if I had asked. She tended to keep her cards close to her chest in all matters. That was my experience, anyway.'

'I still think it's ridiculous to suspect you.'

'I'm glad that's how you feel,' she said with a brief smile. 'I figure Isaac knows how unlikely it would be for me to get over to Dorothy's cabin on my own, but he asked me questions about you. About how far you would go to make me happy.'

That stirred up the feeling of unease in my stomach again. 'He thinks I killed Dorothy for your sake?' Frustration brewed inside of me, but I tried to tamp it down. 'OK, so he doesn't know me, but I still don't get how that would help you. Whoever inherits from Dorothy might not be interested in selling the land to you. Even if it did go up for sale, Ed Grimshaw could probably make a higher offer.'

'That's true,' Aunt Olivia said, but her face had grown somber again. 'The problem is that I wouldn't have to make an offer.'

'What do you mean?'

Olivia reached a hand out to Flossie and the spaniel moved closer so my aunt could pet her. 'Apparently, I inherit the land under Dorothy's will.'

That revelation left me speechless.

'I was as surprised as you are,' Aunt Olivia said. 'I considered Dorothy a friend, but we weren't as close as I am with many of my other friends. I can understand leaving the dogs in my care since I run the sanctuary. Did Isaac tell you about that?'

'Yes.' I ran a hand along Fancy's back. 'I'm relieved.' I smiled at the dogs, though not without a hint of sadness. 'Did you girls hear that? You get to stay here on the farm.'

The dogs wagged their tails as if they understood and approved.

'At least, for now.' I looked to my aunt. 'You'll keep them, right?'

'Of course. It'll be nice to have dogs around again.'

My aunt loved dogs, but hadn't had one on the farm since her golden retriever, Amelia, had passed away two years ago.

'Isaac told me there was a note included in Dorothy's will saying that she left the land to me because she knew I would take good care of it.' Tears appeared in Olivia's eyes. 'I won't let her down. I intend to make sure that it never gets developed.'

My mind whirred as I tried to make sense of everything. 'As a beneficiary, wouldn't you have been invited to the reading of the will?'

'There hasn't been one yet,' my aunt said. 'Dorothy's lawyer is out of town, but the police found a copy of her will in her cabin.'

'Right. Chief Stratton mentioned that. So they think I somehow knew about that bequest and killed Dorothy so you could inherit the land?' That still sounded crazy to me.

'I guess that's the theory, but I'm sure Isaac knows it's a flimsy one. They have to look into every possibility. It doesn't mean we're in any real trouble.'

I hoped my aunt was right, but being a suspect in a murder investigation – even if I sat at the bottom of the suspect list – wasn't pleasant.

Aunt Olivia ate one of Callum's brownies and tried again to convince me not to worry, but when I left the patio a while later, anxiety still hummed through me.

I took the remaining two brownies into the farmhouse kitchen and changed into jeans and my work boots before heading back outside.

On my way to the barn, I passed a large shed which housed the lawn tractor and other gardening equipment. I noticed some shingles missing from the roof and wondered if there was a problem that needed fixing.

I walked around to the far side of the shed and found a wooden ladder lying on its side, resting against the exterior wall. I hauled it up off the ground and leaned it against the edge of the roof. The ladder looked old but seemed sturdy enough.

I took a cautious step onto the first rung. It held, and the ladder stayed steady, so I climbed two more rungs.

Out of nowhere, a dark shape flew at my head. I ducked, hanging on for dear life. Euclid swooped past me, so close I could feel the whoosh of air on my face. I lost my footing, but managed to land on the next rung down. With my heart pounding, I scrambled the rest of the way to the ground.

Euclid perched on the peak of the roof, staring down at me with his yellow eyes.

'What was that about, Euclid?' I asked, pressing a hand to my chest over my thumping heart. 'You almost knocked me right off the ladder!'

'Georgie?' Callum's voice came from off in the distance.

With a last uneasy glance at Euclid, I rounded the shed.

Callum waved to me from near the barn. 'Could you give me a hand with the goats?'

I joined him in a pen which currently held four adorable pygmy goats.

'I want to check them over and make sure they're all doing well,' Callum said.

I picked up the goats, one at a time, and held them while Callum checked their eyes, ears and feet. He used a hoof pick to remove any pebbles from their feet, and a brush to clean off the dirt. When I set down the last of the goats, it galloped off to frolic with its friends.

Callum thanked me for my help and set off to check on the sanctuary's two pigs while I headed into the barn to get started on mucking out stalls. I realized I hadn't mentioned the shed roof to Callum. I decided to go back and take a quick look at it.

Before climbing the ladder, I glanced around for Euclid. The owl didn't appear to be anywhere nearby. I still couldn't believe that he'd nearly sent me falling. I hadn't expected him to act in an aggressive manner. Of course, he was a wild animal. And I wasn't Dorothy.

I climbed up to the fourth rung without any interruptions from owls or anyone else. One more step up and I'd be able to see the roof.

Before I had a chance to raise my foot, the rung I stood on gave way with a crack.

Then I fell.

TEN

I hit the ground before I had a chance to truly register what was happening. I lay on my back in the grass, staring at the blue sky above me, struggling to breathe.

Loud barking sounded from nearby, soon joined by running footsteps.

'Georgie!' Callum knelt by my side. 'Are you OK?'

Flossie and Fancy appeared on my other side. They nuzzled my face with their wet noses and licked my cheek.

Pain reverberated through my body, but it wasn't too bad. The impact had knocked the air out of my lungs, but I was breathing steadily again now.

'I'm all right,' I said.

I sat up and Callum put a hand to my shoulder.

'Maybe you shouldn't move yet,' he cautioned.

'No, I'm OK. Really,' I assured him.

The dogs whined so I ran my hands over their coats.

'No broken bones,' I said. 'Just a few bruises, probably.'

Callum offered me a hand and helped me to my feet.

'What happened?' I asked, rubbing my forehead. I hadn't hit my head, but the surprise of falling had left my thoughts scattered.

Callum examined the ladder. All that remained of the fourth rung was a few splintered bits of wood.

'Looks like the rung was rotten,' he said. 'This ladder is pretty old.'

We both glanced up as Euclid glided in to land on the peak of the shed roof.

'Incredible,' Callum said with a note of awe in his voice.

Euclid ruffled his feathers and took off into the air. He soared toward the forest and out of sight.

'I've seen owls around here before, but never that close,' Callum said.

'He was friends with Dorothy.' I rubbed at an ache in my left arm. 'He'd even sit on her shoulder.'

'I didn't know Dorothy,' Callum said, 'but it sounds like she had a special connection with animals.'

'It certainly seemed like it.' I dropped my hand when I realized Callum was watching me rub my arm.

'Are you sure you're OK?' he asked.

'Positive. A few aches, but nothing to worry about.'

He looked up at the broken rung. 'Why were you climbing the ladder?'

'I was worried about the roof and wanted to see if there was a problem.'

'I had a look at it last week,' Callum said. 'I'm going to pick up some supplies tomorrow and I'll get it fixed over the next couple of days.'

Of course he already knew about the problem. I should have asked him before trying to climb up there. Though, it wouldn't have been a dangerous task if the ladder had been in good condition. Looking it over more carefully would have been wise.

And I should have paid more attention to Euclid.

Maybe it was crazy, but now I was certain that the owl had tried to warn me about climbing the ladder. I didn't mention that to Callum. He'd probably think I was nuts, and I wouldn't be able to blame him.

I shook off the incident and managed to clean out the stalls without too much interference from my minor aches and pains. I spent a couple of hours on my script in the evening, but it wasn't my best work and I knew I'd have to fix it up later. My mind didn't want to stay focused on the story. My thoughts kept drifting back to the fact that Aunt Olivia and I had a cloud of suspicion hovering over us. It bothered me deeply that anyone could suspect me of murder. The fact that Auntie O had ended up on the suspect list upset me even more.

After my aunt retired from her teaching job in her fifties, she'd used the healthy sum of money she and her late husband had accumulated through savvy investments to turn her hobby farm into an animal sanctuary. She'd devoted her life to rescuing and caring for donkeys, alpacas, horses, chickens, and many other creatures. She had a heart of gold. Chief Stratton ought to know that, since he and Aunt Olivia seemed to be well acquainted. I understood that he had to investigate all avenues, but focusing on me and my aunt was a waste of time.

Not that he had focused solely on the two of us. He had to be looking at Ed Grimshaw too. Then there was Marlene Hooper. I wondered if the police knew about her dispute with Dorothy. I recalled Byron saying that it had been documented in the *Twilight Cove Gazette*. In that case, the police must know about it.

The words on the screen in front of me blurred together and a dull thudding in my head joined the other aches in my body. My fall from the ladder had left me with sore muscles and several bruises. A hot shower and some ibuprofen had helped, but hadn't erased the pain completely.

I gave up on getting any more writing done and headed for bed. In my room, I found the amethyst Dorothy had given me sitting on the bedside table. I picked it up and ran my thumb over the smooth surface.

Flossie and Fancy jumped up on the bed and got comfortable. Once they were lying down, they watched me with their brown eyes, and I thought I detected a hint of sadness in their gazes.

My heart aching for them, I gave each dog a pat and a kiss on the head. 'I know you're sad about Dorothy, but you're going to have a good home here with my aunt Olivia. She'll make sure you're always well looked after.'

The dogs rewarded me with kisses and thumps of their tails. Their affection and resilience lifted my spirits.

I set the amethyst back on the bedside table, realizing only then that my headache had disappeared. My other aches didn't feel quite so bad either now. I stared at the purple stone, wondering if it could somehow have eased my pain. Dorothy certainly seemed to believe that it would help with my headaches, but was that really possible?

Some people in town called Dorothy a witch, but surely she was just an eccentric woman who believed in natural remedies and things some might describe as 'out there'.

Pushing those thoughts aside, I crossed to the window to close the curtains. That was when I saw a shadowy form move outside, not far from the barn. I flicked off the lamp so I could see out of the window better.

The moon shone brightly from a clear, star-studded sky, allowing me to identify the shadowy figure as Callum. Until that moment, I'd forgotten about seeing him out after dark on my second night in Twilight Cove.

Just as he'd done the time before, he headed for the woods at the southern edge of the farm and disappeared among the trees. He had something in his left hand, but I wasn't sure what.

Why the heck would he be going into the woods after dark?

I recalled the blue glow I'd seen the other night. I still had no idea what the source of it could have been, but I couldn't see it out there tonight.

I shook my head and closed the curtains.

Being a suspect in a murder investigation gave me enough to worry about. I didn't need to have any other mysteries weighing on my mind.

Even so, as I waited to drift off to sleep, I found myself wondering once again why Callum would make a habit of venturing into the woods at night.

When I saw Callum the next morning, I didn't ask him about his nighttime activities. He'd been cautious enough around me when we first met without me pestering him with questions. If I interrogated him now, he'd probably distance himself from me again, and I'd be left with no more information than I had now. Besides, I'd enjoyed the brief time we'd spent together on the porch steps the day before, and I didn't want to jeopardize the chance to have more of those moments.

Completing the morning chores took me a little longer than usual, thanks to my sore muscles, but I tried not to let on that I was in any pain. I didn't want Callum thinking I couldn't keep up with the jobs he'd given me.

When I finally finished all the tasks on my list, I returned to the farmhouse and took a hot shower, despite the warmth of the sun. My muscles practically sighed with relief when the water hit my skin.

Feeling revived, I dressed in shorts and a T-shirt. For good measure, I dropped the amethyst in my pocket, just in case it could help to further ease the aches in my muscles. After grabbing my keys and sunglasses, I headed into town, leaving the dogs snoozing at my aunt's feet on the carriage house patio.

I'd told Aunt Olivia that I'd drop off her sympathy card at Victor's mansion and then pick up some groceries for her. She would be hosting her Gins and Needles group at the carriage house the next evening and she wanted to start preparing some of the food today.

As I drove through Twilight Cove and headed up the hill toward Victor Clyde's mansion, I rolled down the window so I could breathe in the fresh, salty sea air. I wanted to spend more time at the beach and get reacquainted with the town. I also wanted to visit with Tessa again.

When I first agreed to come to Twilight Cove to help Aunt Olivia, two months seemed like a long time to be away from Los Angeles. Now, I wondered if I'd be able to fit in all the things I wanted to do while I was here. I also found that returning to Los Angeles wasn't something I was particularly eager to do. I'd been here for only a few days so far and already the seaside town was working its way into my heart. Or maybe it had never left my heart.

I didn't have anything against California, and living there made meetings and networking convenient for my screenwriting career, but I often found myself longing for quieter surroundings and a more relaxed pace of life. Even though I'd spent more years living in cities than in the country, I suspected I wasn't a true city girl at heart, and something about Twilight Cove tugged at my soul.

When I reached the black iron gates at the head of Victor Clyde's long driveway, I slowed my car to take in the sight of a small memorial set up by the fence. A few bouquets of flowers leaned up against a simple wooden cross. The nice gesture surprised me, although perhaps it shouldn't have. Aunt Olivia had told me more than once how the people of Twilight Cove were, for the most part, a good bunch with kind hearts.

I continued on through the open gates, thinking that there were definitely some exceptions to that rule. Dorothy's killer, for one. And I wasn't impressed by Marlene Hooper. She didn't seem the least bit sorry that someone had murdered Dorothy. Maybe because that someone was Marlene herself.

I didn't have a good impression of Byron Szabo, either. The only aspect of the murder that seemed to matter to him was the fact that it could give him a juicy story. Would he have killed Dorothy just to have something newsworthy and sensational to write about?

That seemed like quite a leap. I was grasping at straws, hoping that the police would have far stronger suspects than me and Olivia.

When I reached the mansion, I slipped the card into the black metal mailbox next to the door. I decided not to ring the bell. Avery probably had enough to deal with without visitors dropping by. Maybe Tessa and I could check in on her in a few days. At the moment, she was probably overwhelmed with all the things she'd have to take care of in the wake of her stepfather's death.

I was about to climb back into my car when movement overhead caught my attention. Shading my eyes against the sun, I looked up to see Euclid circling overhead. Maybe it could have been another great horned owl, but I didn't think so.

The owl circled lower and then swooped down to land on the roof of my car.

'Hi, Euclid,' I said quietly. 'What are you doing all the way over here?'

That was probably a stupid question. The owl likely covered a large territory. Then again, it was the middle of the day and he was a nocturnal animal.

Euclid blinked his yellow eyes at me and then took off. He circled around overhead again and then soared off in the direction of the center of town and the ocean beyond.

I climbed into my car and quickly buckled up so I could get on my way. It crossed my mind that I could be losing it, because I felt in my bones that Euclid wanted me to follow him. Crazy or not, though, I'd learned from the incident with the ladder that I should pay attention to any signals that the owl might be trying to send me.

Even though I couldn't explain – even to myself – my unusual connection to Euclid and the springer spaniels, I knew I couldn't be mistaken about the owl wanting me to follow him when I glanced out the side window and saw him flying low, at a pace that kept him just ahead of my car. He led me toward the center of town and then off onto a side street. There, he came to rest on the top of a lamppost, so I found a nearby parking spot and got out of my car.

Euclid took off from his perch, dipping down in front of a two-story brick building. Then he winged his way up into the sky and out of sight.

I walked closer to the brick building. The lettering on the window identified it as a lawyer's office. I barely had time to wonder why Euclid would draw my attention to that particular building when I spotted someone familiar through the window.

Ed Grimshaw was inside, and from his wild gestures I gathered that he wasn't having a friendly conversation. My first thought was that it wasn't any of my business what Ed Grimshaw was doing in the office, or what he was saying. But when I took a closer look through the window, I saw a young woman seated behind a desk, cowering in the face of Grimshaw's apparent fury. It didn't appear as though anyone else was in the office. That made up my mind. Whatever was going on inside, I didn't like the thought of Ed Grimshaw bullying the young woman.

Opening the door, I stepped into the reception area.

ELEVEN

'Like I've already said, I can't give you that information,' the young woman at the desk said to Ed Grimshaw. She managed to keep her voice steady, even though she looked as though she wished she could disappear under her desk.

The real estate developer's face was flushed red with anger. 'I can't put my plans on hold simply because you don't want to answer my questions,' he fumed. 'I need to know who inherits Dorothy Shale's land.'

'I don't have that information,' the receptionist said. 'And even if I did, I wouldn't be at liberty to share it with you.'

Grimshaw planted his large hands on the desk and leaned in closer to the young woman. 'Maybe you'd better think twice about that.'

'Is there a problem here?' I asked, stepping farther into the office.

Grimshaw whirled around and narrowed his beady eyes at me. 'This is private business. It doesn't concern you, whoever you are.'

Clearly, he didn't recognize me from when we'd met in the woods. That didn't surprise me. To him, I was probably as insignificant as an ant.

The receptionist pushed back her chair and stood up. 'Actually, this woman has an appointment.'

I managed to hide my surprise.

Grimshaw glared at her and then returned his angry gaze to me. Over his shoulder, I saw the receptionist shoot me a pleading look.

'Right,' I said, catching on. 'Sorry I'm late.'

The receptionist sent me a grateful smile. 'Not a problem.'

Ed turned back to her. 'You told me that Greenaway wasn't in.'

'He's not.' The receptionist seemed more confident now. 'But he asked me to go over a few things with . . .'

'Georgie Johansen,' I intervened quickly, realizing she didn't know my name. I offered my hand to Grimshaw.

He looked at it like it was a smelly piece of garbage. I dropped my hand back to my side, relieved. I didn't actually want him to shake it.

He addressed the receptionist again. 'Tell Greenaway I want to talk to him as soon as he's back in town. I've got deals to make. The man's a lawyer. He should be here working, not off on some vacation.'

Grimshaw pushed his way past me, almost knocking me off balance as he jostled my shoulder. He shoved the door open and stormed his way out of the office. Then he climbed into a silver car parked at the curb and slammed the door. The engine revved a few seconds later and he zoomed off with a squeal of tires.

The receptionist sagged down into her chair and let out a breath.

'Thank you so much for coming to my rescue,' she said. 'Is there something I can help you with?'

'No, I just came in when I saw Grimshaw bullying you. What an awful man.'

'He's a real piece of work.' The receptionist straightened her shirt and then fluffed her chestnut brown hair up off the back of her neck. 'I'm Cassidy, by the way. Cassidy Moore.'

'Georgie Johansen,' I repeated.

'Thanks for playing along with my fib about you having an appointment. I didn't know how else to get rid of the guy.'

'No problem at all,' I assured her. 'He really wants Dorothy's land, doesn't he?'

'Desperately. He knows he could make a killing by building oceanfront condos there.' She grimaced. 'Maybe not the best choice of words.' Her eyes widened and her face paled. 'Wait. I heard Dorothy was murdered. Maybe Ed Grimshaw . . .'

'Killed her?' I finished for her. When she nodded, I added, 'That thought crossed my mind too.'

She swallowed hard. 'And I was in here alone with him until you showed up. Maybe I should keep the door locked, just until Mr Greenaway comes back.'

The door in question opened and Avery Hembridge walked into the office, wearing the same white leather jacket as the day before, but this time over a black jumpsuit. She also wore sunglasses.

Cassidy jumped to her feet. 'Mrs Hembridge, how can I help you?'

'I should go,' I said quickly.

Avery removed her sunglasses. 'Georgie, isn't it? Please, don't feel the need to leave on my account.'

'I only stepped in for a moment anyway,' I assured her. 'I'm so sorry about your stepfather.'

She blinked back tears and offered me a sad but grateful smile. 'Thank you.'

I sent a quick smile Cassidy's way and then ducked out of the office.

I stood on the sidewalk, thinking about Ed Grimshaw. It was all too easy to picture him losing his temper with Dorothy to the point of killing her. Those big hands of his would have easily fit around her neck. I shuddered at the thought.

Except, judging by the location of Dorothy's bruises, I didn't think she'd been strangled.

Nevertheless, if Ed Grimshaw had killed Dorothy, he wasn't doing a very good job of hiding the fact that he had a motive for committing the crime. Hopefully the police would arrest him and put him behind bars in short order. If he really was the killer.

Despite the unpleasant thoughts in my head, my stomach gave a low grumble. Working on the farm had certainly increased my appetite. Summer was doing its best to take over from spring, so I slipped on my sunglasses and decided to enjoy the warm weather as I walked down the hill to the food trucks parked along Ocean Drive. This time I decided to try Shanifa's Lebanese Cuisine. I ordered falafel, stuffed grape leaves, and tabouli salad, planning to share everything with Aunt Olivia when I returned to the farm.

The middle-aged woman working in the truck had dark hair pulled back in a ponytail and toned arms that suggested that she either worked out or engaged in some sort of athletic activity on a regular basis. She introduced herself as Shanifa and started preparing my order as soon as I'd paid for it.

'Are you here on holiday?' she asked as she packed up my food.

A stocky man moved about behind her, his back to me as he worked.

'I'm here helping out my aunt for a few weeks,' I replied. 'She runs an animal sanctuary, but she broke her ankle, so she's not able to keep up with the work.'

'You must mean Olivia van Oosten.'

'That's right,' I confirmed. 'Do you know her?'

'Not well, but I haven't lived here long. She stops by the truck from time to time, and she's always friendly. I know about the sanctuary and I've been past the farm. That Victorian house is beautiful.'

'It's gorgeous,' I agreed. 'I love it there.'

The man joined Shanifa at the serving window. 'It won't be so nice if Ed Grimshaw gets his hands on the witch's land.'

'Mo!' Shanifa admonished. 'Don't call her a witch. Have some respect for the dead.'

The man appeared unrepentant. 'Did you know the old woman?' he asked me.

'Dorothy? I met her a couple of times.'

'Any idea who killed her?'

'Mo!' Shanifa exclaimed again. 'You'll ruin her appetite.'

'No danger of that with all the farm work I've been doing,' I said with a smile, hoping to defuse the growing tension between them.

Shanifa handed me my food and I thanked her. As I walked away, Shanifa lowered her voice and scolded Mo again, but not quietly enough to keep me from overhearing.

'You shouldn't speak ill of the dead!' she said.

'Please,' Mo scoffed. 'Don't pretend you liked her. The woman tried to shoot you!'

I almost stopped in my tracks when I heard that, but I managed to keep going. Unfortunately, that meant I couldn't hear anything else they had to say.

Dorothy had tried to shoot Shanifa? I hadn't noticed a firearm in Dorothy's cabin and I had trouble picturing her shooting anyone or anything. She seemed like such a calm and peaceful woman. I hardly knew her, though, and the gun could have been stored under Dorothy's bed or elsewhere out of sight. Maybe Aunt Olivia could shed some light on that story.

I headed back toward my car, the rumbling of my stomach growing louder as I inhaled the delicious aromas from the packages in my arms. As I turned off Main Street, Avery came out of the lawyer's office.

'Hello, again,' she said with a faint smile as she slipped her sunglasses on.

I thought I caught a glimpse of tears in her eyes before she shaded them.

'How are you holding up?' I asked her.

She let out a heavy sigh. 'I'm doing all right. It's just . . . There are so many arrangements to be made and now I've had a bit of a setback.'

'How so?'

'My stepfather's lawyer, Simon Greenaway, went away for the weekend and hasn't returned. Cassidy, his receptionist, doesn't have the authority to give me his will. I know there's a copy of it in my stepfather's safe, but I don't know the combination. The lawyer has that too, but again, Cassidy can't give it to me without permission from her boss.'

'When will Mr Greenaway be back?' I asked.

'That's the question. He was supposed to be back at work this morning, but Cassidy hasn't been able to reach him.' She glanced around, as if at a loss, but then seemed to make up her mind about something. 'I guess I'll head back to the house and start organizing the funeral.'

'I'm happy to help with that if you need a hand,' I offered. 'Or even if you just want some company.'

Avery gave me a sad but grateful smile. 'Thank you. I'll keep that in mind, but I'm OK for the moment.'

'Will the funeral be held in Twilight Cove?' I figured Aunt Olivia would probably want to attend if that were the case.

'In Chicago,' Avery said. 'That's where most of his friends and family live. I don't think he mixed much with the people here in Twilight Cove, even though he told me the locals did their best to be welcoming and often invited him to various events. He became a bit reclusive in his old age. It was hard to get him out of the house.' She offered me another faint smile. 'Anyway, it was nice to see you again.'

'You too,' I said. 'And if there's anything my aunt and I can do for you, just let us know.'

'I appreciate that.'

She set off down the sidewalk and soon turned the corner onto Main Street.

I drove back to the farm and shared the delicious food I'd bought with Auntie O while the dogs looked on, hoping that we'd drop a morsel or two. They were disappointed that we didn't share, but I promised to feed them their special cookies from the Pet Palace later that day.

I didn't bring up Dorothy or the murder while Aunt Olivia and I ate, but both remained on my mind. One of Olivia's friends phoned her as we finished eating, so I decided to leave my questions about what I'd overheard at the food truck until later.

I spent much of the afternoon working on my script, fortunately with more success than I'd had the day before. Then I helped Callum feed the animals, with Flossie and Fancy supervising my work. I was changing from my work jeans back into shorts, about to head over to the carriage house to help Olivia prepare some of the food for her Gins and Needles meeting the next evening, when I heard a car pull into the driveway. My heart rate ticked up.

Had the police returned with more questions?

TWELVE

The dogs followed me out the door and stuck close to me, as if sensing my apprehension. The tension rushed out of my muscles when I saw Tessa climbing out of a red Toyota Corolla.

Flossie and Fancy ran to greet her. I followed at a slower pace, but with a smile on my face.

Tessa crouched down to fuss over the spaniels, and then straightened up, returning my smile.

'Is this a bad time?' she asked. 'We should have traded phone numbers yesterday.'

'Let's do that now.' I tugged my phone out of the pocket of my shorts. 'And it's not a bad time. You can come with me to the carriage house. Auntie O would love to see you.'

'I'm always happy to see Olivia.'

As we walked, I stored Tessa's number in my phone, and she did the same with mine. The dogs bounded around the back of the carriage house, so we followed them and found the French doors giving access to the patio standing wide open. Flossie and Fancy had already disappeared inside.

I tapped on the French doors before stepping into the living area. A delicious smell greeted me. I thought it came from a mixture of warm bread, cheese and herbs.

Aunt Olivia sat at the kitchen table with her boot-encased foot propped up on an extra chair. She had a bowl in front of her and was mixing its contents with a spoon. Flossie and Fancy had already settled next to her, one on either side of her chair.

'We have a visitor,' I announced as Tessa followed me into the carriage house.

Olivia's face lit up. 'Tessa! What a lovely surprise!'

'Sorry for dropping by unannounced,' Tessa said. 'Georgie and I have so much to catch up on, so I thought I'd come by on my way home from work.'

'You're always welcome, unannounced or otherwise,' my aunt assured her.

'Definitely,' I agreed.

Smiling, Tessa joined Olivia at the table while I peeked into the oven. Some type of tear-and-share bread was baking inside.

'Something smells delicious,' Tessa said.

'That's the cheesy monkey bread.' Aunt Olivia explained that she was getting ready for the next evening's Gins and Needles meeting.

'What can we do to help?' Tessa asked.

Aunt Olivia handed me the bowl she had in front of her. 'This is the smoked salmon spread. Could you pop it in the fridge for me, please, Georgie?'

'Oh, I love this stuff.' I had fond memories of eating crackers slathered with the spread back in my teens. Olivia had made it for me once or twice while visiting me in California as well.

'I was also planning to make chocolate chip cookies,' Olivia said.

'Always a good choice.' Tessa washed her hands at the kitchen sink. 'Georgie and I can do that while you relax.'

Aunt Olivia protested, but with Tessa and I both on the same side, she had to relent. She did so with a smile.

She moved over to an armchair and got her injured foot settled on a stool. Flossie and Fancy joined her, curling up on the area rug and closing their eyes.

With the recipe sitting out on the table, Tessa and I gathered and measured ingredients. As we worked, I asked Tessa about her job. She seemed to enjoy working as a teacher and I didn't doubt that she was great at it. She'd always had a good rapport with pretty much everyone, and that likely extended to her students.

'Do you know Roxy Russo?' I asked as I measured out some flour.

Tessa lined cookie sheets with parchment paper. 'Sure. She's in one of my English classes.'

'She drops by the farm sometimes,' Aunt Olivia said. 'To visit the animals.'

I filled a measuring cup with sugar. 'The one time I saw her here, she ran away as soon as I spotted her.'

'That's always the way,' Olivia said.

Tessa frowned. 'She's a good kid, but she has some troubles, probably because she doesn't have an easy home life. Her mother drinks a lot and doesn't always make the best choices, relationship-wise. Roxy has attendance issue sometimes, but she's very bright and does well with her school work when she actually applies herself.'

I told Tessa about seeing Roxy flee from Dorothy's cabin right before I found the woman dead.

Tessa's face fell. 'Oh no. Poor Roxy. It must have been terrible for her to find Dorothy.'

'I had to tell the police that I saw her there.' I cracked an egg. 'I hope that doesn't cause her much trouble.'

A fierce light showed in Tessa's brown eyes. 'The police had better not suspect her of anything. Roxy's been in a couple of fights at school, but only to stick up for herself when other kids bullied her. I'm sure she'd never intentionally harm anyone.'

'I don't know if the police suspect Roxy,' I said. 'But they're certainly taking a good look at me and Olivia.'

'No!' Indignation quickly replaced Tessa's shock. 'That's crazy!'

'I'm afraid they have their reasons.' Aunt Olivia explained that she would inherit Dorothy's land. 'I had no idea Dorothy had named me in her will, but of course I can't prove that. And because of my broken ankle, they seem to think Georgie might have done the terrible deed on my behalf.'

Tessa shook her head. 'The police are wasting their time if they're investigating either of you.'

I appreciated how strongly she believed that. 'I don't even know how Dorothy died.'

Tessa lowered her voice, even though there was no one around except the three of us and the dogs. 'I have some insider information.'

'Let me guess,' Olivia said from her armchair. 'Your cousin Valentina.'

'Valentina works at the police station,' Tessa said for my benefit. 'In a civilian capacity. And let's just say her lips are a little looser than they should be considering her job.'

I turned the mixer on so it could cream the butter and sugar. 'Sounds like she's a valuable source of intel.'

Tessa added some baking soda to the flour. 'Mostly she just dishes out gossip, but this time it's something a little more solid. She says Dorothy was suffocated, probably with a pillow.'

I remembered the bruises near Dorothy's collarbone. Maybe her killer had held her down, with a hand pressed against that spot.

'They think she died about an hour before you found her,' Tessa continued. 'Dorothy had sedatives in her system at the time.'

'Did she normally take sedatives?' I asked.

Tessa added the eggs to the mixer. 'There was no sign of any such medications in her cabin.'

'So, the killer sedated her to avoid a struggle,' Aunt Olivia surmised.

As I added a teaspoon of vanilla extract to the mixer, I thought back to what I'd seen when I stood in the cabin on the day I found Dorothy's body. 'There was a teacup on the table. Maybe the sedative was put in her tea.'

'Except, the police tested the tea in the cup, which was almost full.' Tessa sat down at the kitchen table. 'No sedative.'

I added flour to the mixing bowl. 'Then the killer must have slipped it to Dorothy some other way. And if the murderer went to Dorothy's cabin prepared to sedate her . . .'

'Then the murder must have been premeditated,' Aunt Olivia finished.

So, if Ed Grimshaw had killed Dorothy, he hadn't lashed out in the heat of the moment. However, he'd been trying to get his hands on Dorothy's land for a while, and I wasn't willing to rule out the possibility that he had come up with a plan to get rid of her.

I shared my thoughts with Tessa and Aunt Olivia.

'Of course, Ed Grimshaw isn't my only suspect,' I said.

'You have a suspect list!' Tessa's eyes gleamed. 'Look at you, turning into Nancy Drew!'

I shook my head. 'I always wanted to be George.'

'She even tried to get everyone to call her George,' Auntie O said. 'You were, what? About nine years old at the time?'

I nodded. 'It didn't work, but I've learned to be happy with Georgie.'

'You should be,' Tessa said. 'I love your name, and it suits you. But, speaking of Nancy Drew and her friends, I bet we could be like them. If we put our heads together, we could probably figure out who killed Dorothy.'

Aunt Olivia didn't look crazy about the idea. 'I'm not sure that's wise. This is a murderer we're talking about, and I don't want either of you ending up in danger.'

'We'll give danger a wide berth,' Tessa said.

I sided with my aunt. 'We should probably leave the investigating to the police.'

Tessa's agreement came reluctantly. 'I suppose.'

After the cookies had finished baking and I'd removed them from the oven, the dogs and I walked Tessa back to her car.

'I know I said earlier that we should let the police handle the investigation,' I said once we were well away from the carriage house.

Tessa's face brightened. 'I knew it! You want to solve the mystery!'

'What I really want is to clear Aunt Olivia's name. Mine too, since the police probably think I committed the crime on her behalf, but I especially hate the thought of anyone suspecting Olivia.'

'No one who knows her truly would, but I understand. The state police are helping out with the investigation. They don't know Olivia like some of our local officers do, and none of the investigators know you.' Tessa stopped by the driver's door of her car. 'Who do you suspect aside from Ed Grimshaw?'

I mentioned Marlene Hooper's dispute with Dorothy.

Tessa nodded. 'I heard about that. Marlene claims that Dorothy cursed her. That's ridiculous, but Marlene seems to believe it.'

'I also overheard something else while I was in town.' I filled her in on my visit to the Lebanese food truck and what I'd overheard as I'd left.

'Dorothy tried to shoot Shanifa?' Tessa echoed with surprise. 'I haven't heard that one before.'

'Do you think it could be true?' I asked.

Tessa considered my question. 'I always thought Dorothy was a peaceful, if somewhat eccentric, woman. It's hard for me to picture her with a gun, but I'll ask Valentina if she knows anything about it.'

'Thanks, Tessa.'

She gave me a quick hug. 'Try not to worry too much about the whole murder suspect thing. You and Olivia are innocent, so there won't be any real evidence against you. And we'll have your names cleared in no time.'

After I thanked her again, the dogs and I stayed to watch her drive off into the growing darkness.

THIRTEEN

After feeding the chickens and cleaning out the stalls in the barn the next day, I got to work on one of my favorite tasks: grooming the donkeys. Aunt Olivia had three donkeys living at the sanctuary at present. She'd told me that there had been five up until a few weeks ago, when she found a new home for two of them, on a farm not far away from Twilight Cove.

There was something about donkeys that I found so charming. They were adorable and full of personality. I loved watching them play with their toys, their favorite being a big rubber ball with a handle for them to grip with their mouths. I planned to give them the ball once I had them all groomed.

I walked Charlie, one of the donkeys, into the barn and tethered him in the aisle so I could brush him.

'I told Tessa that I want to clear Auntie O's name,' I said as I got to work. I often found myself talking to the animals as I groomed them. 'And I really do. But I'm not sure how to go about it. I don't even know anyone in this town, aside from Aunt Olivia and Tessa. And I'm getting to know Callum, slowly.'

Fancy let out a whine from where she lay in the sunshine with Flossie, just outside the open barn door.

'And of course I know Flossie, Fancy, Euclid, and all the animals at the sanctuary,' I amended.

Apparently satisfied with the correction, Fancy rested her chin on her paws.

'But it's a human who killed Dorothy. I'm certain of that. And I don't know many humans in Twilight Cove.'

Both dogs raised their heads, watching something up in the sky. Giving Charlie a pat, I left him tethered in the barn and stepped out into the sunshine so I could look up and see what had captured the dogs' attention.

Euclid circled overhead and then descended to land on the peak of the barn roof.

'Morning, Euclid,' I said, shading my eyes against the bright light. 'Thanks for leading me to the lawyer's office yesterday.'

Euclid lifted off from the roof and glided down to land on a fence post. He stared at me with his intelligent yellow eyes.

Fancy let out a 'wooo'. When I glanced her way, she and Flossie were also staring at me.

Euclid flew up into the air again and disappeared around the side of the barn. The spaniels continued to watch me steadily.

'Don't worry,' I told them. 'I've learned my lesson.'

They jumped up to follow me as I walked around the side of the barn. I drew to a stop as soon as I turned the corner. A teenage girl sat on the fence of one of the paddocks, petting Sundance, a sorrel Quarter Horse.

Roxy Russo.

Hardly daring to breathe, I backed away slowly around the corner again, so Roxy wouldn't see me. The dogs pressed their noses to my legs.

'I know,' I whispered. 'If she sees me coming, she'll run off again.'

I entered the barn and gave the donkey another pat as I passed him. 'I'll be back soon, Charlie.'

I continued straight through to the back door, which also stood open. I stepped outside, trying to make as little noise as possible. When I turned to my left, Roxy was straight ahead, still sitting on the fence, with her back to me. I didn't want to scare the girl, but I also wanted to talk to her, and I couldn't do that if she fled before I got close.

Hoping I wouldn't step on any snapping twigs, I advanced slowly and carefully. Once I was within a couple of strides of the teenager, I stopped being so cautious. I picked up my pace and approached the fence.

'She's beautiful, isn't she?' I asked, looking at Sundance as I rested my forearms on the fence.

Roxy nearly toppled off her perch. As soon as she regained her balance, she hopped to the ground, ready to flee.

'Roxy, wait! Please!' I said quickly.

I could tell she wasn't going to listen to me.

Fancy looked up at Roxy and let out a long 'woo-woo'. Then Flossie jumped up and rested her paws on Roxy's stomach.

The girl remained tense, as if ready to take off at any second, but she stayed put. She stroked the dogs' heads as she eyed me with suspicion. I could see now that she looked to be about fourteen or fifteen and had golden brown eyes, very light brown skin, and a faint smattering of freckles over her nose. She wore her dark brown hair in a ponytail again, with torn jeans and a camouflage hoodie.

'I'm Georgie Johansen,' I said. 'I promise you're not in any trouble. My aunt and I don't mind you visiting the animals. I just want to talk to you for a minute.'

'Why?' Her voice was just as wary as her eyes.

My heart ached for her. It struck me as sad that she was so distrustful and cautious at her age. Then again, maybe a lot of that had to do with the last time we'd seen each other, if she'd managed to get a good enough look at my face to recognize me.

'I'm sorry that you found Dorothy the way you did,' I said.

Roxy's already tense muscles seemed to coil like springs.

'You're not in trouble,' I hurried to say again. 'Not from me, anyway. I'm guessing the police talked to you already, but I know you didn't hurt Dorothy.'

'How can you know that?' she challenged. 'You don't know me.'

'Maybe not,' I said. 'But I know you love animals. That tells me a lot.'

She digested that statement as she sized me up. 'What were you doing at Dorothy's place?'

'Flossie and Fancy led me there.'

We both glanced down at the dogs, who now sat so close to Roxy that they were almost resting on her beat-up green Converse sneakers.

'They showed up here on the farm and wanted me to follow them,' I explained. 'Maybe that sounds crazy, but—'

Roxy cut me off. 'It's not crazy. They're smart.'

'They definitely are,' I agreed.

Flossie thumped her tail and Fancy gave a little woof, as if they also agreed with Roxy's statement.

'Did you see anyone else near the cabin that morning?' I asked.

'No. I already told the cops that.'

'Did you hear anything?' I pressed. 'Or see anything unusual?'

'Why are you asking me all this?' Her eyes narrowed. 'Are you a cop?'

'Definitely not a cop. I'm a writer.' I decided to be open with her. That was probably my only chance of keeping her talking. 'But the police think I might have killed Dorothy to help out my aunt Olivia. Dorothy left her land to Olivia in her will.'

'The cops are stupid,' Roxy said with disdain. 'You didn't kill Dorothy.'

'What makes you so sure?' I asked, genuinely curious.

Roxy rested a hand on each dog's head. 'Flossie and Fancy like you. They know you didn't hurt Dorothy.'

Both spaniels wagged their tails, as if they were again agreeing.

Roxy looked down at the dogs for a moment before asking quietly, 'How did she die?'

I hesitated, not sure I should share those details with someone so young, because despite her suspicious and defiant air, she really did look very young. But if I wanted to build trust with her, I knew I couldn't hold back.

'I heard that she was suffocated, possibly with a pillow, while sedated,' I said.

Roxy's forehead furrowed as she thought that over. 'Did the killer spike Dorothy's tea with the sedative?'

'I wondered that myself, but apparently there were no traces of the drug in the teacup that was on the table.'

A light bulb seemed to go off in Roxy's head. 'There must have been another teacup.'

'There was only one on the table,' I said.

She shook her head, adamant. 'There had to be another teacup. Somewhere.'

'Why do you say that?'

'The teacup on the table, it was a pretty one with pink roses.'

I nodded, able to picture the scene clearly in my head. 'That's right.'

'Dorothy only ever used those teacups when she had company,' Roxy said. 'She told me that. When she was on her own, she drank from one of those plain mugs she had on the shelf.'

I thought back, trying to picture the contents of the cabinet at the time I found Dorothy's body, but I hadn't paid attention to anything on the shelves.

'Do you know how many of those special cups she owned?' I asked.

'Two.'

I wished I knew if one remained in the crockery cabinet.

'Was there one left on the shelf?' Roxy asked, her mind on the same wavelength as mine.

'I don't know,' I admitted. 'All I know is that there was just the one on the table.'

Roxy took a step backward. Flossie and Fancy got to their feet, tails wagging.

'I should go.' Roxy barely had the words out of her mouth before she turned and broke into a run.

'Roxy, wait!'

She didn't even slow down when I called after her.

'Do you want to volunteer here at the sanctuary?' I shouted.

This time she paused, just long enough to call back over her shoulder, 'Maybe.'

Then she tore off around the paddock and disappeared into the woods.

Although tempted to go after her, I hadn't finished my chores, and I'd left Charlie tethered up in the barn, half groomed. I didn't like the thought of Roxy roaming the woods when there was a killer on the loose, but I doubted anything I said to her would change her habits. I was lucky she'd stayed and talked to me as long as she had.

Sundance came over and nudged my shoulder. I stroked her nose and promised to bring her a carrot later. With a spaniel on either side of me, I returned to the barn to finish grooming Charlie.

Once I'd brushed all of the donkeys, I tossed their favorite ball into the pasture. I stayed to watch them play, laughing as Charlie grabbed the ball in his mouth and cantered around, grunting and squealing with glee. The other two donkeys followed after him, making their own noises of excitement as they tried to get a chance with the coveted toy.

Eventually, I tore myself away from watching the donkeys so I could get back to work. As soon as I'd completed all my chores, I stripped off my gloves and left them in the barn's tack room. Without bothering to head over to the farmhouse to change into cooler clothes, I strode into the woods, with Flossie and Fancy on my heels.

I suspected Roxy had already done what I was about to do. I would have liked to believe that she had been in a hurry to get back to school – where she should have been in the middle of a weekday morning – but given that she'd headed into the trees instead of toward the road, and considering our conversation, I very much doubted that was the case.

A frisson of worry passed through my chest. It was one thing for Tessa and me to dig around for information that might help me clear my name – and Aunt Olivia's too. It was another thing entirely for a teenage girl to go poking around the scene of the murder. I fervently hoped that the killer wasn't making a habit of lurking in the woods and instead was steering well clear of the crime scene.

When we reached the clearing where Dorothy's cabin stood, the dogs sat down and whined.

I crouched down and put an arm around each spaniel. 'I know, sweeties. You miss her. I'm so sorry.' I hugged them close before standing up.

While trekking through the trees, I'd worried that I'd find crime scene tape strung around the perimeter of the clearing, but if yellow tape had been there previously, it was now gone. Even so, I stood still for a moment, looking around to make sure that there were no police officers – or anyone else – hanging around.

I couldn't see anyone and all I could hear were the birds twittering in the trees.

A chill ran up my spine and down my arms. This place had seemed so peaceful before the murder, but now it gave me the creeps. I decided to hurry up so I could get back to the farm as soon as possible.

'You can wait here if you want,' I told the dogs.

Flossie touched her nose to my left hand and Fancy pressed her snout to my right one.

'All right,' I said, understanding. 'Let's do this.'

FOURTEEN

When I strode toward the cabin, Flossie and Fancy stayed right with me.

I hesitated at the front door, but then reminded myself that I didn't want to linger. I kept glancing over my shoulder, worried that Dorothy's killer might jump out at me from behind a tree. A silly worry to have, probably, but one I couldn't brush aside.

The door gave a low groan as I pushed it open. A beam of sunlight slanted through one window, highlighting the dust motes in the air, and shining on Dorothy's bed like a spotlight. The quilt and other bedclothes had been removed, leaving the bed stripped bare. The dining table had also been completely cleared and there were signs of other things being moved around and not put back in their proper places.

I crossed the room to the china cabinet and studied its contents through the glass doors. No delicate teacups sat among the mismatched collection of crockery. I opened the cabinet doors for a closer look, wanting to be sure I hadn't missed anything. I still couldn't see any teacups.

I checked every other cupboard in the small cabin without result.

Flossie and Fancy had followed me into the cabin and were lying on the floor by Dorothy's stripped bed, their chins on their front paws and their sad brown eyes watching my every movement.

'The second teacup is missing,' I said. 'Do you think the killer took it?'

Both dogs raised their heads, still watching me.

'That would make sense.' I stared at the dining table, imagining a possible scenario. 'The killer came to the cabin. Someone Dorothy knew. She made tea for them both and served it in the two pretty teacups. The killer slipped a sedative into Dorothy's cup and killed her once she was too groggy to put up much of a fight. They probably left their own tea untouched so as not to leave behind any fingerprints or DNA. Then the killer took the cup with the sedative with them to remove any evidence of the drug and any evidence that a second person had been here. The killer was probably hoping that Dorothy's death would be written off as natural.'

The dogs continued to watch me. I had a funny feeling that they understood every word I was saying.

'Come on, girls.'

The spaniels jumped up and followed me out the door.

I made a slow circuit of the clearing, checking beneath the undergrowth at the perimeter, even though I knew the police would have searched the area as part of their initial investigation. It didn't surprise me in the least that I didn't find the missing teacup. Maybe the police had already found it, but the information Tessa had gleaned from her cousin suggested that only one teacup had been tested for traces of the drug used to sedate Dorothy.

The dogs nosed along with me as I widened my search area. None of us found anything.

'For all I know, the killer could have thrown the teacup into the ocean,' I said to Flossie and Fancy.

The dogs exchanged a glance and then sat down, watching me.

'I guess we could search the beach.' I took my phone from my pocket and checked the time. 'But I need to deliver my completed script to Giselle in a few days.' Giselle was the producer I was working with on my current project. 'I still have several pages to write and then I need to edit. In other words, I'd better get to work.'

I struck off along the path that would lead me to the farm. I glanced back to see Flossie and Fancy still sitting at the edge of the clearing.

'Come on, girls,' I called.

They hesitated for a split second and then came running to join me.

Even though my thoughts kept wanting to return to the missing teacup, I managed to get the final ten pages of my script written in fairly short order. I made a few notes about scenes and plot issues that I already knew I needed to fix, but I decided to leave the actual edits until the next day.

I got up from the kitchen table, where I'd been working, and stretched my arms over my head. The dogs stirred from their naps and got up and stretched too. I wandered over to the kitchen window, which I'd opened to let in the gentle breeze while I wrote. The sun still shone brightly from a cloudless sky. According to the weather app on my phone, the warm, sunny weather was expected to continue for a few more days.

As I stood at the window, Callum emerged from the trees at the southern edge of the property. The small patch of woodland separated the sanctuary from the asparagus farm next door. Why Callum would have been over there, I didn't know. Maybe he was looking for an escaped animal, although he walked at an unhurried pace and didn't appear agitated or concerned. More likely, he'd simply gone for a walk. He was entitled to take breaks from his farm work, after all.

I squinted and realized that he was wearing a toolbelt and had something in his right hand. A drill, maybe.

Perhaps he'd been fixing the shed roof when something in among the trees caught his attention.

I was probably being too nosy. Despite that thought, I kept watching.

Callum headed in the direction of the farmhand's cabin where he lived. As he disappeared from sight, I finally turned my back on the window. Callum's plate sat on the kitchen counter, all clean and waiting to be returned. I dug a carrot out of the fridge and grabbed the plate. I smiled when I saw Flossie and Fancy already waiting by the back door, tails wagging.

'We've got a couple of visits to make,' I said.

The dogs' bodies wiggled with excitement, making me laugh. They pressed their noses to the door and, as soon as I opened it, they burst out onto the porch and down the steps. I was glad to see them happy again, after their sadness at returning to Dorothy's cabin earlier in the day.

With the plate and carrot in hand, I headed first for Sundance's paddock to keep my promise to the Quarter Horse. She saw us coming and walked over to the fence to greet us. I offered her the carrot, which she gobbled up in no time. I spent a few minutes stroking her nose and talking with her softly before Flossie, Fancy and I continued on past the barn to Callum's cabin.

The single-story log cabin had a covered front porch and a red shingle roof. Two rocking chairs sat on the porch and a pair of mud-splattered rubber boots had been left next to the door.

The spaniels ran ahead of me, and seemed to know my destination. They bounced up onto the porch and woofed at me, as if encouraging me to hurry up. I joined them on the porch, not sure if we'd find Callum in the cabin or if he'd gone elsewhere on the farm while I was visiting Sundance.

I soon found out. I didn't even have a chance to knock before Callum opened the door.

'I guess Flossie and Fancy announced our presence,' I said, smiling at the dogs.

Callum grinned. 'Better than a doorbell. Come on in.'

The second Callum stepped back to make room for us, the spaniels charged inside.

'I brought your plate.' I handed it to him as he shut the door behind me.

The cabin had a combined kitchen and living room that took up the front half of the building. I knew from visiting the small dwelling in my teens that two bedrooms and a bathroom occupied the back half. A woodstove stood at the far end of the living room. With a fire going, the cabin was probably nice and cozy in the winter.

I noticed a pair of expensive-looking binoculars hanging from a hook on the wall next to the door. I lifted them off the hook.

'Are you a birdwatcher?' I looked closer at the binoculars, surprised. 'These have night vision?'

Callum set the plate on the counter by the kitchen sink. 'I like birds, but those are mostly for keeping an eye on things at night.'

I remembered the two times I'd seen him out after dark. On both occasions, he'd either been coming or going from the trees at the southern edge of the property, the same place I'd seen him less than an hour ago.

'Don't you ever sleep?' I asked, although what I actually wanted to know was what he'd really been up to with the binoculars. He couldn't exactly keep an eye on the farm when he was off among the trees.

Callum laughed. 'I sleep plenty, but sometimes I like to take a walk before heading to bed.'

I returned the binoculars to the hook on the wall and changed the subject. 'The brownies were amazing, by the way.'

Callum leaned against the counter and folded his arms. 'Did they help fuel your writing?'

I smiled at how the dogs had made themselves at home, lying on the area rug in the living room. 'Definitely, and they helped me recover from the last visit from Chief Stratton.'

'The police have left you alone since then?'

'Yes, thankfully.' My gaze landed on three open boxes sitting on the pine dining table. Distracted, I tried to keep our conversation flowing. 'Hopefully they're focusing their investigation elsewhere.'

'They must be,' Callum said.

I reached for the door, suddenly itching to get away. 'I'd better get going. I want to take the dogs for a walk before dinner.' I stepped out onto the porch. 'I'll see you in the morning.'

I called to Flossie and Fancy, and they burst out of the cabin to follow me. I set a quick pace for us and glanced over my shoulder.

Callum stood in the open doorway, watching us.

I wondered if he'd realized that I'd seen the open boxes on the table.

Boxes that had once held security cameras.

Once within the shade of the woods, I slowed my pace. I'd used the excuse of wanting to take the dogs for a walk to get me out of Callum's cabin so I could think, but I decided I really would take them for a ramble.

Aunt Olivia wanted me to stop by her Gins and Needles gathering to meet the members of the group, but I still had time for some exercise and I figured I could do some exploring and searching at the same time. I wouldn't be able to cover every inch of the woods on my own – that would require an entire team of people and would still take ages – but I could check out the trails that the killer might have taken when leaving Dorothy's cabin. Maybe the murderer had discarded the missing teacup somewhere along the way.

As the dogs alternated between running through the woods and stopping to sniff at interesting smells, I kept an eye out for any flashes of pink or white among the undergrowth on either side of the path. I wanted to stay focused on finding the teacup, but I couldn't stop thinking about Callum and his security cameras.

I should have checked to see if he'd installed the cameras on the exterior of the cabin. I'd have to do that later, on my way back to the farmhouse. It seemed odd to me that he might feel the need for such security measures on the farm, but maybe Dorothy's murder wasn't the only recent crime in the area. I made a mental note to ask Aunt Olivia if she'd had any problems on the farm that would warrant the installation of security cameras.

Although I wanted to believe that Callum had bought the cameras to make the farm safer, I couldn't help but wonder if he had another motive entirely. What that might be, I didn't know. But between the cameras, the night-vision goggles, and Callum's frequent trips into the heavily treed swath of land between the sanctuary and the neighboring asparagus farm, my thoughts had taken a suspicious turn.

I remembered how much I'd enjoyed sitting on the porch steps, chatting with him. My heart was telling my head that I didn't need to worry about Callum, but I couldn't let myself get distracted by his good looks or that one conversation. If he was up to something shady, I needed to be careful. I didn't want Aunt Olivia or the sanctuary to suffer in any way because he wasn't who he claimed to be.

The path ahead of me dipped downward and I smelled salt on the breeze. I'd now trekked farther through the woods than I had since I'd arrived in Twilight Cove. A few more minutes and I would reach the ocean. In some areas along the local coastline, steep cliffs provided a barrier between land and water, but in other parts, like in the center of town and where I was heading, broad hills sloped gently down to the beach.

Water gurgled and rushed somewhere nearby. I rounded a bend and spotted a ravine off to my right. Moving carefully, so I wouldn't crush any plants or get my clothes snagged on branches, I made my way off the path and closer to the edge of the gully. Down below, a creek rushed along, splashing over rocks, heading toward the ocean.

I turned back, intending to return to the path, when Flossie let out a sharp bark. Both dogs bounded down into the ravine.

'Flossie! Fancy!' I called.

They didn't reappear. I picked my way through the underbrush, closer to the edge of the ravine again. Flossie and Fancy stood on some rocks at the edge of the creek. Fancy raised her nose to the sky and let out a long howl.

'What's wrong?' I asked.

Flossie barked and Fancy howled again.

I slid and stumbled my way down the side of the ravine, almost losing my footing a couple of times. When I arrived at the edge of the creek, a bit dirty but unharmed, I saw what had the dogs so worked up.

On the rocks in front of the spaniels were the shattered remains of a pink and white teacup.

FIFTEEN

'You OK down there?'

My head jerked up at the sound of Callum's voice. He stood at the edge of the ravine, looking down at me and the dogs.

'We're fine,' I called back over the sound of the rushing water. 'Come on, girls,' I added to the spaniels.

Flossie and Fancy bounded up the side of the ravine without a problem. It took me a little longer to climb up. When I'd nearly reached the top, Callum offered me a hand and pulled me up the rest of the way.

'Thanks.' I brushed some dirt from my arm.

'What were you doing down there?' Callum's question sounded casual enough, but my heart was beating a little faster than it should have been, and not just from my climb up the ravine.

How had he found us here, off the trail? Had he followed us?

'We were out exploring,' I said, trying not to let my wariness show. 'Then we found a teacup smashed on the rocks by the creek.'

Callum took a step closer to the edge and peered down into the ravine. 'Is that significant?'

I pulled my phone from my pocket. 'I think it was Dorothy's teacup.'

Callum said nothing as I phoned Aunt Olivia, but I could almost see the wheels turning in his head. He'd probably figured out that I thought the teacup had something to do with Dorothy's murder, but I felt like there was more than that going on in his head. I just didn't know what.

I'd left Chief Stratton's business card back at the house, but I got his direct number from Aunt Olivia and dialed it. Even though the information I had was important, I wasn't sure that it qualified as an emergency. If the police chief didn't answer his phone, I would call 9-1-1 to report the teacup. Fortunately, I didn't have to take that step. Stratton answered on the third ring.

After I reported what I'd found, Stratton asked me to stay put until he arrived.

'I'm supposed to wait until the police get here,' I told Callum after I ended the call. 'You can head back to the farm if you want to.'

Callum sat down on a fallen tree. 'I'll keep you company while you wait.'

I wasn't sure whether I should be relieved or disappointed. Hanging around in a spot where Dorothy's killer had likely stood probably would have creeped me out if I were alone, but I wasn't exactly at ease in Callum's company now either.

The dogs approached Callum, sniffing his jean-clad legs and accepting pats from him. That helped me to relax enough to sit down on the same fallen tree, a few feet away from him. Flossie and Fancy liked Callum, so he couldn't be a bad person. Right?

'What brought you to Twilight Cove?' I asked, hoping I could find out more about him while we waited for the police to show up.

'I was looking for a job somewhere quiet, somewhere with a slower pace of life.'

'But Twilight Cove?' I pressed. 'It's not a place everyone's heard about.'

'My grandparents used to live here,' Callum explained. 'I used to spend two or three weeks with them every summer when I was growing up, until . . .' He shifted his weight on the log, as if no longer quite so comfortable.

'Until?' I prodded.

He shrugged. 'As I got older, I started spending the summers at sports camps. That sort of thing.'

'What sports were you into?' I asked.

He rubbed the back of his neck and kept his gaze away from mine. 'I played soccer for a while. A little bit of hockey.'

Silence fell between us as I studied his face. For whatever reason, he didn't seem comfortable talking about himself. Whether that was because he had something to hide or because it was simply his personality, I didn't know. I hoped it was the latter, but the suspicious part of my mind believed it could well be the former.

Fancy put her paws on Callum's knees so she could lick his face. He laughed, relaxed and at ease again.

'How about you?' he asked me. 'Have you spent a lot of time in Twilight Cove?'

'Not for years.' It was my turn to feel uncomfortable with the direction of the conversation. I didn't have anything to hide, but I didn't know how to adequately explain why I'd stayed away for so long. Maybe because my reason for doing so seemed flimsy now that I was back here again.

I turned the conversation to the animals at the sanctuary, a much safer topic. It could have been my imagination, but I thought Callum was relieved by the change in subject too.

After another five or ten minutes, Chief Stratton called me back. He'd parked his vehicle by Dorothy's cabin and wanted directions to my current location. I realized I didn't actually know how to get to where I was from Dorothy's cabin. I knew the general direction, but not which trails to follow. Callum stepped in to help out, taking my phone and guiding the police chief along a route that would bring him our way. Callum clearly knew the woods well, and I couldn't help but wonder yet again about his nighttime excursions.

It didn't take long for Stratton to find us, and he hadn't come alone. Officer Brody Williams and a balding man in a suit followed him through the woods toward me and Callum. Stratton introduced the man in the suit as Detective Fernandez of the state police.

I directed the officers to the remains of the shattered teacup. Officer Williams made it to the bottom of the ravine without any trouble, even though he carried an expensive-looking camera down with him. The two older men made the descent more slowly, and with less grace.

Eventually, Stratton and Fernandez climbed their way back up the ravine while Officer Williams snapped photos of the smashed cup. Detective Fernandez asked me questions about how I'd found the teacup. I told the same story I'd told Callum, making it sound like I'd happened upon the shards of porcelain while exploring the woods with the dogs. That was mostly true, but I wasn't about to say that I'd specifically been searching for the teacup. I doubted that would go over well with the cops.

When the detective dismissed me, I decided to carry on with my plan to walk to the beach. Callum returned to the farm, so the dogs and I walked on our own, which was exactly how I wanted it. While questioning me, Fernandez had mostly maintained a bland expression, but I thought I'd detected a hint of suspicion in his eyes now and then. That made sense, since I was a suspect in the murder case, but it made me feel slightly ill. I worried that the detective thought I'd killed Dorothy and disposed of the teacup by throwing it into the ravine as I fled the cabin. Maybe he believed I'd returned today to make sure that the remains of the teacup and sedative had been carried away by the creek.

That theory might not have made sense if not for Callum's presence. The police might think that I'd been forced to call them and report the teacup because Callum had happened upon me checking on the evidence.

I wondered what Callum thought about everything. Did he suspect me of killing Dorothy?

Maybe the fact that he was holding back, and the fact that he thought he needed security cameras and night-vision binoculars, had to do with his suspicions of me.

Almost as soon as I had that thought, I realized it couldn't be entirely true. The first time I'd seen Callum out after dark was before Dorothy died.

I stopped in my tracks as an unpleasant thought occurred to me.

Could Callum have killed Dorothy?

I shook my head, as if trying to rid myself of such thoughts, and started walking again.

Callum wouldn't have killed Dorothy. He had no reason to.

Did he?

The fact was that I didn't know nearly enough about Callum to answer that question. That left me distinctly uneasy, but as I broke free of the tree line and stepped onto the sandy beach, I drew in a deep breath and immediately felt a little better. Another half-hour spent on the isolated strip of beach helped to calm my spinning thoughts even more. I laughed as I watched Flossie and Fancy splash about in the shallows and gallop along the wet sand, chasing seagulls and salty spray from the crashing waves.

By the time we returned to the farm and I'd hosed down and dried off the spaniels, several cars had parked in the driveway. I fed the dogs their dinners and then the three of us walked across the driveway to the carriage house. I could hear voices and laughter coming from around back, so we followed the sounds and found my aunt and the members of her Gins and Needles group gathered on the patio. The French doors stood open and I could see a generous spread of food set out on the kitchen table. It looked as though some of the group members had brought dishes to add to Aunt Olivia's offerings.

As soon as my aunt noticed me, she waved me over and introduced me and the dogs to everyone.

'Grab yourself a plate and some food,' Dolores Sanchez urged me. She wore a bright blue muumuu and had her black hair tied back in a bun. 'We chat and nibble before we stitch.'

'More like feast and gossip,' Leona Powell amended.

The other ladies laughed, and Leona joined in. She was a tall, wiry white woman with short gray hair and a loud laugh.

Flossie and Fancy stayed out on the patio, enjoying all the attention they were getting from Aunt Olivia's friends, while I filled a plate with food in the kitchen.

'Are you related to Cynthia Yoon from the Pet Palace?' I asked a petite woman whom Olivia had introduced as Esther Yoon.

She beamed. 'I'm Cynthia's mother. You look to be around the same age. Thirty?'

'Thirty-two,' I said.

The smile remained on her face. 'Close enough. Maybe you'll be friends.'

'That would be nice,' I said, sincere, 'but I won't be here long. Just a few weeks.'

Esther patted my arm. 'Ah, but maybe you'll be back for visits.'

'I hope so.' More than hoped. I planned to make sure I came back regularly from now on. I'd stayed away for far too long.

Once I'd added a sampling of each dish to my plate, I took my food and one of the kitchen chairs out to the patio to join the group.

'Rumor has it that you've inherited Dorothy's land,' Vera Jackson said to Olivia. Vera, a tall Black woman with close-cropped hair, looked to be in her late fifties.

'Did you see that coming?' Leona asked.

'I never had a clue.' Auntie O tasted a mini quiche. 'I'm still in shock, to be honest. About Dorothy's death and the bequest.'

'I heard her talking to Ed Grimshaw in town one day,' Clara Olmstead said. A tiny woman with pale skin, snowy hair and cornflower blue eyes, Clara appeared to be the oldest of the group. 'She told him that even if she would consider selling, she'd never let the woodland fall into hands like his. She wanted the property preserved.'

'And she knew how you feel about animals,' Esther added. Flossie and Fancy wagged their tails as she continued, 'She probably thought you'd keep the woodland as is for the wildlife.'

'And that's exactly what I plan to do,' Aunt Olivia said.

The spaniels came over and rested their chins on my aunt's lap. She gave them each a pat, careful to keep her plate of food out of their reach. 'And these two will always have a home here.'

I smiled as Flossie and Fancy gave my aunt's hand a lick. Then they wound their way around chairs and people to come and sit by me. When they looked up at me with adoring brown eyes, my heart cracked and nearly broke. I didn't want to think about leaving them in a few weeks' time, even though I knew they would have a wonderful home with my aunt.

'I still can't believe Dorothy was murdered,' Dolores said.

The other ladies shook their heads and murmured their agreement.

'And now there's been another death,' Vera said.

'You mean Victor Clyde?' Olivia asked. 'At least his death was natural.'

Vera balanced her empty plate on her lap. 'There was Victor's death, yes, but I'm talking about Simon Greenaway.'

I stopped short of taking a bite of the cheesy herb bread Auntie O had made. 'The lawyer?'

'That's him,' Leona confirmed. 'Damn shame.'

'What happened?' Aunt Olivia asked the question before I had a chance.

Clara sadly shook her head of white hair. 'He had an accident while at his cabin up in the mountains. His cousin drove up there to look for him and found him dead on the shore of the lake.'

SIXTEEN

'**A**re you sure it was an accident?' I asked as I digested the news about the lawyer.

Esther Yoon's eyes widened. 'You think Simon was murdered?'

'He was up at his cabin alone,' Leona said. 'He slipped on the rocks by the lake and hit his head. A tragic accident.'

'That's so sad,' Dolores said. 'He was only in his fifties. He should have had so many years ahead of him.'

'Three deaths in one week in Twilight Cove.' Vera paused to take a sip of coffee. 'We don't usually have so many at once. It's a sad time.'

'And I don't like the fact that there's a murderer running around loose.' Worry clouded Clara's bright blue eyes. 'Makes it hard to sleep at night.'

'I've got a baseball bat stored under my bed,' Leona said.

Vera smiled. 'Anyone who knows you knows better than to try breaking into your house.'

'You've got that right.' A fierce glint showed in Leona's gray eyes.

I'd just met the woman, but her expression made me never want to get on her bad side.

The ladies spent several minutes speculating about who might have killed Dorothy. The general consensus was that Ed Grimshaw had committed the crime.

'Just you wait,' Dolores cautioned my aunt. 'He'll be on your doorstep any day now, trying to get you to sell the land you inherited so he can build his beachfront condos.'

'He'll be wasting his breath,' Olivia said.

A thought occurred to me, one that I should have considered earlier. 'You don't think Ed Grimshaw would try to harm you too, do you?' I asked my aunt. 'He'd give himself away as the killer if he did.'

I was hoping Grimshaw would think things through that far and see how foolish it would be to harm Auntie O.

'You should ask for police protection,' Vera advised.

Leona grinned. 'Preferably from Officer Williams. I wouldn't mind having him stationed at my house twenty-four-seven.'

'Leona, Brody Williams is far too young for you,' Clara chided.

'That's up for debate,' Leona shot back.

All the ladies laughed.

Leona sent a sly smile my way. 'But he's definitely not too young for Georgie.'

All eyes turned to me. My cheeks warmed and I knew they'd flushed red.

My aunt came to my rescue. 'The police are already keeping an eye on me and Georgie, but not to protect us.'

Clara gasped. 'They think you killed Dorothy for her land?'

'I think it's me they actually suspect of committing the crime,' I said.

I appreciated the indignant exclamations and murmurs of disapproval that followed my statement.

'Stuff and nonsense,' Aunt Olivia declared.

'I still think you should ask Brody Williams for police protection.' Leona winked at me. 'You'd make a good-looking couple, Georgie.'

I felt my cheeks flush again.

'You don't even know that she's single,' Esther said.

A series of questions about my love life (or lack thereof) followed. I answered a couple, dodged a few more, and then made my excuses and left the gathering as the cocktails started to flow.

As I walked around the carriage house, I heard Dolores say, 'It's customer appreciation night at Siren Beauty tomorrow evening. Who's going?'

At my side, Fancy let out a 'woo-oo' and Flossie barked in agreement.

'All right,' I conceded. 'I guess I have plans for tomorrow evening.'

That night, before going to sleep, I turned out the lights in my bedroom and stuck my head out the open window to survey the farm. No mysterious lights caught my eye and I didn't spot Callum out and about. I noticed a flash of headlights and heard the low rumble of a vehicle's engine coming from the asparagus farm next door, but otherwise all was quiet.

I waited a minute or two, breathing in the fresh night air, waiting to see if Callum would appear, flitting from shadow to shadow, but nothing stirred.

From off in the distance came the hoo-hoo call of a great horned owl.

I smiled and whispered, 'Good night, Euclid.'

Then I closed the window all but a crack and climbed into bed.

I spoke to Callum as little as possible during morning chores the next day. That wasn't hard to do since he didn't seem to be in the mood to chat either. It was as if we'd fallen back into the dynamic of the first day we'd met. Although part of me regretted that and wanted to somehow dispel the uneasiness that sat between us, I instead kept my distance. No matter how much I wanted to believe that Callum was a good guy, I couldn't trust him, so I stayed focused on the animals and got through my chores quickly.

After checking in on Aunt Olivia, who seemed none the worse for wear after her Gins and Needles meeting the night before, I hopped in my car with Flossie and Fancy and drove into the center of town. As I slowed down on Ocean Drive, preparing to turn onto Main Street, I spotted Shanifa over by her food truck. The truck wasn't yet open for business, but probably would be soon. At the moment, Shanifa stood by the back corner of the truck, deep in conversation with reporter Byron Szabo.

The last thing I wanted was for Byron to chase after me, hounding me for an interview. If he hadn't yet heard that I was a suspect in Dorothy's murder, he soon would. I'd have to stay on my toes if I hoped to continue avoiding him.

I left the dogs in the car with the windows half open while I popped into the bakery to buy some bread for myself and for Aunt Olivia. On a whim, I added some fresh croissants to my order. I always had trouble resisting temptation when faced with croissants and I knew my aunt loved them too.

With the baked goods stowed safely in my car, Flossie, Fancy and I paid a visit to the Pet Palace to pick out two dog beds and a toy for each spaniel. Fancy chose a squeaky ball for her toy while Flossie jumped up and pawed at a not-yet-inflated soccer ball with tabs on it. On the way to the sales counter, I picked up a bag of treats, much to Flossie and Fancy's approval.

I was storing all the purchases in the trunk of my car when my stomach sank at the sound of a familiar voice.

'Ms Johansen, I've been wanting to speak with you.'

I bit back a sigh as I closed the trunk of my car. Apparently, Ed Grimshaw remembered my name. I wished he'd go back to failing to even recognize me.

'I'm afraid I'm busy,' I said, even though that wasn't quite the truth. I'd planned to take a leisurely walk on the beach before heading back to the farmhouse to write.

Beside me, the dogs tensed and Fancy let out a low growl.

Ed Grimshaw eyed the spaniels nervously. He stepped close enough to shove a business card in my hand and then put some space between himself and the dogs again. 'I understand your aunt has inherited Dorothy Shale's land. I'm sure she'll want to unload it quickly, and I can give her a good deal.'

I wanted to tell him that Aunt Olivia had no intention of selling the land, and certainly not to him, but I bit my tongue. If Grimshaw had killed Dorothy over the woodland, I didn't want him hatching a plot to harm my aunt. Even if going after Olivia as the new owner of the land would make him seem all the more suspicious, I couldn't count on that to hold him back. If he was the killer, his greed was likely far more powerful than any sense of reason.

'I'll pass on your message,' I said instead.

A satisfied smirk twitched at his lips. 'You do that. I'll drop by to see her tomorrow.'

'She's busy tomorrow.'

'The next day, then.'

The dogs remained tense and stood so close to me that they had their bodies pressed against my legs.

'My aunt won't be able to do anything with the land until after probate,' I pointed out, hoping to keep Grimshaw away from the farm.

'That doesn't mean we can't be prepared for the moment she can make a move. I'll bring some papers with me when I visit the farm. You advise your aunt that making a deal with me is the right choice. The only choice.'

I had to hold my tongue again to keep myself from telling him where to go. Fortunately, he turned away and climbed into a silver car parked in front of mine.

'What an odious man.' Avery Hembridge came to stand next to me as Grimshaw's vehicle squealed away from the curb and shot off along Main Street. 'Was he bothering you?'

'He was, but at least he's gone now.' For the moment, I didn't bother to add.

I looked at the business card in my hand. If there'd been a garbage can nearby, I would have tossed it immediately. Since the nearest trash receptacle was half a block away, I tucked the card in the pocket of my jeans to dispose of later.

I turned my full attention on Avery. 'How are you doing?'

Her blue eyes filled with tears.

'I'm so sorry!' I said with dismay as Fancy whined at my side. 'You're probably tired of people asking you that question.'

'No, it's OK,' she assured me, blinking away the tears. 'I appreciate you asking. It's just . . . the last few days have been a lot.'

'I heard about Simon Greenaway. I guess his death complicates matters.'

'A little.' She blinked again. No tears fell but her eyes were still shiny. 'Are you busy? I could use some company.' She shook her head. 'I'm sorry. I'm sure you have things to do.'

'I've got some free time,' I said. 'Do you want to go for a walk with me and the dogs?'

'Would you mind coming up to my stepfather's place? I have a few groceries in the car and some of them need to go in the freezer. But I'd love it if you could come for a drink.' She smiled at the spaniels. 'And the dogs too.'

'Sure,' I said. 'I'll meet you there.'

We set off in our individual cars and I followed Avery up the hill to her stepfather's mansion. I wondered if it would now be her mansion. If so, would she keep it or sell it? Although I was curious to know the answer, I didn't want to be rude, so I wasn't about to bring up the subject.

Avery parked in the driveway, right in front of the mansion, and I pulled in behind her car. I kept the dogs on their leashes, not wanting them to roam freely through the mansion, even though they were likely to stick close to me. I didn't want to take any chances, since I imagined that such a stately home was likely filled with expensive objects.

Avery set down her two bags of groceries while she unlocked the front door. 'Come on in, all of you.'

The dogs stayed sitting outside the door until I encouraged them to cross the threshold. We stepped into a spacious, two-story foyer with white marble floors, white walls, and a large crystal chandelier overhead. A curving staircase led up to the second floor and the foyer was furnished with a settee and console table – both of which looked like antiques. A large porcelain vase sat on the table, holding a giant bouquet of lilies and greenery. I knew lilies were poisonous for dogs, so I was glad the table was high enough to keep the flowers away from curious canine noses.

The housekeeper I'd seen on my first day in Twilight Cove walked toward us along a hallway that led deeper into the mansion. Fancy whined as she looked around, but she quieted when I gave her a pat on the head.

'Abigail,' Avery said to the housekeeper, 'I've brought a friend, Georgie Johansen. Could you please bring drinks to us in the parlor?'

'Of course,' Abigail answered in a deferential tone.

She shot what I thought was a disapproving glance at the dogs, but otherwise ignored them. Flossie and Fancy watched her with their brown eyes but stayed quietly at my side.

'What would you like to drink?' Avery asked me. 'Coffee? Soda?'

'We also have lemonade,' Abigail added.

'Lemonade would be great, thank you,' I said.

'I'll have a coffee. And bring a dish of water for the dogs, please,' Avery requested.

Abigail hesitated ever so slightly before nodding and heading back down the hallway.

'Would you like a tour of the house before we have our drinks?' Avery asked.

The offer surprised me, but I was definitely curious to see more of the mansion. 'Only if you'd like to give me one,' I said, not wanting to put her out, despite my curiosity. 'It's a beautiful place.'

'I'll show you around,' she said. 'And bring the dogs. You can let them off their leashes. My stepfather would have wanted them free in the house.'

I unclipped the leashes and the spaniels stayed at my side.

'Victor loved dogs,' Avery continued, 'but after he lost his sweet whippet, Zelda, five years ago, he didn't get another one. He was having too many health issues by that time.'

As she talked, Avery led me through a door to the left of the foyer and into a large and immaculate sitting room. The large, dual-aspect windows let in plenty of light. Together with the white walls, that made the room bright and airy. A large oil painting of a seascape hung over a marble fireplace and beautiful antiques furnished the room. I spotted two more vases full of fresh flowers and wondered if the mansion was always filled with fresh bouquets, or if these ones had been sympathy gifts.

'This place was built nearly a hundred years ago,' Avery explained as she led me through another door into a large dining room with a table that would easily seat a dozen people. 'Back then Twilight Cove was really just a little fishing hamlet.'

From the dining room, she led me into a state-of-the-art kitchen that was probably twice the size of my Los Angeles apartment. 'I'm just giving Georgie a quick tour before we have our drinks,' she told Abigail as the housekeeper passed us on her way to the parlor, carrying a tray with our drinks.

Avery continued showing me the various rooms and luxuries on the main floor, including an indoor swimming pool, a billiards room and a library. To complete the circuit of the ground floor, she led me into a large study.

'And this was Victor's home office.' She ran her hand over the mahogany desk with a sad, wistful smile. 'He loved working. It was hard on him when he had to sell off some of his businesses when his health began to fail.'

'What kind of business was he in?' I asked.

'A little of this and that, but he started out in real estate and lately he mostly focused on importing high-quality wine and liquor,' Avery replied. 'Check this out.'

She walked over to a floor-to-ceiling bookcase holding several thick binders and a few photographs. She pressed a spot on the edge of the bookcase. There was a click, and she tugged at one of the shelves. The entire unit swung away from the wall to reveal a doorway.

'A secret room?' I asked with fascination. I'd always loved the idea of houses with hidden passageways and rooms.

'I would have loved this when I was a kid,' Avery said. 'But Victor just bought this place two years ago.'

She passed through the doorway, and I followed. I was a little disappointed to find the small room completely empty.

'He didn't use it?' I asked.

'He used to store some valuables in here, things that were too big to fit in the safe in his study, but he got rid of those things a while ago.' Avery led the way back into the study and returned the bookcase to its place against the wall.

My gaze landed on an oil painting of a rugged coastline. It hung on the wall behind the desk.

'That's a beautiful painting.' I moved closer for a better look.

The artist had captured the energy of a stormy day on the Oregon coast.

Avery joined me by the painting. 'I'm not sure if Victor truly liked the painting or simply kept it there because of this.'

She pulled at the right side of the frame. It turned out it was on hinges, rather than hanging from a picture hook. The painting swung away from the wall to reveal a safe.

'The safe that you haven't been able to open?' I guessed, remembering what she'd said to the receptionist at the lawyer's office.

She sighed. 'That's it.'

A phone rang, and Avery dug the device out of the pocket of her black pants. She checked the screen. 'I'm so sorry. Please excuse me for a minute. I need to take this call, but I won't be long.'

'No problem,' I assured her.

She hurried out of the study and across the foyer into the parlor.

I wandered over to the floor-to-ceiling windows that looked out toward the ocean. I could see the water sparkling in the distance. The mansion definitely had gorgeous views.

I turned around at the sound of Fancy whining. She sat in the middle of the study, watching as her sister jumped up on the sturdy chair behind the desk. Once up on her perch, Flossie stood up on her hind legs and rested her front paws on the wall below the large oil painting.

'Flossie, what are you doing?' I crossed the room toward her, hoping she wasn't leaving dirty pawprints on the pristine white walls.

She pressed her nose to the edge of the ornate frame and gave it a nudge. It swung away from the wall again.

'Flossie!' I whispered.

I'd almost reached her when she touched a paw to the safe's dial.

I grabbed her collar, but let go when I heard a clicking sound come from the safe.

Fancy gave a soft 'a-woo' of encouragement, and Flossie butted the safe with her nose.

To my astonishment, the door opened.

SEVENTEEN

'What the . . .' I stood staring at the safe door, wondering if my eyes could be deceiving me.

Flossie pressed her nose into the crack of an opening and gave the safe door a push so it swung open wider.

'Flossie!' I whispered again.

I glanced over my shoulder, worried that Avery might come back, but I could still hear the low murmur of her voice coming from across the foyer.

As if understanding my worries, Fancy trotted across the study and sat down at the door, like she was standing guard.

Flossie was still on her hind legs on the chair, nosing around in the safe.

I grabbed her collar. 'Flossie, you can't be doing that!'

I caught a glimpse of papers piled in the safe, along with some bundles of cash and what might have been velvet jewelry boxes.

Flossie grabbed a manila envelope with her teeth and hopped down from the chair. The envelope fell from her mouth, and some of the contents spilled out onto the floor.

Casting another frantic look at the door, I dropped to my knees to gather up the fallen materials. Flossie stood by, watching me.

'Why on Earth did you do that?' I asked in a hushed voice.

The dogs had been so well behaved up until now that Flossie's stunt with the safe and envelope had completely taken me by surprise.

I was about to stuff everything back in the envelope when I paused. The materials included a yellowed newspaper clipping and an old photograph that featured a young, smiling couple dressed in clothes that dated the photo to around the 1970s. I glanced at the headline of the newspaper clipping. It related to a bank robbery that took place in Tennessee in 1974.

Fancy gave a quiet whine. I stuffed everything back in the envelope, thrust it into the safe, closed the door, and turned the dial. I moved the painting back in place and then scooted over to a framed photograph sitting on the bookshelf. It showed a man I presumed was Victor – probably when he was in his fifties or early sixties –

with a blonde woman around his age and a teenage Avery, all smiling at the camera, with a backdrop of palm trees and glittering turquoise waters.

My heart jumped when Abigail stepped into the room.

'Everything all right?' the housekeeper asked, her gaze traveling over me and then to each of the dogs.

'Yes, thanks,' I said, hoping I sounded completely at ease rather than guilty and breathless. 'I'm just waiting for Avery to finish a phone call.'

Abigail nodded and disappeared down the hall.

I barely had a chance to take in a deep, relieved breath when Avery breezed back into the room.

'Sorry about that.' She tucked her phone into her pocket.

'No need to apologize,' I said.

She gave me a grateful smile. 'Shall we have our drinks now?'

The dogs and I followed her across the foyer to the parlor. I took a seat on an antique settee while Avery settled in a wingback chair. I watched the dogs closely, hoping Flossie wouldn't try to pull any other stunts. To my relief, the spaniels took a drink from the bowl of water Abigail had left on the floor, and then they lay down by my feet.

My mind was spinning, wondering how the heck Flossie had managed to open the safe, but I couldn't focus on that at the moment.

'What will you do now that Victor's lawyer is dead?' I asked, hoping I wasn't being too nosy. 'Will that cause problems with dealing with the estate?'

'It won't hold things up for long,' Avery said as she added a splash of cream to her coffee. 'Simon had a partner at the law firm. She's semi-retired and splits her time between Twilight Cove and Carmel-by-the-Sea, but she's on her way here as we speak. She'll be able to access Victor's will and give me the combination to his safe.'

My gaze flickered to the open study door across the foyer. 'I don't suppose your stepfather left the safe unlocked?'

'He was too careful to do something like that.' Avery took a sip of coffee. 'Although, I did check, just in case. I even tried a few combinations. Family birthdates, things like that. None of them worked.'

I took a long drink of lemonade to cover my confusion. Either Avery was lying and the safe was unlocked when Flossie opened it, or someone else had unlocked it since Avery last tried to open it. Those seemed like the only rational explanations.

'Anyway, I expect this place will go on the market soon,' Avery said before taking another drink of coffee.

'You won't keep it?' I asked, glad she'd brought up the subject.

'I doubt it'll be mine. Victor talked to me about his will a while back. He didn't give me all the details, but he knew that my husband and I have a successful business in Chicago, and he was very focused on philanthropy in his later years, especially since my mother passed away from cancer twelve years ago.'

'I'm sorry about your mom,' I said.

'Thank you. I think her death was part of the reason my stepfather moved here. A new place without all the reminders of what he'd lost.' She set her cup on the coffee table. 'Victor told me he would leave me his Chicago condo and my husband would get one of his classic cars. I assume the rest will go to various charities.'

Those charities would likely be very pleased in the near future, once they found out what they'd be getting from Victor's estate.

Avery's phone rang again. She checked the screen and sighed. 'I'm sorry. There are so many arrangements to be made.'

I set down my empty glass and got to my feet. 'No worries. The dogs and I will head out now.'

Flossie and Fancy jumped to their feet and trotted after me as I made my way out of the mansion. I didn't see Abigail as we left. I hoped the spaniels hadn't left too much dog fur behind for her to clean up.

I spent most of the afternoon editing my script. In the early evening, I helped out with the farm chores and then took a quick shower. Afterward, I put on a simple green dress and tamed my short, wavy hair. Silver hoop earrings, a touch of makeup, and a pair of strappy sandals completed my look.

I explained to the dogs that they most likely wouldn't be allowed in Marlene's store, so they had to wait at home. They did a good job of making me feel guilty, simply by looking at me with sad brown eyes.

'I'm sorry,' I said as I backed out the door. 'I won't be long.'

My heart hurt as I walked down the porch steps without them. That wasn't a good sign. How would I ever be able to say goodbye to them when it came time for me to move back to Los Angeles?

I pushed those thoughts aside. I needed to stay focused on clearing away the cloud of suspicion hanging over Aunt Olivia and me.

I drove over to the carriage house and helped my aunt into the front passenger seat. She was going stir-crazy at home, so when I'd told her I wanted to find out more about Marlene and her dispute with Dorothy, Auntie O had wanted in on the plan. Although she'd previously said that we should leave all investigating to the police, an entire day spent cooped up in the carriage house had made her decide that a bit of observation and a touch of gossip gathering wouldn't hurt.

All the parking spots in front of Siren Beauty had already been claimed when we arrived on Main Street, so I double-parked and helped Olivia get out of the car. Dolores Sanchez came along the sidewalk, dressed in a purple muumuu this time, and waved when she saw us.

'I'll make sure Olivia gets inside all right,' Dolores assured me.

I thanked her and hurried back to my car before I caused a traffic jam. I managed to find a parking spot around the corner on Ocean Drive and, a couple of minutes later, I joined my aunt and Dolores in the cosmetics store.

Quite a crowd had already gathered for the customer appreciation event. Every product on the shelves was on sale, and a folding table had been set up at one end of the store. It held an array of finger foods and a bowl of what looked like orange punch. The crowd consisted mostly of women, but a couple of men were present as well. Many customers had a paper plate of food or a cup of punch in hand as they wandered around the shop, some showing interest in the various cosmetics and skincare products, while others seemed to be there for the food and socializing. Despite the latter, Marlene had a steady stream of people purchasing items at the sales counter near the back of the store.

The first fifteen minutes we spent in Siren Beauty didn't help me with my plan. I indulged in the finger foods and wandered around the shop. Aunt Olivia couldn't move very fast on her crutches, but she spent a lot of time in one spot, with a stream of people coming over to talk with her.

While trying to tune into all the conversations going on around me, I picked out some mineral-based mascara and eyeshadow. As I browsed and eavesdropped, I didn't hear anything of interest.

When there was a lull in people greeting Aunt Olivia, I made my way over to stand with her and Dolores.

'My plan has been a bust so far,' I admitted in a quiet voice.

'What plan?' Dolores asked with interest.

I glanced at Auntie O, not sure how much I should say. If Dolores and Marlene were friends, I didn't want to ruffle any feathers by revealing that Marlene was one of my murder suspects.

'We want to know if there's any chance that Marlene could have killed Dorothy,' Aunt Olivia whispered.

Dolores shot a suspicious, sidelong glance in the shop owner's direction. Definitely not friends, then.

'She certainly hated Dorothy,' Dolores said in a quiet, conspiratorial whisper. 'She thought Dorothy cursed her.' Dolores rolled her eyes. 'When her car broke down and her basement flooded, Marlene blamed both things on Dorothy, in addition to her minor loss of customers. The woman simply can't handle a bit of healthy competition. She still had plenty of customers coming here for her products.'

'So she had a motive,' I said, keeping my voice quiet. 'But what about opportunity?'

'Leave that to me,' Dolores said. She had a bottle of moisturizer in hand and strode over to the sales counter with it.

Aunt Olivia and I followed a short distance behind her. My aunt stationed herself in front of a display of face masks, while I got into line behind Dolores with my makeup.

When it was Dolores's turn to be served, she got right down to business.

'Such a good turnout, Marlene,' she said. 'It's so nice to see. I'm betting this event helped draw back the customers you lost to Dorothy.'

The shop owner smiled with self-satisfaction. 'I always knew they'd be back. Snake oil won't fool anyone for long.'

'Still, it doesn't hurt that Dorothy's gone.'

'I'm not one to speak ill of the dead,' Marlene said as she scanned the bottle of moisturizer, 'but that witch was a blight on this town.'

'It's scary knowing there's a murderer in Twilight Cove, though.' Dolores tapped her credit card to pay for her purchase. 'Don't you go walking early each morning? Maybe you passed the killer the day Dorothy died and didn't even know it.'

Marlene shook her head as she placed the bottle of moisturizer in a bag. 'That was the weekend I went to my favorite spa in Portland with my sister. My assistant ran the shop for me. I didn't even know about the murder until someone texted me about it the next day.' She tore the receipt off the printer. 'Would you like the receipt?'

'No, thanks.' Dolores picked up her bag. As she turned away from Marlene, she gave me a wink.

I paid for the makeup I'd picked out and then joined Aunt Olivia and Dolores over by a display of lip balm.

'How was that?' Dolores asked me.

'Smooth and impressive,' I said.

She smiled. 'Just call me Jessica Fletcher.'

We laughed and headed in the direction of the food table again.

'But how do we know if she's telling the truth about her alibi?' I whispered when we reached the table.

'My brother's ex-girlfriend, Lily, works at that spa,' Dolores said as she picked up a paper plate from the end of the table. 'I'll get her to check the records and see if Marlene really was booked in.'

'If she's your brother's ex, will she want to help?' Aunt Olivia asked.

Dolores waved off that concern. 'She'll help. We're still on good terms. Besides, Lily is the nosiest nosy Parker I've ever known. She won't be able to help herself.'

Dolores fired off a text message to her brother's ex before following us along the food table. We sampled a couple of the desserts, which were delicious, and enjoyed some punch. By the time we'd finished the treats, I could tell that Aunt Olivia was growing weary.

After saying goodbye to Dolores, my aunt and I made our way around a crowd of ladies who were chatting and laughing together while drinking punch. Our route took us past the sales counter, where Abigail – Victor Clyde's housekeeper – was next in line to pay.

When it was her turn, she stepped forward and said, 'Hello, Marlene. What a wonderful event.'

'Abigail,' I heard Marlene say as I walked away. 'One of my most loyal customers. I'm so glad you were able to make it here this evening.'

The store had grown even more crowded and it took another couple of minutes to get Aunt Olivia safely out the door. I fetched the car while she waited, leaning on her crutches, and I soon had her back at the carriage house, where she planned to read for a short while before going to bed.

Although going to sleep sounded tempting, I felt too guilty to head straight for my bedroom when I got back to the farmhouse. Flossie and Fancy greeted me as if I'd been gone for a year, and my guilt at leaving them behind made a strong comeback.

I traded my sandals for flip-flops and the three of us piled into my car and drove down to the beach so the dogs could run around and get some exercise. I took them to the stretch of beach below Main Street rather than the isolated strip of sand on the other side of the woodland from the farmhouse. I wasn't about to go trekking through the forest after dark. Even if there weren't a killer on the loose, I wouldn't have been keen to do that.

While the dogs ran down to the water's edge, I checked my phone and found a text message from Auntie O. She'd heard from Dolores, who'd already received a response from her brother's ex. Marlene had indeed stayed at the spa on the weekend that Dorothy was killed. Not only did the spa's records confirm that, but Lily remembered Marlene and her sister, both repeat customers. Lily also recalled seeing Marlene on the morning that Dorothy was killed. She and her sister took a yoga class and then had breakfast in the dining room.

As I walked through the cool sand in my bare feet, my flip-flops held in one hand, I watched the dogs run and play while I thought over that information.

It seemed beyond dispute that Marlene had an alibi for Dorothy's murder.

That meant I had to strike her off my list of suspects.

It also meant Aunt Olivia and I weren't yet free of that hovering cloud of suspicion.

EIGHTEEN

While working on the farm in the morning, I made sure to check for security cameras on Callum's cabin, the barn, and the other outbuildings. I didn't spot a single one. I fed the chickens, cleaned out stalls, and then got to work grooming the donkeys. Callum wasn't far away. I could see him fixing a section of fencing.

He finished up and headed over my way as I was combing Hamish the donkey's mane.

'Need help with anything?' Callum asked as he ran a hand along Hamish's back.

'I'm fine,' I assured him. 'I'm almost done here.'

'I'll be in the barn then.' He gave Hamish a pat. 'I need to fix one of the stall doors.'

'Callum,' I said to stop him before he could leave. I tried to keep my voice casual so he wouldn't think I was harboring any suspicions about him. 'I couldn't help noticing that you had boxes for security cameras in your cabin. Are the cameras for the farm? Because I haven't seen any around.'

He hesitated for a split second before answering, 'I'm using them at the perimeter of the property.'

'Because of the murder?' I pressed. 'Or have there been other problems?'

He took a step backward. 'No problems here on the farm. Just being proactive.' He turned toward the barn. 'Holler if you need anything.'

He strode away, faster than he usually walked.

'What do you think, Hamish?' I asked the donkey as I ran the comb through his short mane one last time.

He swished his tail.

I sighed. 'I know. He's hiding something. I just hope it's not something terrible.'

I finished up with the donkeys and then returned to the farmhouse and changed into clean clothes. I had a phone meeting scheduled for the afternoon to talk about script rewrites and I wanted to start brainstorming for a new project, but I decided to take the dogs down to the beach before I got started. They'd followed me around the farm all morning, but that didn't burn off their energy the same way as running along the beach would.

To save time, I decided to drive the dogs to the main beach, like I'd done the night before. I told them where we were heading, and they seemed to understand. As soon as I opened the farmhouse door, they burst outside and ran to my car. They waited impatiently, tails wagging, for me to open the back door so they could pile into the vehicle.

When I climbed into the driver's seat, Fancy threw her head back and let out a howl of excitement.

I laughed. 'Are you turning into a couple of beach bums?'

Flossie gave a woof that sounded like an affirmative response.

After we arrived at the beach, I walked at a leisurely pace along the water's edge while the dogs bounded off ahead of me, sometimes on the sand and sometimes in the shallows. Unlike the night before, we didn't have the beach to ourselves this time. An older couple walked two golden retrievers at the far end of the cove, two mothers watched as their young children played in the sand with shovels, and a middle-aged man was out jogging. I wondered if I should take up jogging on the beach. The farm chores kept me fairly active, but I still spent a lot of hours sitting at my computer.

I reminded myself that I'd be heading back to Los Angeles before long. I sometimes jogged in the city, but nowhere so nice and peaceful as this stretch of coastline. Even when sharing Twilight Cove's main beach with others, it was still far quieter than any of the places I frequented in LA.

After we'd walked the full length of the cove and back to the parking lot, I did my best to wash the sand off the dogs at the outdoor shower. Fortunately, I'd thought to stash a couple of old towels in the trunk of my car so I could dry the spaniels off before they got back into the vehicle.

We were driving along Larkspur Lane, getting close to the farm, when I saw someone emerging from the woods. I nearly hit the brakes when I realized the person was Byron Szabo. I stole a few glances at him through the rearview mirror as I continued along the road. Just as I took the final curve before reaching the farm, I saw Byron stash something in the trunk of his car.

This time I did pull over and stop the vehicle. Had the reporter gone nosing around Dorothy's cabin?

Another thought struck me, kicking my pulse up a notch.

What if he was the killer and had gone back to make sure that the discarded teacup had been carried away by the creek?

He wouldn't have found it, since the police had it. So, what had he stowed in his car?

'Go home and write or turn around?' I voiced the question out loud.

Fancy let out an 'a-woo' and Flossie added a woof.

Maybe I was simply interpreting their vocalizations the way I wanted to, but I thought they were encouraging me to go with my gut.

I made sure that the road was clear and then executed a quick U-turn. I drove slowly around the bend and then increased my speed when I saw that Byron had already pulled away from the side of the road. I almost lost sight of his vehicle, but I stepped on the gas and managed to get close enough to keep track of him again.

Most likely, following the reporter wouldn't lead me to any clues, but maybe if I were lucky, I'd see him removing the object he'd put in his trunk. Whatever it was had been larger than a camera. Had he stolen something from Dorothy's cabin?

I didn't know why he would do that since there wasn't much there to steal, but I definitely didn't trust Byron.

I expected the reporter to drive to the newspaper office – wherever that was located – and simply get back to work, leaving me with no more information than I already had. He turned off Larkspur Lane and onto Ocean Drive, heading south along the coastline. I realized that downtown Twilight Cove wasn't his intended destination when he left Ocean Drive for a residential neighborhood.

A minute later, he pulled into the driveway of a beige, two-story house with brown trim. I drove past his driveway and pulled up to the curb two houses away. I twisted around in my seat and peered back toward the beige house. Byron climbed out of his car and headed straight up to the front door. He unlocked it and disappeared inside.

Whatever he had in the trunk of his car remained there.

I drove to the end of the street and around the corner, parking the car out of sight.

'This is probably pointless, but let's take a walk past Byron's house,' I said to the dogs as I opened the back door.

They jumped out of the car eagerly. I snapped their leashes to their collars and noticed that an alley ran along the back of the properties on Byron's street.

'We'll walk up the street and down the alley, and then give up,' I told Flossie and Fancy.

They trotted along happily as we walked toward Byron's house. I tried to walk slowly enough to allow myself a good look at his place while not appearing suspicious. The dogs helped out by stopping to sniff here and there, so I had an excuse to pause and scope out the property. Not that it did any good. I couldn't see through the windows from this distance and nothing about the front yard shouted, 'A killer lives here!' The grass needed to be mowed, but otherwise the place seemed reasonably tidy and well-maintained.

We'd almost made it past Byron's house when the front door opened. Suddenly, I didn't want to be there any longer. If he recognized me, he'd probably pelt me with questions about Dorothy and my role as a suspect in the murder investigation.

The dogs and I picked up our pace, and I only allowed myself a glance over my shoulder once we'd reached the end of the street. Byron climbed into his car – without opening the trunk – and started the engine. As we turned the corner, Byron's vehicle backed out of the driveway and onto the street. He drove off in the opposite direction from where we stood.

I'd given up on finding any clues or helpful information, but we carried on down the alley as planned since that would be the quickest route back to my car. When we passed by the back of Byron's house, I stopped dead in my tracks.

A girl dressed in jeans and a black hoodie darted across the yard to Byron's back door. When she sent a furtive glance over her shoulder before trying to open the locked door, I recognized her immediately.

Roxy Russo.

NINETEEN

'What the heck is she up to?' I said under my breath.

Roxy moved from the locked door to a window she could reach from the porch. To my dismay, it opened when she gave it a push.

I glanced around to check if anyone might be watching us. Thanks to the trees growing at the back of the surrounding properties, I didn't think any of the neighbors could see us.

By the time I returned my attention to the back of Byron's house, Roxy was climbing in through the window.

I hated the thought of the teen getting into serious trouble, so I made a quick decision and opened Byron's back gate.

Flossie and Fancy darted through ahead of me and I barely had time to quietly close the gate before they were tugging on their leashes, urging me forward. Desperately hoping that no neighbors would spot us, I hurried after the dogs. They scrambled up the steps to the back porch and I followed, trying to move quickly but silently.

When we reached the open window, I poked my head through it.

'Roxy!' I said in a loud whisper.

She was nowhere in sight, and I heard no response.

I pulled my head back out of the window and hesitated, not sure what to do. If I followed Roxy inside and we got caught, we could both end up in trouble with the police.

Fancy whined quietly at my side. I rested a hand on her head as I continued to wonder if I should go inside after Roxy or retreat to the alley and wait for her to reappear.

Flossie, apparently, didn't share my internal dilemma.

In an impressive display of agility and grace, she leapt up onto the windowsill and into the house. Her leash slipped out of my hand before I could tighten my grip on it.

'Flossie!' I whisper-yelled.

She didn't reappear.

That made up my mind. I scrambled through the window, my long legs giving me a bit of trouble. When I got all my limbs through and my feet hit the floor, I stuck my head back out the window.

'Wait there, Fancy,' I said as I dropped her leash.

She gave a soft 'a-woo'. At first, I thought it was a sound of acknowledgement, but as soon as I moved away from the window, I realized it was more likely an apology, because she leapt up onto the sill and followed me into the house.

I ran my hands through my hair, on the verge of panicking.

Get it together, I admonished myself. *This isn't a good time to freak out.*

I closed the window all but a crack in case Byron came home before I had a chance to get Roxy out of there. I didn't want an open window to alert him to our presence in his house.

Flossie was nowhere in sight. I unclipped Fancy's leash and she stayed by my side as I took note of the fact that I was standing in Byron's kitchen. He'd left dirty dishes stacked in the sink and crumbs on the laminate countertop. Straight ahead of me, across the room, a doorway led into a dining room. I could see from my vantage point that the dining table held messy stacks of papers, books, and what looked like electronics.

Halfway along the right-hand wall, another doorway led to a hall. I couldn't see Flossie or Roxy in the dining room, so I took the door to the right and crept into the hallway. One branch led straight ahead while the other stretched toward the front of the house. Flossie sat in the middle of the latter branch. She jumped up when Fancy and I joined her in the hall.

'Come on, Flossie,' I coaxed. 'We need to get out of here.'

To my dismay, she trotted toward the foyer and then disappeared around a corner. Fancy bounded after her.

'Fancy!' I whispered, wishing I'd kept her on the leash.

She disappeared around the same corner.

I picked up my pace and reached the foyer in time to see the spaniels bounding up the stairs to the second floor, Flossie's leash trailing behind her. Letting out a few choice words under my breath, I hurried after them. When they reached the upstairs hallway, the dogs sat down. I'd just joined them at the top of the stairs when Roxy emerged from a bedroom off to our right.

Her eyes widened when she saw me and the dogs. She froze, and I could tell she was about to bolt. Not that she had anywhere to go, since I was blocking the stairs. Although, as freaked out as she appeared, she might try to escape out a window.

'Roxy, wait!' I whispered. 'I'm here to get you *out* of trouble, not *in* trouble.'

Flossie nuzzled Roxy's hand with her nose.

The teen relaxed enough that she no longer appeared ready to flee, but she remained wary, and defiance replaced the fear in her eyes. 'Why do you care if I get caught?'

'Does that matter right now?' Every second that passed left me more convinced that Byron or the police would soon be at the door.

'Why are you whispering?' Roxy pushed past me, heading down the hall to my left. 'We're the only ones here.'

'At the moment.' I followed her, with the dogs between us, and grabbed the end of Flossie's leash on the way.

On this side of the staircase, the hall had three doors, one on either side and the third at the end. The door on the right stood open, revealing a bathroom. Roxy opened the one on the left. The bedroom held nothing but some dumbbells and a treadmill. Roxy shut that door and tried the one at the end of the hallway. It was locked.

'If I'm going to end up in jail for coming in here after you, can I at least know why you're here?' The mere thought of getting caught in Byron's house made me feel faint. I put a hand to the wall to steady myself. Clearly, a life of crime didn't suit me.

Roxy rattled the doorknob, obviously frustrated. The door didn't budge. She gave up and whirled around to face me.

'Byron's a creep,' she said. 'Dorothy was my friend, and he murdered her.'

Flossie and Fancy whined at the sound of Dorothy's name.

'How do you know that?' I asked with surprise.

'I've seen him sneaking around in the woods. Sometimes he has a shovel with him. I bet he's buried a whole bunch of bodies out there.'

That news sent a chill slinking through me. 'Have there been any missing persons from Twilight Cove who might be his murder victims?'

Roxy shrugged and tried the door again. It still wouldn't open. 'He could be finding victims in other towns.'

'If Byron's a murderer, that's all the more reason not to be here in his house,' I pointed out.

'I want to find evidence so he doesn't get away with it.'

'Even if we find evidence here, that won't help the police,' I said, trying to keep my voice calm. That wasn't easy. 'It's not like we can tell them that we broke into the house.'

'I'll leave one of those anonymous tips.' She pushed past me again. 'I'm going to check the basement.'

Great. That's exactly what I wanted to do: check out a suspected killer's basement.

As I let out a huff of air, Flossie went up on her hind legs and touched a paw to the door at the end of the hall.

The lock clicked.

She sat down and looked at me expectantly.

Thinking I might be losing it, I tried the doorknob. It turned easily.

Roxy turned back at the sound of the opening door. 'How did you do that?'

I shrugged, not sure what to say. My mind was spinning too fast to come up with any sort of explanation.

Roxy stared at me with a mixture of suspicion and respect. 'You're a lock picker.'

'No.' I didn't think she heard my denial.

She was too busy making a beeline for the door. She pushed it open wider and stepped into the room. The dogs followed her and I did the same. Roxy wasn't going to leave until she'd had a good look around the house, and I didn't want to leave her there on her own, even if that meant going into the basement. The police and jail time aside, if Byron was a murderer, I didn't want him finding Roxy in his house and harming her.

I tried to calm my pounding heart, but without success. I'd just have to put up with my racing, dizzying pulse until I could convince Roxy to leave. I hoped I wouldn't pass out. The jumble of thoughts swirling in my head like a dust devil was only adding to my wooziness.

'Holy . . .' Roxy's voice distracted me from my anxiety.

I stepped farther into the room so I could see what she was looking at. My eyes widened when I saw the walls of what was apparently Byron's home office. They were covered in papers, newspaper clippings, and photographs. Some items were connected to each other with pieces of red string held down by thumbtacks.

Roxy perused the display on the wall to the left of the door, so I unclipped Flossie's leash and headed for the far wall. We stood there in silence, reading headlines and looking at the photos. There was so much to see, so much to take in, that my heart finally slowed its frantic thudding.

'It looks like Byron has an obsession with cold cases,' I said after studying the far wall for close to a full minute.

'He's seriously obsessed,' Roxy agreed. 'It's totally creepy.'

We both turned around when the dogs whined. They were sitting by the wall across the room from me, staring up at it. We joined them there and continued our perusal.

My pulse picked up again as I read one of the newspaper clippings.

'Hold on . . .' I gave my head a shake, trying to clear my thoughts. We'd stumbled upon something important. I just wasn't quite sure what to make of it yet.

Roxy ignored me and continued her own examination of the items on the wall.

I whipped out my phone and snapped several photographs of the clippings. Byron had also added sticky notes with handwriting on them. I took photos of those as well.

Roxy stepped back from the wall, taking in the sight of the office as a whole. 'Some of these are murder cases. I bet Byron's the killer in all of them.'

'I'm not so sure,' I said.

I was about to explain why I had my doubts, but I didn't get a chance.

From the front of the house came the sound of a key in a lock.

TWENTY

Roxy spun around to face me, her brown eyes so wide they might have been comical if we weren't in such a perilous situation.

'What do we do?' she whispered, frantic.

I made a quiet dash for the office window. The two-story drop to the ground ruled it out as an escape route. I shouldn't have even wasted time looking out the window. There was no way Flossie and Fancy could go out that way, even if Roxy and I could.

Below us, the front door opened and closed. Footsteps sounded in the foyer and then disappeared deeper into the house. That allowed me to breathe more easily, but not by much. Byron might not be heading upstairs – yet – but we had to go downstairs to get out of the house.

Even though my heart was galloping like a wild horse on the run, I forced myself to take a deep breath. I had to get all of us out of the house, safely and without being seen.

I touched a finger to my lips and Roxy nodded. Her eyes still shone with fear, and that made her look so young that a wave of protectiveness hit me. No matter what happened, I'd do everything in my power to defend her and the dogs.

I took a careful step toward the door, relieved that the floor didn't creak beneath me. I continued to tiptoe out of the room and into the hallway. Roxy followed, mimicking my careful, soft steps. Flossie and Fancy brought up the rear.

Once we were all out of the office, I pointed at the open door. Roxy caught on and grabbed the doorknob, easing the door shut. We both flinched when the latch clicked. I refocused on the path ahead of us, but I glanced back again when I heard another click. Flossie had a paw on the door, near the knob. She dropped back down to all fours and then joined Fancy at Roxy's heels.

Maybe I was crazy, but I was sure she'd locked the door. Just like she'd unlocked it a few minutes ago.

Breaking and entering and now thinking a dog could unlock safes and doors. I really was losing it.

But that was a worry for another time.

I crept forward.

Lucky for us, the office and upstairs hallway were carpeted. I wasn't sure what we'd do once we reached the main level. Flossie's and Fancy's claws would likely click against the hardwood floors.

I decided to worry about that when we made it that far.

I paused at the top of the staircase, listening. Water ran somewhere in the house. Then it shut off. Byron was likely in the kitchen or the bathroom. If he was in the bathroom, this might be our best chance to escape.

Carefully, I lowered one foot onto the top stair. I realized I was holding my breath and forced myself to draw air into my lungs. Passing out wouldn't help us get out of the house un-detected.

The first stair didn't creak beneath me, so I picked up my pace, just slightly. The fourth stair down gave a groan when I settled my weight onto it. I winced and froze, expecting Byron to appear at the bottom of the staircase at any moment, demanding to know what we were doing in his house. Instead, I heard only the sound of a cupboard door closing, probably in the kitchen.

Glancing back at Roxy, I pointed at the stair I stood on. She nodded in understanding. I continued downward and Roxy followed, skipping the creaky stair. She nearly lost her balance and put a hand to my shoulder to save herself. I grabbed the railing to keep us both steady. We recovered and continued our slow progress down the stairs with the dogs creeping along behind us.

Flossie and Fancy seemed to understand that we had to be as quiet as possible. When we reached the hardwood floors of the foyer, they moved with great care so their nails made hardly any noise against the floor.

I could still hear Byron moving around in the kitchen. Although leaving through the front door didn't strike me as the best idea, since we might be seen by neighbors, we couldn't leave through the kitchen window with Byron in that room. I took a step closer to the front door, hoping it wouldn't make much noise when I unlocked and opened it. If it did, we'd have to make a run for it, but I doubted we had much chance of getting out of sight before Byron got a look at us. Roxy could pull up her hood to hide her face, but I had no such handy disguise, and the spaniels were distinct enough to make it easier to figure out our identities.

Unfortunately, we didn't have much choice but to take our chances.

I settled my hand on the deadbolt lock, working up the courage to turn it. Before I could do anything more, Roxy's hand clutched my arm in a painful grip. I knew what had scared her. Byron's footsteps were coming toward the front of the house.

I realized that he was entering the dining room from the kitchen. Any second now, he'd be able to see us in the foyer.

We moved faster than I thought possible while making little noise. I gripped Roxy's hand and pulled her along the hallway toward the back of the house. The dogs stayed on our heels.

Byron began whistling random notes as he moved about in the dining room. I heard papers shuffling as I paused by the kitchen door. Roxy's eyes were as wide as saucers. Mine probably were too. Only the dogs seemed perfectly calm as they stood waiting for our next move.

I chanced a peek into the kitchen. Byron stood just past the doorway to the dining room, looking through the books and papers piled on the table. I ducked back into the hallway, my heart once again pounding like the bass beat of a fast-paced song turned up too loud. There was no way we could creep across the kitchen, open the window, and climb out without Byron hearing us. As soon as he turned around, he'd spot us.

I slipped around Roxy and peeked into the main floor bathroom. My hope of finding an escape route there shattered when I saw the tiny window, only half of which could open. None of us would fit through it.

Turning toward Roxy and the dogs, I pointed at what I assumed was the basement door. That appeared to be our best option now. At least the windows would be close to the ground. I just hoped they wouldn't be painted shut, and that we wouldn't stumble across any dead bodies.

Roxy reached for the basement door, but halted with her hand on the knob. By the sound of his footsteps, Byron was back in the kitchen and coming our way.

Grabbing Roxy's arm, I pulled her into the bathroom. Flossie slipped inside with us, but my heart dropped like a heavy stone. Fancy was still out in the hall. She wasn't going to make it into the bathroom in time.

I had no choice. I shut the door all but a crack and hoped that

Byron would think that Fancy had somehow managed to slip into his house all on her own. In the best case scenario, he'd herd her out of the house and we could escape while he was busy doing that. If he got angry at Fancy and tried to harm her, I knew I'd be out of my hiding spot in a flash to defend her, no matter what the consequence.

Fancy stood by the basement door, just two feet away from us. I held my breath as Byron came into the hallway from the kitchen. I blinked and couldn't believe my eyes.

Fancy had disappeared.

Byron began whistling again as he stopped at a closet in the hallway. He opened the bifold doors, grabbed something, and closed up the closet. From there, he headed along the hallway to the front of the house. Then his footsteps pounded up the stairs to the second floor.

I stared at the spot where Fancy had stood moments before.

How had she vanished?

Then I saw it: an outline of the spaniel against the white paint of the basement door. As I watched, more of her form filled in until she was once again a fully visible, brown and white dog standing in the hall.

She hadn't vanished, I realized.

Somehow, she'd managed to camouflage herself.

My brain wanted to go numb with shock and disbelief, but I didn't have time for that. I opened the bathroom door wider and motioned for Roxy to follow me. We scurried into the kitchen, where I opened the window and ushered Roxy out of it. Flossie and Fancy then jumped out onto the porch one after the other. I climbed out last, clutching the bundled leashes in my hands, my legs nearly getting tangled in my haste. Luckily, I managed to land on my feet without making much noise. I lowered the window and ran after Roxy and the dogs, who were already making a dash for the back gate.

When we reached the alley, I latched the gate behind us and chanced a glance up at the second-story windows. I couldn't see Byron looking out at us. Maybe we'd made a clean getaway.

Not waiting around for that to change, we ran along the alley like we had hell hounds on our heels. I led the way to my car and pushed the button on the key fob so the doors would unlock.

'Get in!' I said to Roxy as I opened the back door for the dogs.

They piled in while Roxy clambered into the front passenger

seat. I zipped around the back of the car and jumped in behind the wheel. Seconds later, we pulled away from the curb and zoomed off down the street.

When we'd put half a mile between us and Byron's house, I finally started to breathe a little easier. My fingers ached, and I forced myself to relax my death grip on the steering wheel.

'We never got a chance to check his basement for bodies,' Roxy said. 'We should go back.'

I nearly slammed on the brakes.

'You've got to be kidding.' I glanced her way to find her smiling. It was the first time I'd seen her face lit up like that.

'I am. Sort of.' She laughed. 'You should see your face!'

I pressed a hand to my chest before replacing it on the steering wheel. 'I don't think my heart can handle anything more today.'

Needing some fresh air, I pulled into the parking lot at Twilight Cove's main beach. We climbed out of the car and the dogs ran straight for the water. I shut the driver's door and rubbed my forehead. My brain was struggling to process everything that had happened, everything I'd seen.

Roxy had been tucked behind me while we'd hidden in Byron's bathroom, so I knew she hadn't seen Fancy camouflage herself. Although that brought me a sense of relief, it also disappointed me. If we'd both seen it happen, I'd know I hadn't imagined it.

Yet, I knew it really had happened. There was no way that Byron could have missed seeing her otherwise.

Then there was the way Flossie had unlocked the door to Byron's study. And the safe at Victor Clyde's mansion.

It was time for me to accept that the spaniels had special powers, gifts, abilities – whatever the best word was for the things they could do.

Maybe Dorothy really was a witch. Perhaps she'd bestowed the powers upon the dogs. Or had they been born with their special abilities?

I had no idea, and with Dorothy gone, I'd likely have to accept that I would never get answers to those questions.

Thinking about the dogs' powers felt like too much at the moment.

I bought ice-cream cones for Roxy and myself at the shop on the corner of Main Street and Ocean Drive, and we walked down to the water as we ate. We watched the dogs splashing about in the shallows, playing and chasing seagulls.

'How are we going to get the police to look at Byron as a suspect?' Roxy asked as she licked the last of her ice cream off her fingers.

'I'm not sure,' I said as we sat down on a log.

'Maybe I should leave an anonymous tip.' She didn't sound as confident about that as she had back at Byron's house. 'I don't want the cops tracing it back to me, though. They say it's anonymous when you call those tip lines, but are they really?'

'I don't know,' I admitted. 'Let's take some time to think things over.'

I almost told her to forget about Byron and let the police do their job without any input from us, but that would have been hypocritical of me to say that. After all, the only reason I'd seen her breaking into Byron's house was because I myself was poking around. Plus, I didn't want to alienate Roxy now that she was talking to me. Getting anywhere close to lecturing her would probably do just that.

'Promise me that you really won't go back to Byron's house,' I pleaded.

She huffed out a sigh, but then relented. 'Fine. I promise. But you think he's the killer, right? You saw all that creepy stuff in his office, and I swear he's been digging in the forest.'

'There's definitely something up with him,' I said. 'And, yes, he very well could be the killer. All the more reason to stay away from him.'

Roxy stared out at the ocean. I couldn't tell what she was thinking, but I hoped she wouldn't be breaking into any more houses in the future.

I stood up and brushed the sand from my shorts. 'How about I give you a ride to school?'

She gave me an award-worthy eye roll, but she didn't protest.

When I dropped her off at the local high school, I waited until I saw her disappear into the building. Whether or not she would actually go to class, I didn't know, but during the car ride she'd agreed to start volunteering at the animal sanctuary, and I counted that as a win.

TWENTY-ONE

After dropping Roxy off at school, I returned to the farmhouse and parked myself at the kitchen table with my laptop in front of me. My thoughts wanted to bounce around in all different directions, but with my phone meeting coming up, I had to focus on my job. Although I'd always been self-disciplined, I impressed myself with my ability to concentrate on going over my script before my conversation with Giselle, the producer.

During the phone meeting, my attention never wavered from the subject of our discussion. Once it ended, however, my brain had reached its capacity for ignoring the day's earlier events.

Since I didn't want to think about the dogs' special abilities (my mind still wasn't ready to process any of that), I focused on what we'd found in Byron's study. Maybe Roxy was right and Byron had collected newspaper clippings for crimes he'd committed, but that couldn't be the story behind all of the items he'd posted on his walls, because some of the crimes dated too far back.

I accessed the photos I'd taken in Byron's home office and zoomed in on several of the newspaper stories. While a few were original copies clipped from a newspaper, others appeared to be photocopies or printouts from the Internet or digital archives. A couple of the crimes had taken place in the past decade. Others were far older. Some of them dated so far back that Byron either wouldn't have been born or would have been a young child when they were committed.

Byron probably just had an obsession with cold cases. Although, that didn't explain why he kept his home office locked. Maybe he had a lodger whom he didn't fully trust. I didn't check all of the bedrooms so I didn't know if more than one appeared to be occupied. Roxy had looked into at least one of the rooms I hadn't seen. She'd given me her cell phone number before getting out of the car at the high school. I wondered if I should text her and ask what she'd seen in the other bedrooms. I didn't want to encourage her to stay focused on Dorothy's murder, but the information would be helpful.

Making up my mind, I sent her a quick text message. Then I zoomed in on the photo of the newspaper clipping that had really caught my attention. The story related to a bank robbery that took place in Tennessee back in 1974. The text of the clipping was a little bit blurry in the photo I'd taken, but not so bad that I couldn't read it again. I'd felt certain back at Byron's house that the story related to the same robbery as the one mentioned in the clipping I'd seen in Victor Clyde's safe. Now, having read the story again, I was more certain of that than ever.

I poured myself a glass of iced tea and sat down at the kitchen table again with my laptop in front of me. It didn't take long for me to find some information online about the robbery. The crime took place in a small town in the spring of 1974. A man wearing a ski mask to disguise his face entered the bank with a gun and demanded money. He made off with more than a hundred thousand dollars in cash. A vehicle and getaway driver waited outside the bank and took off as soon as the robber climbed in with his loot.

Although the police set up roadblocks, they failed to nab the robber and getaway driver. A week after the robbery, the getaway car was found abandoned on the edge of a logging road. The car had been stolen in Kansas and had been wiped clean of fingerprints. However, based on the bank tellers' description of the robber's build and voice, and the concurrent disappearance of a young local man named Jeffrey Herring, the police believed that Herring was the culprit.

Herring was in his early twenties at the time and was dating a local teenage girl named Ellen Dudek. The police believed that Ellen was the getaway driver. When officers showed up at her family's home to question her, she sneaked out of the back door and took off in her father's car. While fleeing, the vehicle went off the road and into the local river, which was swollen from the spring run-off. The police came across the accident scene shortly after it happened, but they were unable to save Ellen. Her boyfriend, the suspected robber, was never located.

I sat back in my chair and took a long drink of iced tea. Was it a coincidence that both Byron and Victor had newspaper clippings related to the 1974 robbery? The case didn't seem high-profile enough to make such a coincidence likely. Then again, if Victor and Byron were cold case buffs, maybe it wasn't so unusual that they'd both taken an interest in the crime. Could I really conclude that Victor was a fan of unsolved cases, though? I hadn't gone through the entire contents of his safe, but I hadn't seen any evidence that he'd taken an interest in past crimes aside from the robbery.

Car tires crunched over the driveway, making Flossie's and Fancy's ears perk up. The dogs jumped up from where they'd been snoozing and ran for the back door. I got up to see who'd arrived at the farm. My shoulders tensed when I opened the door and saw Ed Grimshaw climbing out of his car.

I strode across the grass with the dogs at my side. 'You're not welcome here,' I called out to Grimshaw.

The front door of the carriage house opened and Aunt Olivia emerged on her crutches.

'I'm not here to see you,' Grimshaw said to me.

'I agree with my niece.' Aunt Olivia's blue eyes didn't shine with their usual friendly light.

'Hear me out,' Grimshaw said to her. 'I think you'll like what I have to say.'

'I already know what you're going to say.' Olivia leaned on her crutches. 'And I won't be selling the woodland to you, or to anyone else. Dorothy entrusted it to my care so I could protect it, and that's exactly what I intend to do.'

Grimshaw's expression darkened. 'Foolish notions won't keep a roof over your head when times get tough. And they will get tough if you don't make the right choice.'

'Are you threatening my aunt?' I demanded.

The dogs shifted restlessly at my side.

Grimshaw shrugged. 'I'm just saying that I've got friends in high places.' He returned his attention to Olivia. 'You might find that you end up having trouble with your mortgage. This is a nice place you've got here. I'm sure you wouldn't want to lose it.'

Beside me, the dogs growled. I clenched my fists at my side, ready to explode.

Aunt Olivia spoke again before I had a chance to blow up at Grimshaw.

'Leave now or I'm calling the police,' she said, a hard edge to her voice that I hadn't heard before.

'You don't want to be doing that,' Grimshaw said with a smirk.

I pulled my phone from my pocket. 'I'll make the call.'

The smirk fell from his face when I started punching buttons on my phone. 'You'll regret this.' He aimed the threat at both of us.

He got into his car and slammed the door. The engine revved and dirt and gravel sprayed up as he stomped on the gas pedal and careened around in a wide U-turn. I had to jump out of the way as he tore onto the grass before returning to the driveway and shooting out onto the road.

I moved over to stand next to my aunt as we watched his car disappear.

'Don't worry,' Auntie O said, sounding far calmer than I felt. 'I don't even have a mortgage on this place anymore. I own it outright. Ed Grimshaw is all bluster and empty threats.'

'Unless he's the one who killed Dorothy.'

My aunt frowned at that.

Something occurred to me. 'It looks like Dorothy had tea with her killer before she died. Do you think she would have let Grimshaw into her home and sat down with him? He was so threatening toward her when I saw them in the woods together the day before she died. Why would she invite him into her cabin?'

And did that mean that Grimshaw wasn't the killer?

'Would it be his style to sedate someone before killing them?' I asked before my aunt had a chance to answer my first question.

'If Ed Grimshaw was planning a murder, I can imagine him doing it in a way that would ensure he would keep his hands relatively clean. So, yes, he might have used a sedative to drug his victim. To answer your first question, I have trouble picturing Dorothy letting him into her home. At the same time, she mentioned once that forgiveness and tolerance were important to her. She fell for Marlene's bait and argued with her once – that's the time she supposedly cursed Marlene – but I know Dorothy regretted that later. She told me she planned to apologize to Marlene, for the purported curse, not for helping people with her natural remedies. I don't know if she ever got the chance.'

I mulled that over. Apology or not, Marlene couldn't have killed Dorothy because of her alibi. I still wasn't sure about Ed Grimshaw. Maybe he pretended to change his tune and asked to have a reasonable conversation with Dorothy. I couldn't picture Grimshaw doing that sincerely, but as a way to try to get what he wanted, that was far more likely. I didn't know that Dorothy would have fallen for such an act though.

It was all so confusing and troubling. If not for the fact that Aunt Olivia and I had been dragged into the murder case as suspects, I would have gladly left all the investigating and theorizing to the police. The unsolved mystery, and the fact that a killer was roaming free, would have still troubled me, but I could have stayed out of the investigation. In the present circumstances, however, I couldn't sit back and do nothing.

As much as I disliked Ed Grimshaw, he might not be Dorothy's killer. Roxy was convinced that Byron was the culprit. I wasn't so sure about that. I needed to find out if anyone else might have committed the crime.

My thoughts immediately zeroed in on Shanifa.

'Do you know anything about Dorothy shooting at Shanifa, the owner of the Lebanese food truck?' I asked as I accompanied my aunt back into the carriage house.

The dogs came too. They'd seemed agitated while Ed Grimshaw was present, but they had since settled down and quickly made themselves comfortable on the rug in the living room.

'That's the first I've heard of any such thing,' Olivia replied as she made her way across the room. 'It doesn't sound like Dorothy at all. Where did you hear about it?'

'The guy who works there with her, I'm assuming it's her husband?'

'Mo, yes. That's her husband,' Aunt Olivia confirmed.

'I overheard him saying that Dorothy tried to shoot Shanifa once.'

My aunt lowered herself into an armchair, her forehead furrowed. 'That couldn't have happened right in town. Everyone would have known about it if it had. And Shanifa must not have reported it to the police, either. Otherwise, again, the news would have spread like wildfire.'

'Tessa's cousin never heard about it either.' Tessa had told me that in a text message. 'Maybe Shanifa didn't report it because she had something to hide,' I speculated. 'How well do you know her and her husband?'

'Not very well. They've been in Twilight Cove for less than a year. Shanifa seems friendly enough. I've talked to her a few times, and I know she volunteers at one of the local retirement homes. Mo doesn't seem like much of a conversationalist.'

I decided I needed to find out more about Shanifa and the shooting incident. Since I hadn't eaten anything for lunch other than ice cream, my rumbling stomach gave me an excuse to stop by the food truck. I needed to stop eating so much takeout if I wanted to stay healthy while in Twilight Cove, but I decided I could be healthier starting tomorrow. Right now, I needed both food and information.

TWENTY-TWO

After parking in the beach lot for the second time that day, I opened the back door of my car and the dogs almost tripped over each other in their rush to get out. I laughed as they ran for the water. It seemed they loved the ocean as much as I did.

Even though I'd come into town for information, I took a moment to face the water and breathe deeply while enjoying the view. Sunlight danced on the waves and the salty breeze ruffled my hair. Seagulls cried from somewhere nearby and a sailboat with a red and white sail cut across the cove. Farther out, a fishing boat bobbed on the water.

A few people dotted the beach and cars passed along Ocean Drive now and then, but the cove was still quite peaceful.

'I could get used to this,' I said under my breath.

Then I reminded myself that I shouldn't.

I also reminded myself why I was there by Ocean Drive. I called to the dogs and they came splashing out of the water. Flossie stopped and gave a great shake, spraying water in every direction. Fancy copied her and then they bounded over my way. I snapped their leashes onto their collars, not wanting to take any chances when we were going so close to Twilight Cove's busiest road.

Three food trucks sat parked along the edge of Ocean Drive, but I went straight for Shanifa's Lebanese Cuisine. It looked as though Shanifa was working on her own, unless her husband had stepped away for a break.

After greeting Shanifa, I ordered the vegetarian stuffed grape leaves again. I handed over some cash to pay for the food and she got busy preparing my order.

'Those are beautiful dogs,' she said with a glance and a smile at the spaniels.

I patted Fancy and Flossie. 'They were Dorothy's,' I said, glad that Shanifa had given me an opening for talking about the murder victim.

'I thought so.' She packaged up my stuffed grape leaves. 'Dorothy didn't spend a lot of time here in town, but when she did she always had the dogs with her.'

'Is it true that Dorothy once fired a gun at you?' I asked.

Shanifa frowned as she handed me my food, but she quickly smoothed out her expression. 'Where did you hear that?'

I had hoped she wouldn't ask me that question. 'I couldn't help overhearing when your husband mentioned it the other day.'

Again, a frown appeared on her face before she quickly replaced it with a neutral expression. 'She didn't actually shoot at me. It was a warning shot fired into the air.'

'Why would she do that?' Dorothy hadn't struck me as the type to fire off a gun for no good reason.

Shanifa's gaze darted away from mine. 'I was trespassing on her land, although I didn't mean to do it. I was just taking a walk in the woods and didn't realize I was on her property. Dorothy over-reacted.' She tapped her fingers on the counter, still not meeting my eyes. 'Sorry, I think I hear my phone.'

She disappeared deeper into the truck.

Food in hand, I wandered back toward my car. Shanifa's cooking skills were top-notch, but her ability to lie definitely wasn't in the same league. If Dorothy really had fired a gun in Shanifa's presence, it wasn't to scare off a mere accidental trespasser. The problem was that I didn't know how to find the truth of the matter. If Aunt Olivia, as one of Dorothy's neighbors and someone who was plugged into the local gossip network, didn't know about the incident, then who would? Shanifa's husband, Mo, might know more, but would he be willing to tell me? It might be worth asking him, although I didn't hold out much hope.

I leaned against the hood of my car and munched on my food as I thought things over. Despite the fact that I felt better for eating, the questions bouncing around in my head still troubled me as much as ever.

The dogs watched me as I ate, their eyes hopeful. I finished off the last bite and looked down at them.

'Sorry, girls. You can have dinner when we get home.'

Fancy wiggled in her seated position and let out her characteristic 'a-woo'. Flossie gave a woof of agreement. I interpreted that to mean they wanted to eat now rather than later.

Two more seconds of them staring at me with pleading eyes and my resolve cracked.

'All right,' I said. 'You win.'

Fancy let out a 'woo-woo' of happiness while Flossie bounced around in circles.

I laughed as I tossed my empty food container onto the passenger seat to be recycled later.

'Come on then.'

I had to tighten my grip on the leashes when the dogs charged ahead of me. They knew exactly where they were going, and led me straight to the ice-cream parlor. I'd noticed earlier that the shop had pup cups on the menu, so I bought two of those. Each small cup held a single scoop of lactose-free vanilla ice cream.

Flossie and Fancy wiggled and waggled just outside the door, with Fancy talking the entire time, urging me to hurry up. The young man working behind the counter laughed at their antics, and so did I. When I had the cups in hand, I returned to the beach and sat on a log, holding a cup in each hand while the dogs stuck their snouts inside and busily lapped up every last trace of the ice cream. Once they cleaned out the cups, they swished their tongues around to clean the droplets off their muzzles.

After that, they seemed satisfied with heading home. When we got back to the farmhouse, I set out their dinners. I wondered if the ice cream would have ruined their appetites, but that definitely wasn't the case. Both dogs gobbled up every last crumb from their dish. I answered a couple of emails while they ate and then I took a book out to the swing on the back porch and read while the dogs lounged in a shady spot on the grass.

Eventually, I set the book aside. Flossie and Fancy lifted their heads, watching me.

'How about we go for a walk in the woods before it gets dark?' I suggested.

The spaniels were on their feet in an instant. Fancy let out an encouraging howl as I got up from the swing. She and Flossie charged toward the woods, only stopping to wait for me to catch up once they reached the tree line.

In the woods, away from the evening sunshine, I detected a hint of a chill in the air. Goosebumps popped up on my arms and I wished I'd thought to grab a hoodie before leaving the farmhouse. I picked up my pace, hoping that would warm me up. The dogs trotted along ahead of me, sometimes on the path, sometimes weaving in and out of the trees and underbrush.

After about twenty minutes of walking, I was almost ready to turn back. Dusk had arrived and the light in the woods was fading quickly. I didn't want to get caught out there in the darkness. The mere thought made me jumpy.

A twig snapped somewhere off to my left, well away from where the dogs trotted along ahead of me. My heart rate picked up. Maybe I needed to stay out of the woods until the police caught Dorothy's killer. What was supposed to be a relaxing walk was now making me nervous and paranoid.

I was about to call Flossie and Fancy back to me when I drew to a halt, listening. I heard a strange noise, but I wasn't sure yet where it had originated.

On the path ahead of me, the dogs paused, their ears twitching. I heard the sound again.

The dogs tensed.

'Wait,' I whispered to them.

As quietly as possible, I crept forward until I was standing right behind the dogs. Flossie held one of her front paws up off the ground, her nose forward, in a pointing stance. Fancy had all four paws on the ground, but was just as alert, her nose twitching.

The sound came yet again. I couldn't quite place it, although it struck me as familiar.

I rested a hand on each dog's head. 'Let me go first,' I said quietly.

I squeezed between the dogs and moved forward, silent step by silent step. Even though I didn't look back, I knew the dogs were following right behind me.

We rounded a bend in the path and I dropped down into a crouch. Ahead and to my left, the trees thinned and opened onto a clearing. A man stood hunched over in the middle of the open space. He held something long. When he jabbed at the ground, making the sound I'd already heard several times, I realized he was digging with a shovel, stabbing it into the earth and then flinging the dirt away.

The man paused and straightened up, wiping his arm across his brow. In that moment, I got a good look at his profile.

Byron Szabo.

Roxy had mentioned seeing him digging in the woods.

A lightbulb flicked on in my head. The shovel was the item I'd seen Byron stashing in his trunk at the side of the road. That time, he must have been leaving after one of his digging expeditions.

But why would he be digging out here?

I didn't have a great view of the clearing floor, but I didn't spot anything that might be a dead body. Besides, if he was burying bodies every time he was out here digging, he must have killed several people recently. That didn't make sense. Even if he'd found his victims beyond the borders of Twilight Cove, surely news of so many missing persons in the area would have reached the town grapevine.

Was he digging holes to hide something else?

As Byron got back to his work, I carefully eased up out of my crouched position, my legs burning. I straightened halfway up and rested my hands on my knees. Now that I could see over some of the underbrush between me and the clearing, I spotted a backpack on the ground, but nothing else. Maybe he had stolen goods in the backpack and was stashing them until he could sell them.

That theory didn't have me convinced.

Whatever Byron was up to, I didn't want him to know I'd seen him. The best course of action was to get the heck out of there.

I took a step backward. My heart almost lurched to a stop when a twig snapped beneath my shoe.

Byron's head whipped around in my direction.

'Who's there?' he demanded.

He raised the shovel like a weapon and took a menacing step in my direction. That's all it took to kick me into action.

I spun around on my heel and ran.

Flossie and Fancy darted ahead of me, galloping along the path. I could hear Byron crashing through the underbrush behind us. That pushed me to pick up my pace.

The gathering dusk made it difficult to see, so I stayed focused on the white ends of the dogs' tails. We careened around a bend in the path and I tripped on a rock. I stumbled but managed to stay on my feet. I pressed onward.

At a fork in the path, the dogs veered off to the left, heading along a narrow and overgrown trail that was barely visible from the wider path. That direction would take us away from the farm, but I didn't hesitate to follow the spaniels. I trusted that they knew what they were doing.

Branches scratched at my arms and face as I ran behind the dogs. Flossie and Fancy easily leapt over a tree that had fallen across the path. On the other side, they stopped, their tongues hanging out as they panted. I clambered over the trunk to join them. They dropped down on their bellies and I did the same, taking cover behind the fallen tree.

I tried to quiet my gasping breaths as I listened for Byron. I heard his footsteps pounding against the hardened dirt of the path and the occasional snap of a branch or twig. Then his footsteps stopped. I thought he was close to the spot where the overgrown trail branched off from the wider one.

Digging my fingers into the dirt, I kept my head down, hoping with desperation that Byron would stay on the main trail. A second later, the sound of him crashing through the brush dashed that hope into pieces.

With my chin a mere inch above the ground, I glanced around, looking for something I could use as a weapon. It was growing darker by the minute, and the lack of light obscured the details of my surroundings. I spotted a branch about four feet away. I couldn't tell if it would come free of the undergrowth with a tug or if it was hopelessly tangled, but it looked like the only potential weapon within reach.

I wanted to grab the branch, but I knew that any noise or movement could give away our position. I dug my fingers into the dirt again and waited, my pulse beating in my ears like a bass drum.

Despite the pounding in my ears, I could hear Byron drawing closer. If he was trying to move quietly, he wasn't doing a good job of it. Maybe he didn't care how much noise he made. If he knew where the dogs and I were hiding, he might believe he had enough of an upper hand that he didn't need the element of surprise.

My heart beat so hard in my chest that I worried it might give out. Flossie pressed her nose to my arm. I slid my hand over and rested it on one of her front paws.

Fancy wriggled closer to me and kissed my cheek.

Then she jumped up and darted off into the undergrowth.

TWENTY-THREE

'Fancy!' I hissed with panic.

Flossie let out a soft whine and licked my arm.

The sound of Fancy running through the woods quickly faded away. I hoped she would run back to the farm. As much as I didn't want to be alone, I wished Flossie had gone with her. I wanted them both somewhere safe, far away from the man who might well be a murderer.

My limbs felt like jelly as I listened to Byron getting closer and closer. When it sounded like he was a mere stone's throw away, the sound of his movements stopped.

I held my breath.

'What the . . .' Byron muttered. Then he chuckled. 'You shouldn't have turned on your phone.'

He started moving again, but this time it sounded like he was walking away from me and Flossie.

I chanced a peek over the fallen tree. Byron really was heading away from us.

I got up onto my knees but then froze as Byron drew to a stop, partially visible to me through the trees and scraggly bushes. Something to his left caught his attention. He broke into a run, crashing through the undergrowth, not bothering to stay on the trail.

I clambered to my feet, my legs trembling beneath me, and spotted what Byron had thought was my phone.

A blue light glowed through the trees, way off in the distance. As I watched, the light moved, dancing along, getting fainter and fainter until I could no longer see it. Byron followed the light and he soon disappeared from sight as well.

I sank down onto the fallen tree, taking a moment to gather myself. Flossie put her front paws up on the trunk next to me. I wrapped an arm around her and gave her a hug and a kiss on the top of her head.

'We'd better get out of here.' I whispered the words, even though Byron was a long way off now. 'I hope Fancy is OK.'

Flossie licked my cheek as if trying to reassure me.

I gave her a shaky smile. 'Let's go.'

Darkness had fallen for real now and all I could see were dark shapes and shadows.

I nearly jumped out of my skin when something swooped down toward me from the dark sky. I exhaled with relief when Euclid landed on the fallen tree, right where I'd been sitting a moment ago. Pressing a hand to my chest, I tried to calm my racing heart.

'Euclid. I'm glad it's you.'

The owl spread his wings and flew up to a tree branch not far above my head. Then he moved to another tree and paused on a sturdy branch, as if waiting. He continued to do that, moving from branch to branch, tree to tree, while Flossie and I made our way along the trail. I followed in Flossie's footsteps, always listening for any sign that Byron might be coming back our way.

If not for Flossie and Euclid leading me, I probably would have become hopelessly lost. Thanks to them, I soon made it out of the woods and on to the farm. I still feared running into Byron, so I stuck to the darkest of shadows and scurried across the nearest paddock to the barn. I crept along the exterior wall, always watching and listening. When I reached the front of the building, I paused to prepare myself to leave the shadows and cross the lawn to the farmhouse.

As I stood there, Euclid landed on the nearby fence.

'Thanks for your help,' I whispered to the owl.

He let out a hoo-hoo and then took off, disappearing into the inky sky.

I crouched down next to Flossie and gave her a hug. 'I hope Fancy's nearby. Do you think it's safe to make a run for it?'

Flossie answered that question by darting forward as soon as I released her. She trotted across the grass toward the farmhouse as if she didn't have a care in the world. I took that to mean that Byron wasn't lurking somewhere nearby.

I almost cried with relief when I made out the form of Fancy sitting at the bottom of the porch steps. Dropping to my knees in front of her, I gave her a big hug and kissed her snout. She wriggled with happiness and licked me all over my face.

I laughed. 'Let's get inside.'

I still didn't like the idea of lingering out in the darkness.

The three of us climbed the steps to the porch. I slipped a hand into my pocket, reaching for my keys, but then my gaze landed on

Flossie where she waited next to me. I wanted to test one of my theories.

I tried the door, confirming that I'd left it locked.

'Flossie,' I said quietly, 'could you unlock the door for me, please?'

Flossie stood up on her hind legs and touched one of her front paws to the doorknob. The lock clicked.

This time when I tried the door, it opened easily.

The dogs rushed into the house ahead of me.

I might have stayed standing out on the porch, staring at the open door, if not for the fact that I was still scared about the possibility of Byron being somewhere nearby. I hurried into the house and locked up behind me.

Instead of flicking on the kitchen light, I decided to test another theory.

'Fancy, could you light the way, please?'

Slowly, the brown and white spaniel began to emit a soft blue light. Her whole body glowed, like some sort of bioluminescence. The light brightened until it was strong enough that I could have made my way through the darkened house without any other source of illumination.

'Thank you,' I said, resting a hand on her head before crossing the kitchen.

Out in the hall, I turned on the overhead light and Fancy's glow faded away to nothing. I could hardly believe what I'd seen and yet there was no doubting it. I shook my head and made my way into the living room.

Flossie and Fancy followed me as I made a circuit of the house, checking to make sure that all the doors and windows were locked up tight. Once I was certain that the house was secure, I took a quick shower. The warm water helped to ease my tense muscles and to soothe my mind.

Dressed in my pajamas, I sat cross-legged on my bed as the dogs jumped up to join me. They circled around and lay down at the foot of the bed. They kept their eyes open, watching me. Instead of the racing thoughts I expected to hit me now that I was safe, I felt a sense of calm and acceptance settling over me.

Flossie and Fancy weren't ordinary dogs.

Flossie could undo locks and Fancy could glow with blue light and camouflage herself with her surroundings.

I didn't know how the dogs could do those things and I doubted I ever would.

Dorothy might have had something to do with their abilities, or they could have been born with them.

I thought of Euclid and wondered if the owl had special powers too.

Maybe I'd find out in time.

I gave the dogs a pat on the head and climbed beneath the covers.

I didn't know how to explain the dogs' extraordinary talents, and I didn't know if Byron was a killer or up to something else in the woods. I also didn't know if I should tell anyone about Flossie and Fancy. The only person I would consider telling about their abilities was Aunt Olivia. She wouldn't believe me, unless the dogs gave her a demonstration of their powers. Would they be willing to do that? I really wasn't sure.

Hopefully the dogs would be discreet about their unique skills. If word got out to the general public about what they could do, there would be a media circus, and all sorts of people – many with greedy or nefarious intentions – would probably want to get their hands on the spaniels. I couldn't let that happen.

I'd take some time to think about whether I should share the secret with Aunt Olivia. I might have to before heading back to Los Angeles and leaving Flossie and Fancy with her.

The thought of leaving Twilight Cove and the dogs behind sent a piercing ache through my heart.

I shut off the lamp next to my bed and burrowed deeper beneath the covers.

As I drifted off to sleep, my hazy mind toyed with the possibility of staying in Twilight Cove for good.

TWENTY-FOUR

The sense of calm and acceptance that had found me the night before stayed with me into the next day. As I fed the chickens and ducks, talking quietly with them now and then, I pondered the information Roxy had shared with me by text message. She'd sent the message while I was sleeping so I hadn't seen it until I checked my phone while eating breakfast. I'd asked her if she'd seen any sign of anyone living in Byron's house with him, whether it was a roommate, family member, or romantic partner. Roxy told me in her text message that it looked like a bachelor's house, with no signs of any other residents. That meant that Byron hadn't locked his study to keep out a nosy housemate. So why take that precaution?

Maybe he had a housekeeper come in to clean and didn't want them to stumble upon his true crime obsession. The question was whether that was because he believed others might think it macabre, or because he was a murderer and didn't want anyone figuring that out.

Flossie and Fancy trotted along with me as I headed back to the barn after feeding the ducks and chickens. On the way, I spotted Callum over by the alpaca pasture, his forearms resting against the top rail of the fence. He had his eyes on Daisy, one of the latest additions to the animal sanctuary. The daughter of a recently deceased farmer had brought Daisy and her mother, Rosie, to the sanctuary three weeks ago because there were no family members who could care for the animals. Daisy had arrived pregnant and not far off from giving birth.

My curiosity and concern for Daisy overrode any misgivings I had about Callum. I returned the feed bucket to the barn and then joined him by the fence, where I had a good view of the pregnant alpaca. Flossie and Fancy walked with me to the pasture but then wandered off to explore all the smells around the outside of the barn.

'Is Daisy OK?' I asked Callum.

The expectant mother stood away from the other three alpacas, humming and moving about restlessly.

'She's in labor, but she's doing all right,' Callum replied.

'When do you think she'll give birth? Today? Tonight?' I watched her with concern. 'I wouldn't want her to be alone. Besides, I've never witnessed the birth of an alpaca – or any animal, for that matter – and I don't want to miss it.'

Callum smiled without taking his eyes off Daisy. 'She won't be alone. Even if the unpacking – the birth – happened at night, I'd stay with her, but most alpacas give birth during the day. Given her current behavior and how much she's dilated, I think the cria will be on its way soon.'

I wasn't familiar with the term 'cria' but assumed it was the word for a baby alpaca. I might know how to feed chickens, groom donkeys and clean out stalls, but I still had a lot to learn about the animals at the sanctuary.

I kept my eyes on Daisy as she wandered to and from the manure pile, still humming. 'Will you move her to the barn?'

'That might stress her out. I think it's best to keep her here, close to Rosie.'

As if on cue, Rosie ambled over to her daughter and sniffed at her rear end before touching her nose to Daisy's neck.

'Should we call the vet?' I asked, not sure how worried I should be.

Callum seemed at ease, though he was watching Daisy closely.

'Not unless a problem comes up,' he said. 'Most alpaca births go smoothly without much or any human interference. I'll keep a close eye on her, though.'

I winced as I realized I'd practically been interrogating him. 'Sorry for all the questions.'

He laughed and my stomach swooped at the sound. 'Don't worry about it. I'm happy to answer them.'

Relaxing, I settled more of my weight against the fence. 'I just have one more. For now, anyway,' I amended. 'Can I stay and watch?'

Callum's eyes crinkled at the corners when he smiled. 'Sure. I'm going to grab the cria kit from the barn. I'll bring a couple of camp chairs with me when I come back.'

He disappeared into the barn, with Fancy and Flossie trotting at his heels. When he came back, he carried two folded chairs under one arm and held a large, hard-plastic toolbox in his other hand.

The cria kit, I assumed. I helped him set up the chairs just inside the paddock. Then I ran to the farmhouse to grab us some cold drinks, with the dogs following me.

On my way back, I stopped in at the carriage house to tell Auntie O that Daisy was in labor. She wanted to be there to watch the birth, but decided it would be too difficult for her with her broken ankle. Instead, I promised I'd film the birth and drive her out to the paddock later, once the baby was born.

Flossie and Fancy decided to stay at the carriage house with Aunt Olivia while she worked on a needlepoint project. Maybe that was for the best, I mused as I walked back across the yard. They'd have to get used to being with my aunt instead of me if I returned to Los Angeles.

Again, the thought of facing that day filled me with sadness. I needed to think seriously about what I wanted to do in the near future – or, more precisely, where I wanted to live – and I needed to talk to Auntie O about that too. But not until after Daisy's baby was safely in the world with us.

'Did I miss anything?' I asked when I settled into the camp chair next to Callum's.

'It's just been more of the same,' he assured me. 'Restless and humming.'

I passed him one of the cold cans of iced tea I'd grabbed from the farmhouse refrigerator. He thanked me as he opened it and then took a long drink. I found myself watching him out of the corner of my eye. Maybe admiring was a better word for it. I told myself to stop. The last thing I wanted was for him to catch me checking him out. Besides, falling for him wasn't a good idea when I was leaving in a few weeks. Never mind the fact that I didn't know if he was trustworthy or not.

I pushed those thoughts aside and popped open my own can of iced tea. 'How did you learn so much about caring for animals?'

As soon as I voiced the question, I remembered that he didn't like talking about himself. I couldn't help being curious about him, though. The hint of mystery surrounding him only made him all the more intriguing. Maybe it was the writer in me, but I wanted to know his story. I also wanted to know if my heart was right in telling me that he was a good guy.

I wondered if he'd clam up on me or change the subject, but he remained relaxed in his chair and answered without hesitation.

'I grew up on a ranch.'

'In Colorado.'

He nodded. 'Near Manitou Springs.'

'I have no idea where that is,' I admitted.

He laughed, and my stomach did that funny swooping thing again.

'Not far from Colorado Springs.' He glanced my way before returning his gaze to Daisy. 'Have you ever been to Colorado?'

'It's one of the few states I haven't visited. Or lived in.'

'You've moved around a lot?'

I held back a sigh as I looked down at the can in my hand. 'Growing up, I did.'

'Because of job situations? Were your parents in the armed forces?'

I was glad I wasn't the only one asking questions. Maybe he was just trying to keep me talking about myself so I wouldn't pester him for information about his life, but whenever he took his eyes off Daisy to look my way, there was something in his gaze that told me he was truly interested.

'Not in the armed forces,' I replied. 'But my dad's job took him all around the country.' I ran my finger up the side of my can of iced tea, condensation gathering on my skin. 'My mom died when I was three and my dad changed jobs soon after. I think he wanted to get away. Too many reminders, that sort of thing.'

His green eyes met mine. 'I'm sorry about your mom.'

'Thanks.' I looked down again. 'I don't really remember her. Sometimes I feel guilty for that.' I couldn't believe I'd said that last part out loud. I'd never admitted it to anyone before.

I silently scolded myself as I fiddled with the tab on my drink can. I didn't know enough about Callum to go pouring my heart out to him. But I wanted to get to know him. And I really wanted him to be a good guy without any dangerous secrets.

My breath caught in my throat when Callum rested one of his large, callused hands over mine, stilling my fidgety fingers.

'You were only three, Georgie. It's not your fault that you can't remember her. Even when we lose someone when we're older, memories fade. It gets harder to picture their face, to remember the sound of their voice.'

I could breathe again when he slipped his hand off mine, but I immediately missed his touch.

'It sounds like you're talking from experience,' I said.

A shadow of sadness passed across his face. 'I mentioned my grandparents lived here in Twilight Cove.'

I nodded, remembering.

'They both passed away a few years ago, within six weeks of each other.'

'I'm sorry,' I said with a pang of compassion for him. 'That must have been really difficult.' I remembered the pain of losing my own grandparents all too well.

He gave the barest nod of acknowledgment. 'I think my grandma died of a broken heart. My grandpa died first, and they'd been together since they were eighteen. Never a day apart. They were completely in love right till the end.'

This time I rested my hand on his. 'That's sad, but also beautiful.'

He let our fingers entwine and gave mine a gentle squeeze before I slid my hand away.

He smiled, his sadness ebbing away. 'Hashtag relationship goals, my grandma would have said.'

I smiled too. 'She was a techie grandma?'

'Even had an Instagram account. She took a lot of photos and videos that I can hang on to. They help, when the memories threaten to fade.'

I understood that. I didn't have much in the way of my own memories of my mom, but many times over the years I'd gone through the photos and videos of her that my dad had kept.

Callum stilled beside me. I glanced his way and then followed his line of sight to Daisy.

'This might be it.' Callum set his empty can aside and leaned forward. 'Here it comes.'

I grabbed my phone and started filming.

Daisy had turned so she was facing away from us. Now we could see the birthing sack emerging. Daisy pushed and pushed. Then the cria's head emerged. A few moments later, the baby's front legs pushed forward and burst the birthing sack.

I drew in a sharp breath as I got my first look at the cria unobscured by the sack. The baby moved around as it hung there, not quite half out. Daisy shifted a few steps now and then, staying off to the side of the paddock. Rosie sniffed at the new arrival and the other alpacas moved in to see what was happening. They stayed a little farther back than Rosie, but still sniffed with interest at the cria's head.

'Is everything OK?' I whispered to Callum when the cria had hung there for several minutes without coming out any farther.

'We'll give her a little longer,' Callum said, also keeping his voice quiet. 'If needed, I can help get the shoulders out.'

That turned out to be unnecessary. After another minute or so, the cria's shoulders emerged. Then, with one final push from Daisy, the entire baby slithered out and plopped to the ground.

My heart soared at the sight and I had a big smile on my face. Callum's smile wasn't quite as wide as mine, but I could see in his green eyes that he was just as happy and delighted.

Daisy still stood facing away from the cria. Callum got up from his chair and quietly moved in and knelt next to the baby. He gently wiped at the cria's nostrils and then scooped up the small animal and shifted it so it was lying in front of Daisy. Then he backed off again, and grabbed a towel to wipe his hands on.

'It's a girl,' he said. Now his grin was full-fledged.

We watched as Daisy sniffed at her baby girl, along with all the other alpacas.

After a few minutes, Callum moved back in and gently toweled off the cria. She went from looking like a slimy alien creature to a fluffy, cute baby, all spindly legs and big eyes.

Pausing the video app on my phone, I quickly texted Auntie O to let her know that all was well and that Daisy had a baby girl.

Callum and I stayed there, watching, and eventually the baby got her long, gangly legs under her and tried to stand. I started filming again, so my aunt would be able to see the cria take her first steps. The baby alpaca toppled over, but gamely tried again. She teetered her way up onto her feet and then staggered forward a couple of steps before collapsing.

I continued to watch with delight as she made further attempts. After a few tries, she managed to stay upright, swaying a little and still staggering when she moved, but no longer collapsing.

I stopped recording for a few minutes, and then started again when the cria began nursing for the first time.

Callum crouched next to mother and cria, making sure that the baby latched on and began to drink. Satisfied that all was going well, he came back over to sit next to me.

I stopped filming and set my phone on my lap.

'So,' Callum said, tearing his gaze from Daisy and her baby so he could look my way, 'what do you think of your first alpaca unpacking?'

My smile brightened. 'It was one of the most amazing things I've ever seen.'

TWENTY-FIVE

I kept my promise to Auntie O and drove her out past the barn to meet the cria. With the help of her crutches, she hobbled right up to the fence and got a good view of mother and baby. The cria was standing up on her spindly legs, nursing.

'Do you have a name picked out?' I asked my aunt as I leaned my forearms on the fence.

'I think you should name her,' Olivia said.

'Maybe Callum should,' I countered. 'He's looked after Daisy since she arrived.'

Callum stood on my aunt's other side. 'I'm not great with names. You go ahead and pick one, Georgie.'

I studied the little white alpaca for a moment. 'If her grandma is Rosie and her mom is Daisy, she should have a flower name.' I ran through some possibilities in my head. 'Violet,' I finally decided. 'She looks like a Violet to me.'

'Good choice,' Aunt Olivia said with a smile.

Happiness glowed warmly in my chest as I watched Violet. She finished nursing and tried out a few steps on her gangly legs. She was much steadier now than shortly after her birth, but she still hadn't quite mastered smooth movements.

Eventually, after taking at least a dozen photos each with our phones, Aunt Olivia and I returned to the carriage house. I decided not to bother trying to write that day. I was too keyed up after watching Violet's birth and didn't think I'd have any success with sitting still and focusing on the plot of my latest screenplay. Aunt Olivia had a hair appointment that afternoon and I'd already planned to drive her into town. Originally, I thought I would take my laptop and work while she had her hair cut, but now I decided to explore the heart of Twilight Cove instead.

After dropping Auntie O off at Scissor Me Timbers, the dogs and I wandered along the side road where the salon was located and on to Main Street. We headed down the south side of the street first, with the spaniels investigating all the smells and me checking out the shops we passed. A store called Beachside Books caught my eye. I was tempted to go in for a look, but I doubted that Flossie and Fancy would be allowed to join me, especially since two cats sat in the window. I didn't want to leave them outside on their own for long, and I had a tendency to lose track of time while browsing the shelves of bookstores and libraries.

Continuing along the south side of the street, we passed the Pet Palace, though not without Fancy and Flossie trying to tug me in the direction of the shop's door. I promised them we'd visit their favorite store again sometime soon, and they relented, carrying on down the street with me.

We strolled past a souvenir/gift shop, a photography studio, and a sporting-goods shop that appeared to have everything from golf clubs and baseball gloves to paddleboards and lifejackets. At the corner of Main Street and Ocean Drive, we passed by the ice-cream parlor.

As the spaniels and I waited for a safe moment to cross Main Street, I caught sight of Shanifa standing near her food truck, talking with Byron Szabo. I had to take a deep, steadying breath to calm my suddenly racing heart. Had Byron recognized me in the woods the night before? If so, would he dare come after me in broad daylight?

A car turned onto Main Street from Ocean Drive. After it had passed us, the road was clear. Clutching Flossie's and Fancy's leashes in my hand, I hurried to the other side of the road. When we reached the safety of the sidewalk, I glanced over toward the food truck again. Shanifa and Byron quickly turned their heads away, but not fast enough for me to miss that they'd been watching me.

Unease crept across my skin like a thousand tiny bugs. I realized then that I hadn't worried about my encounter with Byron, the murder, or the fact that I was a suspect since before Daisy had given birth. Watching Violet come into the world had taken my thoughts to a much happier place, but now Byron's suspicious activities and Dorothy's murder came crashing back to the forefront of my mind.

I started up the north side of Main Street, heading away from Shanifa and Byron. I pretended to study the window display of a cute chocolate shop while I darted sidelong glances back toward Ocean Drive. Byron was walking away, along the top of the beach, and was nearly out of my sight. I thought Shanifa had left too, until I spotted her lurking behind the shuttered food truck, peeking out from around the back corner, her eyes on me.

At least Byron wasn't still watching me, but had he asked Shanifa to spy on me in his stead?

You're being paranoid, I told myself.

After all, if Byron had asked Shanifa to keep an eye on me, he probably would have had to tell her why. And would he really want anyone to know that he'd been out digging in the woods? He certainly hadn't liked it when I'd shown up near the clearing.

I passed the coffee shop and the Moonstruck Diner, which I remembered from when I'd lived in Twilight Cove when I was seventeen. I'd often visited the retro diner with Tessa and other classmates after school or in the evenings, enjoying the creamy milkshakes and the music playing on the vintage jukebox. I paused on the sidewalk and sent a text message to Tessa, suggesting that we meet up at the diner sometime soon. The dogs had found an interesting scent beneath one of the diner's front windows, but when I said their names, they abandoned their investigation and joined me in continuing along the street.

At the next corner, I turned left onto a quiet road lined with shops and other businesses like a dentist's office, a small fitness center, and an accountant's office. Across the road, located in an old Victorian house, was a tea room. The house had been there back in my teens, and long before that, but I didn't recall it being home to a tea room. It was another place I wanted to visit while in town.

When Flossie and Fancy paused to sniff the base of a slender tree, I sent a casual glance over my shoulder. Shanifa hovered back at the corner. When she realized I was looking her way, she darted out of sight.

The skittering of unease I'd felt back on Main Street returned, stronger this time. Whether or not Byron had put her up to it, Shanifa was definitely following me.

Before she had a chance to peek around the corner and see what I was up to, I backtracked a few paces and dashed down the alley behind the Main Street businesses. Flossie and Fancy ran along with me. Three cars sat parked behind the Moonstruck Diner, with a dumpster on the far side of them. I didn't fancy squeezing myself into the narrow space between the dumpster and the exterior wall of the building, so instead I ducked down behind the front bumper of the middle car. The spaniels crowded in with me and lay down, as if understanding that I was trying to hide.

A full minute ticked by and I wondered if I'd overreacted. I doubted Shanifa would try to harm me in broad daylight. Byron, maybe, but not Shanifa. Then again, what did I really know about the woman? Maybe she and Byron were in on something together and she was just as dangerous as him.

My legs burned from staying down in my crouched position. I hoped no one would come out the back door of the diner and see me huddled there with my dogs. It would probably strike them as odd, if not outright suspicious. I glanced up at the back wall of the diner and breathed a sigh of relief when I didn't spot any security cameras.

I was about to give up on hiding and get back to touring the town when I heard footsteps in the alley. I peeked around the car and quickly hunkered back down. Shanifa was wandering along the alley, looking left and right.

From my hiding place, I heard her swear under her breath. I chanced another peek around the car and saw her heading back out of the alley. Bracing a hand against the exterior wall of the diner, I carefully eased up out of my crouch. Shanifa turned out of the alley, heading back toward Main Street.

I shook out my burning legs and decided to turn the tables.

'Let's go,' I said to Flossie and Fancy.

I jogged out of the alley, with the spaniels trotting along next to me. I paused before turning onto the side street, checking around the corner before moving out into the open. Shanifa had just taken a right onto Main Street.

I hurried after her, stopping close to the shop on the corner of Main Street so I could dart out of sight at any moment. Shanifa walked at a quick pace, heading toward Ocean Drive. When she was two-thirds of the way there, I continued to follow her, hoping she wouldn't look back.

She did, once, just before crossing Ocean Drive, but the dogs and I had taken shelter in the recessed doorway of the chocolate shop and she showed no sign of having spotted us. She crossed Ocean Drive and jogged toward her food truck, pulling keys from her pocket on the way. When she reached the truck, she unlocked the door and disappeared inside.

With no traffic in sight, the dogs and I quickly crossed the street and hurried over to the food truck. The serving window was still shuttered, but the back door stood open a crack. I moved as close as I dared while trying to appear casual. Fortunately, Flossie and

Fancy helped me out by sniffing around one of the back wheels of the truck. To any onlooker, I probably appeared to be an innocent dog walker who'd paused to let the spaniels sniff for a minute.

In reality, I was straining my ears. Shanifa was talking to someone. On the phone, probably, since her voice was the only one I could hear.

'I lost her,' Shanifa said as I listened.

A long pause followed, likely because the person on the other end of the line was speaking.

'She was probably just walking the dogs,' Shanifa said after a moment. 'OK,' she added a few seconds later. 'We'll have to keep an eye on her.'

Shanifa's voice sounded closer now, so I hurried away from the food truck, the dogs abandoning their sniffing investigation to stay at my side.

It was most likely Byron on the other end of the phone call, and it sounded like Shanifa really was in cahoots with him.

But what were the two of them up to?

They wanted to keep an eye on me, probably because of what I'd seen in the woods last night, but would they stop at surveillance or would they try to silence me?

Despite the warm sunshine, goosebumps popped up along my arms.

If Byron really had killed Dorothy, and Shanifa was his accomplice, I needed to be very, very careful. Otherwise, I could end up as their next victim.

TWENTY-SIX

That evening I left Flossie and Fancy at the carriage house with Auntie O while I drove back into town to meet Tessa for dinner at the Moonstruck Diner. I hadn't told my aunt about my encounter with Byron in the woods, or the fact that Shanifa had followed me that afternoon, because I didn't want to worry her. At the same time, I knew it would be prudent to tell somebody. Maybe that somebody should have been the police, but I didn't know if they would believe me. I worried that they might think I was simply trying to deflect suspicion away from myself and my aunt.

I decided to share everything with Tessa over dinner. As a lifelong resident of Twilight Cove, she might have a better idea of whether or not the local police would believe my story about Byron.

The Moonstruck Diner looked exactly as I remembered it. The restaurant's interior had a checkered, black-and-white floor, turquoise and chrome stools at the counter, and turquoise and white bench seats at the booths. The walls were still bubblegum pink and covered with vintage posters and black-and-white photos. The jukebox stood in its same place of honor, to the right of the door.

When I stepped inside, it was almost like being transported back to my junior year of high school. The only thing that didn't appear the same were the faces of the people seated at the counter and in the booths. I didn't recognize any of them except one. Tessa waved to me from the booth at the back of the diner. I smiled and hurried to join her, slipping onto the bench across from her.

A teenage girl wearing a retro turquoise dress with a white apron came over to take our orders, her brown ponytail swaying when she walked. I ordered fish and chips and a chocolate milkshake while Tessa requested a burger and a strawberry shake. Once the waitress had brought us our milkshakes and left our table, I quietly filled Tessa in on my encounter with Byron in the woods the night before and what I'd experienced in town during the afternoon.

I wanted to tell her about Roxy and me being in Byron's home office and what we'd seen there, but I didn't dare talk about that in public, even in whispers. Instead, I simply told her that he had an apparent fascination with cold cases and promised I'd let her know how I knew that after we left the diner.

'You should tell the police,' Tessa said after the waitress brought us our food.

'Do you think they'll believe me?' I asked. 'I'm still a suspect, as far as I know. What if they think I'm just trying to throw suspicion on someone else?'

Tessa considered that for a moment. 'I don't know how the state police would react, but I think Chief Stratton would hear you out. Brody Williams too. Have you met him?'

I nodded. 'A couple of times now. I'll try to talk to him or the chief tomorrow.'

I told her what the Gins and Needles ladies had said about Officer Brody Williams during their last meeting.

Tessa laughed. 'Those ladies are incorrigible. But they're right – Brody is cute. And single. And only a year younger than us.' She waggled her eyebrows at me.

I laughed this time. 'I didn't come to Twilight Cove looking for someone to date,' I said. 'Besides, I'm just here for a few weeks.' Unless I decided to change my plans. I kept quiet about that for now.

'Doesn't mean you can't enjoy some fine male company while you're here.' Tessa waggled her eyebrows again.

I balled up my napkin and tossed it at her. She tossed it back, hitting me right on the nose. We both laughed, and for the second time that evening I felt like I'd gone back in time. I hadn't realized just how much I missed Tessa's friendship until I'd come back to Twilight Cove.

'Brody's a really talented painter and wood-carver,' Tessa said. 'He sometimes sells his Native American art at the local farmers' market.'

'Hmm.' I eyed her with amused suspicion. 'You seem to be a fan. Maybe you should be the one enjoying his company.'

'We're just friends,' she said, but I detected a hint of a blush on her cheeks.

I didn't press the subject but I filed that observation away in my mind.

'Brody's not the only good-looking man around our age here in town,' I said before taking a sip of my milkshake.

Tessa's eyes lit up with interest. 'Ooh. Tell me more.'

'Not much to tell,' I said. 'Let's just say that Auntie O's farmhand is easy on the eyes.'

Tessa looked at me with a level of perception I hadn't anticipated. 'I think you should say more, because I'm sensing there could be sparks.'

I pretended to zip my lips shut.

'We'll come back to that,' she said.

'Or not,' I countered, spearing my last bit of fish with my fork. 'What about you?' I asked before she had a chance to disagree. 'Are you dating anyone?'

Tessa took a sip of her strawberry milkshake. 'Nope, and that's fine by me. Life is simpler without juggling a relationship along with everything else.'

The look in her eyes didn't quite match the conviction in her voice, but I wasn't going to bring up the subject of Brody again. Not yet, at least.

Instead, I said, 'I'll drink to that.'

As I took a long sip of my milkshake, my thoughts strayed to Callum with his green eyes, golden hair, and broad shoulders . . .

Don't go there, I silently scolded myself.

Hoping for a distraction from those thoughts, I asked Tessa to fill me in on the classmates I could remember from my year of school in Twilight Cove.

After we'd finished eating, we strolled down to the beach, with me telling Tessa how the dogs and I had followed Roxy into Byron's house. I didn't mention Flossie's and Fancy's special abilities, but I shared everything else.

'OK, he's creepy,' Tessa said about Byron when I'd finished the story. 'And Roxy!' She shook her head. 'She's so lucky that you're the only one who caught her in the act. I wish that girl could see all the potential she has. I worry she's going to do something to jeopardize her future.'

'She's going to volunteer at the sanctuary,' I said. 'She clearly loves animals. Maybe by spending a few hours per week at the farm, she'll have less time to get into trouble.'

'That would be amazing.' Tessa tucked her arm through mine as we reached the beach. 'Thank you, Georgie.'

'I don't know her well yet, but I like her. She's a good kid.'

'She really is,' Tessa agreed. 'If only she had more people in her life telling her that.'

I filled Tessa in on my most recent conversation with Shanifa, the one where I'd asked about the shooting incident.

'Shanifa says it was a warning shot because she accidentally wandered onto Dorothy's land while out walking in the woods,' I recounted, 'but I swear she was lying when she told me that story. Some of it might be true, but not all of it.'

'Do you think she was doing something more than simply walking in the woods that day?' Tessa asked.

'It could be.' I told her how I suspected that Shanifa had followed me that afternoon with Byron's knowledge and possibly at his behest.

'So whatever Byron's up to in the woods, Shanifa's probably in on it,' Tessa surmised. 'Dorothy caught her in the act of . . . whatever it is they're doing, and thought it was threatening enough that she brought a gun into it.'

'That's what I'm thinking.'

The breeze blew a strand of hair into Tessa's face and she brushed it aside. 'You need to look into those cold cases that Byron's obsessed with. They could be the key to figuring out what he and Shanifa are up to. Even if neither of them killed Dorothy, they're definitely up to something.'

'That's for sure.' I kicked off my sandals so I could walk barefoot in the cooling sand. 'And you're right about the cold cases. I'll see if I can learn more about them.'

We spent a few minutes more on the beach, chatting about this and that while gentle waves crashed ashore and the moonlight danced on the water. Then we walked back up to Main Street together and hugged goodbye before returning to our respective vehicles.

I was about to climb into my car when a great horned owl glided down from the dark sky and landed on the top of a nearby lamppost.

'Euclid,' I whispered, having no doubt that it was him and not another owl.

I stood with the driver's door open, looking up at Euclid, until an approaching car distracted me. With a last glance at the owl, I got into my car and shut the door. I leaned forward over the steering wheel and craned my neck so I could look up at the lamppost. Euclid unfolded his wings and took off into the night. I wondered if he wanted me to follow him, but he disappeared into the darkness overhead rather than staying within sight and trying to lead me somewhere.

Maybe he just wanted to say hello, I thought as I started my car's engine.

Although I didn't yet know if Euclid had any special powers, he certainly had a unique intelligence. He'd led me to the lawyer's office, where I'd seen Ed Grimshaw bullying the receptionist. Did the owl know who had killed Dorothy?

I shook my head at the thought and pulled out onto the road. If Euclid did know the killer's identity, he probably would have led me straight to that person. Although, maybe he already had if Grimshaw was the murderer.

I decided I needed to stick to facts and evidence. Yes, I believed that Euclid had tried to point me in a certain direction investigation-wise, but I didn't know exactly why. Ed Grimshaw might well be the killer, but I had other suspects I couldn't forget about. Tessa was right. I needed to dig into the cold cases that held Byron's interest. Hopefully, I'd have a chance to do that the next day. For the moment, I would try to put thoughts of the murder aside and focus on getting a good night's sleep.

As I turned into the farm's driveway, I smiled at the thought of Flossie and Fancy waiting at the carriage house to greet me. I was looking forward to giving them each a good hug and then settling in for the night at the farmhouse. I hadn't yet raised the subject of possibly staying in Twilight Cove with Auntie O, so I added that to my mental list of things to do the following day. Maybe it was foolish to move to the small town instead of remaining in Los Angeles, but something told me that the opposite might be true.

I pulled up next to the farmhouse and parked.

I was still sitting in the car when a dark figure darted off the back porch and ran away.

TWENTY-SEVEN

I sat frozen, gripping the steering wheel, my heart thudding, as the figure ran around the far corner of the farmhouse and disappeared from sight. Releasing the steering wheel, I grabbed my phone and called 9-1-1, silently cursing myself for forgetting to leave the porch light on. The farmhouse was completely dark, and the illumination from the security lights out at the barn barely reached the lawn behind the house.

At least I'd left all the doors and windows locked. I'd spent most of my life living in cities and tended to lock doors out of habit, even here on the outskirts of sleepy Twilight Cove. Hopefully the intruder hadn't broken a window and made it inside the house.

Aunt Olivia had left the light on over the front door of the carriage house. I gathered up my courage and climbed out of my car, quickly darting over to the smaller dwelling, hoping the prowler hadn't tried to break in there as well. I found a sticky note posted to the door. My aunt had left it to let me know that she'd gone to bed. The dogs were inside, waiting for me.

When I'd first arrived at the farm, Auntie O had given me a set of keys that included one for the carriage house, in case of emergency. I slipped the key into the lock and quietly opened the door. I shut and locked it behind me, deciding I'd feel safer waiting for the police in the carriage house than in my car. A single lamp near the back of the carriage house sent a glow of warm light through the living room.

I crouched down as Flossie and Fancy jumped up from the rug and bounded over to greet me. I kept our reunion shorter than I normally would have, giving each dog a kiss and a pat on the head before creeping over to the ground-floor bedroom and peeking through the half-open door. Aunt Olivia was tucked up in bed, sound asleep and breathing steadily.

Letting out a sigh of relief, I backed out the bedroom door and moved to the front window in the living room. As far as I could see, nothing moved out in the driveway or near the farmhouse. I still didn't want to risk going outside before the police arrived.

Fortunately, it didn't take long for a patrol car to pull into the driveway, its lights flashing but with the siren turned off. Quietly, so as not to wake my aunt, I switched off the lamp and slipped out the front door with the dogs, locking up behind me before tucking the key ring into the pocket of my shorts.

Officer Brody Williams got out of the cruiser and I hurried over to greet him, the spaniels happily trotting along with me. I explained what I'd seen when I arrived home, and Williams instructed me to wait in my car while he had a look around. Flossie and Fancy wanted to follow the officer over to the farmhouse, but I managed to coax them into the back seat of my car. With the doors locked, I tapped my fingers against the steering wheel, waiting and hoping that the prowler hadn't broken a window and gained access to the house.

Aided by a bright flashlight, Williams made a full circuit of the farmhouse. I climbed out of my car when he returned to the driveway. Flossie and Fancy ran for the back porch and began sniffing around. They probably knew that someone had been there, someone who didn't belong, but they didn't seem worked up or anxious about the scent. They soon gave up their investigation and lay down on the porch to wait for me.

'Whoever it was, they didn't gain entry to the house,' Williams reported. 'Everything's locked up tight and there's no sign of an attempted forced entry. Either they were just casing the place or you scared them off before they had a chance to break in.'

'That's a relief,' I said.

Callum came striding across the farmyard from the direction of the barn. At least I knew he wasn't the prowler. The creeping figure had been shorter and stockier than Callum. I knew of someone else who matched that description.

Callum broke into a jog and quickly joined us by my car. 'What's going on?' He looked at me with concern. 'Are you OK, Georgie?'

'I'm fine.' I rubbed my arms, the cool night air adding to the chill that the prowler had triggered. 'Someone was creeping around the farmhouse when I got home.' I returned my attention to Officer Williams. 'I might have an idea who it was.'

I told Williams about my encounter with Byron in the woods the previous evening. Callum tensed beside me as he listened, but he stayed quiet. Williams took out a notebook and pen and jotted notes as I spoke.

After recounting the events of the night before, I shared what had happened in town that afternoon. I wished I could tell the police about the cold case room in Byron's house, but there was no way I could do that without getting Roxy and myself in serious trouble.

'You think Byron recognized you in the woods last night and that's why he and Shanifa want to keep an eye on you?' Callum asked as soon as I finished talking.

I had a feeling Williams had been about to ask the same question, but Callum had beaten him to it.

'That's the only explanation I can think of,' I replied. 'I just got a brief glimpse of the prowler tonight, but going by the person's height and build, it could have been Byron.'

I was almost convinced that it was the reporter. Too bad I couldn't prove it.

'Will you talk to Byron?' Callum asked Williams.

'I'll talk to the chief first,' Williams said. 'I don't want to jeopardize the murder investigation by tipping Szabo off.'

'So he's a suspect?' I asked.

Williams jotted something in his notebook and closed it. 'I can't answer that question, but I'll certainly be letting the chief and the state police know about Byron's activities in the woods.'

I thanked Williams and he left soon after. I stood watching as he turned his cruiser around and drove out onto Larkspur Lane.

Callum put a hand to my back. 'Are you sure you're OK, Georgie?'

I realized that I was hugging myself and shivering. I dropped my arms to my sides. 'I'm all right. Just a little spooked.'

Callum removed his hand from my back and I immediately missed its warmth.

Together, we walked toward the back of the farmhouse. The dogs raised their heads, but didn't get up from the porch. I sank down onto the steps, not quite ready to go inside. I was glad when Callum sat down next to me. I wanted his company for a while longer.

He looked over toward the carriage house. 'Is Olivia all right?'

'She's sound asleep,' I said. 'I checked on her before the police got here.'

'Maybe you should stay with her at the carriage house,' he suggested. 'I don't like that you've got people after you.'

'I don't know for sure if anyone's actually after me. Although, I'm pretty sure it was Byron creeping around the house.'

Flossie gave a woof, as if confirming my suspicions.

I smiled at her over my shoulder and added, 'I'll be fine here with the dogs.'

'You'll keep the doors locked?' he checked.

'The windows too,' I promised.

We sat in silence for a moment. The cool breeze lifted a curl of hair off my forehead and cut through my thin T-shirt, sending a shiver through me.

Callum must have noticed. 'Are you cold?' he asked.

'A little.' I rubbed my arms. 'I'll go inside soon.'

Callum shrugged out of the plaid flannel shirt he wore unbuttoned over a T-shirt. 'You can borrow this.'

'But then you'll be cold,' I protested.

He draped the shirt over my shoulders. It was soft and wonderfully warm from his body heat.

'I'm fine,' he assured me.

I couldn't bring myself to protest further. I slid my arms into the sleeves and immediately felt cozier and warmer. 'Thank you.'

For some reason, sitting there in the dark emboldened me.

'Did you follow me into the woods the other day?' I asked before I could lose my nerve. 'The day I found the smashed teacup.'

Callum hesitated before responding, 'Not exactly.'

I raised my eyebrows, wondering what that meant.

'I was already out in the woods,' he clarified. 'I heard someone nearby and followed the noises. I thought it might be Dorothy's killer, but then at the ravine I saw it was you.'

'Do you think I might be Dorothy's killer?' I asked, not sure if I truly wanted to know the answer.

The surprise on his face reassured me even more than his response.

'Of course not.'

'But you barely know me,' I said, wondering if he might have some doubts lurking deep inside. 'What makes you so sure I'm not a murderer?'

'I've seen you with the dogs.' He glanced over his shoulder at the snoozing spaniels. 'And with the farm animals. I can tell you've got a good heart.'

Maybe it was silly, but his words warmed me up even more than his shirt had. Then I finally registered what he'd said about already being in the woods on the day I found the broken teacup.

'You go into the woods a lot.' I tucked my hands inside the

sleeves of his shirt, hoping I wasn't going too far with my questions. 'Why is that?'

'Ah.' He rubbed the back of his neck. 'I guess you were bound to notice that.'

'You don't have to tell me,' I said, suddenly regretting that I'd raised a question that made him uncomfortable, even though I wanted to hear the answer to it.

'No, it's fine. I trust you.'

Again, his words warmed me. I knew I should try to temper my growing feelings toward him, but I was too focused on what he was saying.

'My grandparents used to own the asparagus farm next door,' he explained. 'When they passed away, they left the property to me and my sister.'

'Did you sell it?' I asked, wondering why he was living and working on Aunt Olivia's farm instead of next door.

'No,' he replied, 'though we probably will in the near future. Neither of us wants to run the business, but we also didn't want to sell the property back when we first inherited it. It would have felt like severing a connection to our grandparents when our grief was still too raw. I hired someone to live there and manage the farm, a man named Gary Woodberk. But after a while I got suspicious. The profits from the harvest had dropped significantly compared to when my grandparents ran the place.'

'You think Woodberk is mismanaging the farm?' I guessed.

'That was my first thought, so I dropped by a couple of times to get a feel for how things were going. What I saw didn't match up with the numbers Woodberk was sending me. Between that and having a chat with your aunt, I began to think Woodberk was selling some of the crop on the sly so he could keep the profits for himself instead of splitting them with me and my sister, as our arrangement dictated. But all I had were suspicions. This year I'm trying to get some evidence.'

'That's what the security cameras are for,' I said with sudden understanding.

A hint of a grin showed on his face. 'I was kicking myself for leaving the boxes on the table for you to see.'

'You could have just told me what you were doing.'

'I should have,' he conceded, 'but at the time I was still getting to know you and I'm trying to keep it a secret that I'm here so

Woodberk doesn't realize what I'm up to. I'm sorry I didn't tell you sooner.'

'I get why you didn't,' I said. 'We still don't know each other very well.'

Even in the darkness, I felt the intensity of his gaze. 'I'd like to change that.'

A shiver ran through me, one that had nothing to do with the cool night breeze. A sudden case of nerves followed. I averted my eyes from his and scrambled to come up with something to say.

'Does Aunt Olivia know about the situation with the asparagus farm?' I asked.

To my relief and disappointment, Callum shifted his gaze away from me. 'She's known about it from the start. Olivia was the one who suggested I work at the sanctuary while keeping an eye on my farm. It's the perfect set-up. I asked her to keep it between us, but when you showed up, I wasn't sure how much she would tell you.'

'She really didn't tell me much about you other than the fact that you're from Colorado.'

If I'd asked her more direct questions about Callum, she wouldn't have lied to me, but now I understood why she'd changed the subject when I'd brought up Callum in conversation.

'So have you got the evidence you need?' I asked.

'Not yet. There's been some suspicious activity at the asparagus farm after dark. Trucks coming and going. Next time that happens, I'm planning to follow one of the trucks when it leaves.'

'Please be careful,' I implored. 'You never know what lengths someone will go to in order to keep their secret under wraps.'

'I'll be careful,' he promised. He paused before saying, 'Georgie, there's something—'

Flossie put her front paws on the top step and pushed her head between us.

I laughed and gave her head a pat. 'Are you trying to tell me something?'

Fancy jumped to her feet and gave a short 'a-woo', while Flossie trotted to the back door.

I scrambled to my feet, worried that she might unlock the door right in front of Callum. 'I guess we'd better get inside.'

I hesitated on the porch when Flossie sat down, waiting for me to unlock the door. Once again, I felt emboldened by the darkness surrounding us.

'There's a seafood restaurant on Ocean Drive that I was thinking of trying,' I said. 'Do you want to go with me? Maybe tomorrow, or another day?'

Despite the darkness, I saw his hint of a grin slide from his face. 'I'd like to, Georgie, but—'

'It's OK!' I said in a rush, taking a step backward. 'No worries.'

I fumbled with my keys and got the door unlocked and open. The dogs hurried in ahead of me.

'Georgie . . .' Callum said from where he now stood on the steps.

I forced a smile. 'Good night! See you in the morning!'

I shut and locked the door before leaning my back against it, my face burning with embarrassment. I stayed there with my eyes closed until Fancy pressed her nose against my bare leg. She gave me a nudge and looked up at me, her eyes luminous in the shaft of moonlight shining in through the kitchen window.

It wasn't until I started up the stairs to the second floor that I realized I was still wearing Callum's shirt.

TWENTY-EIGHT

I tossed and turned for much of the night. Between the prowler and my conversation with Callum, I didn't have much of a chance of shutting my thoughts off. My mind was still spinning as I ate breakfast the next morning, but at least I managed to focus on writing projects as I munched on my jam-slathered toast. Byron's cold case room and his mysterious activities out in the woods had given me ideas for a new thriller. I didn't plan to write the pitch for it until my current script was finished, but I jotted down some notes so I wouldn't forget the story taking shape in my head.

When I left the house through the back door, with Flossie and Fancy on my heels, all thoughts of story ideas flew out of my head, leaving me to once again dwell on the subjects that had kept me awake for far too long during the night. I double-checked that I'd locked the door behind me and then paused on the porch to scope out the farm. Nothing looked out of place and not another soul was in sight.

I had Callum's shirt with me, but I tied it around my waist for the time being. When I reached the barn, I could see him through the open back doors. He was out checking on Daisy, Violet and the other alpacas. As much as I would have liked to visit Violet, I wasn't quite ready to swallow my embarrassment and face Callum. Instead, I grabbed some feed and left through the barn's front door to go tend to the chickens.

Once I'd finished that task, I moved on to cleaning out the stalls in the barn. I worked up a thirst, even though the weather was cooler than it had been in recent days. When I emerged from the barn, my chores complete, dark gray clouds had moved in to hide the sun. The breeze swirled through the barnyard, carrying with it stray bits of straw.

I wandered over to the alpaca pasture to visit Violet and Daisy now that Callum had moved on to another part of the farm. Leaning against the fence, I talked quietly to the alpacas. Violet was cuter than ever, with her fluffy white fleece, her big dark eyes and her spindly legs. As she began nursing, I lapsed into silence and my thoughts strayed to Callum.

It was for the best that we wouldn't be having dinner together at the restaurant on Ocean Drive. At least, that's what I told myself. Even if I decided to stay in Twilight Cove – and that was still very much up in the air – I didn't want to develop feelings for Callum. Auntie O had said from the beginning that he was here temporarily. That made sense now that I knew what he was up to. Once he had the evidence he needed to prove his theory about what Woodberk was up to, he wouldn't need to stay at the sanctuary any longer. And since he had no interest in running the asparagus farm, he'd probably sell the property and move on somewhere else.

I wouldn't let his green eyes and heart-swooping smile get to me, I decided. I was completely immune to such things.

That was a whopper of a lie, but maybe if I kept repeating it to myself it would become true.

When Violet finished nursing, I snapped a few photos of her to share with Auntie O.

As I tucked my phone back in my pocket, Callum appeared by my side. I'd been so engrossed in photographing Violet that I hadn't heard him approach.

'Mother and baby are doing well,' he said as we watched the alpacas.

'Violet is adorable.' I shot a brief, sidelong glance at Callum as my embarrassment from the night before made a comeback. I untied his shirt from around my waist and offered it to him. 'Thanks for the loan.'

He tugged off his work gloves and accepted the shirt, those green eyes that I was supposedly immune to having a funny effect on my heart. 'You made a quick getaway last night.'

My cheeks burned. 'I'm sorry. I made a mess of things. When I mentioned the restaurant, I didn't . . . I thought we could go as friends . . . I didn't . . .' I shut up and closed my eyes. Talk about making a mess of things. I couldn't even get a complete sentence out of my mouth.

My eyes opened when Callum's hand touched my back for a brief moment.

'Georgie.' The way he said my name drew my gaze to his like a magnet. 'I'd love to have dinner with you.'

'You would?' The question came out heavy with skepticism and laced with surprise.

'Of course,' he said, his eyes still on me. 'I just don't want to be seen in town, because word might get back to the asparagus farm.'

I nodded with understanding. 'And you don't want Woodberk knowing you're here.'

'Exactly.'

'Do you know people in town?' I asked, thinking he must if he was worried about the word spreading about his presence in Twilight Cove.

'I don't,' he said, 'but someone might recognize me. I had a decent career as a major league baseball player for fourteen years. I retired at the end of last season.'

'Oh.' I hadn't expected that explanation. I'd had no idea that he was a sports celebrity.

My embarrassment came rushing back. He probably dated supermodels and Hollywood actresses, not totally *not* famous screenwriters.

'I'm trying to lie low until I've got everything sorted with the asparagus farm,' Callum continued as he hung the flannel shirt over the fence. 'That's what I wanted to tell you last night.'

'But I didn't give you a chance,' I said with chagrin.

He grinned. 'You did make a hasty exit.'

'I was embarrassed.' *I still am*, I added silently.

'There was no need to be. Like I said, I'd love to have dinner with you.'

'You're leaving,' I blurted out. 'I mean, once you've got the evidence you need to do whatever it is you're going to do about the situation at your farm.'

He leaned his forearms on the top rail of the fence. The short sleeves of his black T-shirt left his tanned, muscular arms on full display. I averted my eyes so he wouldn't catch me staring.

'I'm not sure what I'll do once I've sorted that out,' he admitted. 'I'll need a job of some sort.'

'You played in the big leagues for fourteen years. Do you really need a job?' I slapped a hand to my forehead, wishing I had a better filter. I usually did, but not in Callum's presence, apparently. 'I'm sorry. That's so not my business.'

He laughed and I silently cursed the way my stomach swooped at the sound.

'I definitely need a job,' he said. 'Not for the money, but to keep myself from going crazy. I'm just not sure yet what that job will be.'

'Or where?'

He nodded as his gaze met mine and held it. I felt like he was searching for something in my eyes, but I didn't know what that might be or whether he found it before he looked away, watching the alpacas again.

'You're leaving in a few weeks, aren't you?' he asked. 'When Olivia's ankle is better?'

I studied his profile for a moment. There was a slight bump in his nose that I hadn't noticed before. I wondered if it had been broken by a baseball.

'That was the plan,' I said, following his lead and returning my eyes to the animals in the pasture. 'But now that I'm here, I don't want to go back to Los Angeles.' I tipped my face up to the sun as it broke through the dark clouds, gracing us with its warmth. 'I'm happier here. More relaxed.'

'Do you need to be in LA for your career?' Callum asked.

I shook my head as the sun disappeared again. 'I can write from anywhere. I'd go back now and then for meetings, or if I'm ever needed on set, but there's no reason I can't live in Twilight Cove.'

As I said the words, I knew more than ever that staying here was what I wanted.

'I haven't broached the subject with Aunt Olivia yet,' I continued. 'Not that I have to live here on the farm. She'll be moving back into the farmhouse once her ankle has healed.'

'I don't think Olivia is going to have a problem with you staying in Twilight Cove,' Callum said. 'I doubt anything would make her happier. She talks about you all the time.'

'That's embarrassing,' I said, but with a sensation of warmth spreading through my heart.

'It shouldn't be. She does it because she loves you and she's proud of you.' Callum nudged his hat higher on his forehead. 'She had me liking you before I'd even met you.'

I shot him a sidelong glance full of skepticism. 'That can't be true. You didn't like me when we first met.'

His green eyes darkened with regret. 'I didn't mean to give you that impression. I was wary, that's all.'

'Because you thought I might recognize you?' I guessed.

He confirmed that with a nod. 'I didn't know if you were a baseball fan or not.'

'I don't really watch sports,' I confessed. 'Please don't hold that against me.'

He grinned, and the corners of his eyes crinkled. 'Don't worry. You're forgiven.'

I watched as Violet pranced around Daisy and Rosie, her movements awkward and completely adorable. 'Maybe you can convert me.'

'I'd like to try.'

Something in his voice drew my gaze back to him. The intensity in his eyes stole the breath from my lungs, and I had to look away so I could breathe again, but I did so with a smile on my face.

'Wait,' I said, my thoughts bouncing around like my heart was doing in my chest. 'Does Aunt Olivia know about your baseball career?'

'That's another thing I asked her to keep under her hat.'

'You two have been keeping a lot of secrets,' I said without reproach.

He shifted his weight. 'I didn't mean to put Olivia in a difficult position.'

I rested a reassuring hand on his arm until I realized what I'd done and pulled it away. 'Don't worry about it. She wouldn't have lied to me if I'd asked her direct questions. She just dodged the subject of you.'

'I'm glad everything's out in the open now.'

I smiled. 'Me too.'

My thin T-shirt fluttered in the brisk breeze and a lock of my short hair blew into my eyes. I was about to flick it away when Callum beat me to it. His rough, warm fingers whispered across my skin as he gently brushed the curl back where it belonged. I suppressed a shiver as pleasant tingles followed in the wake of his touch.

My thoughts had scattered, so it took effort to refocus when he spoke again.

'Since I'm not ready to be seen in town, how about we have dinner here on the farm instead?' he suggested.

'As friends?' I asked, reminding myself that he probably wouldn't be here much longer. My heart wasn't keen on listening to that warning.

'As friends.'

I thought he'd left the words 'for now' unspoken, but maybe that was nothing but wishful thinking. Clearly, my head wasn't listening to my warning either.

'How about a barbecue?' Callum said. 'I've got some mean grilling skills.'

'Maybe I do too.'

He sized me up, the warmth of his gaze almost palpable against my skin. 'We could have a grill-off.'

I laughed at that idea. 'Actually, I've never grilled anything in my entire life.'

'How is that even possible?'

I shrugged. 'Never owned a barbecue.'

Growing up, it would have been just another thing to take with us every time we moved. Now, my apartment balcony was so tiny I could barely fit a few small pots of herbs on it.

'Maybe it's time you learned the art,' Callum said.

'I'm happy to watch the master at work for now.'

A slow grin took shape on his face as he pushed off from the fence. 'Tonight?'

'Works for me.'

He tipped his cowboy hat at me. 'Looking forward to it.'

Callum headed into the barn and I walked back to the farmhouse with a smile on my face. Tessa was right. There was no reason why I couldn't enjoy Callum's company while we were both in Twilight Cove. The giddy feeling in my stomach didn't have to lead to heartache.

Despite telling myself that, a small voice in my head reminded me to be cautious. So many times in my life I'd grown attached to people, only to have to leave them behind, or have them leave me. I'd moved repeatedly growing up, and I'd lost my mom at a young age and all my grandparents by the time I was twenty-two. I'd never managed to get used to the pain that losing friends or loved ones caused, so it was best avoided whenever possible.

I decided to go ahead with the barbecue anyway. If I thought I was growing too attached to Callum, if my feelings for him were getting too strong, then I could back away. That was something I was good at. I'd done it plenty of times in my life when attempting to protect myself.

Yet, something told me that hardening my heart against Callum would be easier said than done.

I spent a couple of hours writing and editing before taking a break for lunch. As I munched on a sandwich, I tugged my laptop closer and opened the Internet browser. I couldn't resist typing Callum's name into the search bar. So many results popped up that it would have taken me days to go through them all. I clicked on the first couple of links and it quickly became clear that Callum had downplayed the success of his career. He had impressive stats and multiple Gold Gloves and Silver Slugger awards under his belt. I knew he had impressive stats only because an article told me so. The actual numbers and acronyms didn't mean much to me.

Maybe I should have ended my search there, but my curiosity got the better of me. It surprised me that a guy as successful and good-looking as Callum would be single. He'd never actually told me he was single, I realized, and since I'd emphasized that we were having dinner as friends, maybe there was no reason to tell me otherwise. He didn't wear a ring, but that didn't mean he wasn't dating someone.

It didn't take long to dig up information on his relationship history. For a time in his mid-twenties, he'd dated a pop singer whose name was vaguely familiar to me and he'd married an actress named Vanessa Lee Raine at age twenty-seven. I'd never heard of Raine, but the photos I found of her and Callum sent my heart sinking. She was a leggy bombshell of a blonde, with her hair, makeup and clothes utter perfection in every photo, even those taken in more casual settings.

I navigated away from the pictures, not wanting to torture myself, though I continued to read. The marriage, it turned out, had lasted barely three years. In more recent times, online articles referred to Callum attending charity galas, sometimes with a brief mention of his date, but the last such mention was from more than two years ago.

I refocused on much safer territory: Callum's career. He'd spent the last four years of it playing for the Toronto Blue Jays, and he'd played for three other teams before that. Against my better judgement, I looked up photos of the pop singer he'd dated. Glamorous and gorgeous, just as I'd expected.

Humiliation burned through me. I couldn't believe I'd basically asked him out.

I dropped my face into my hands, but then raised my head as my thoughts turned.

Callum seemed sincere about wanting to spend time with me and hadn't once made me feel like I wasn't good enough in any way. We could still be friends while we were both living on the farm.

Twinges of guilt haunted me while I read about him online, so I closed those tabs on the browser and instead started looking deeper into the cold cases that held Byron's interest, consulting the photos on my phone. I read brief articles about a couple of the unsolved murders, but nothing stood out to me as particularly significant, and I couldn't find any obvious ties to Byron, other than his interest in the cases.

I turned my attention to the Tennessee bank robbery and conducted an online search for more information about the case. I sifted through the search results and found an article I hadn't seen before. A black-and-white photo accompanied it. The picture showed a young man, probably in his early twenties, standing with his arm around a pretty girl who looked to be in her late teens.

I was almost certain they were the same two people depicted in the old photograph I'd seen in Victor Clyde's safe. According to the article I found online, the two people in the picture were Jeffrey Herring, age twenty-one, and Ellen Dudek, age seventeen – the suspected robber and getaway driver. Like the previous articles I'd read, this one stated that Ellen had perished when her car went off a bridge while she was leaving town, and that Jeffrey might have died in the same accident, though there was no evidence of that. Otherwise, he simply disappeared. The stolen money was never located.

I zoomed in on the photo and studied the faces of the two young-sters. Then I conducted another quick search and came across several photos of Victor Clyde. The oldest one I could find dated back about twenty-five years. I arranged the two photographs so I could study them side-by-side. Jeffrey vaguely resembled Victor, particularly around the eyes, but their noses and mouths were different.

Those were both features that could have been changed by plastic surgery.

And something told me that Jeffrey and Victor were one and the same.

TWENTY-NINE

When I turned my full attention on Ellen Dudek, I knew I was onto something. Even though I'd met Dorothy Shale only a couple of times, I had a clear enough picture of her face in my head to know that seventeen-year-old Ellen Dudek bore a striking resemblance to Dorothy. I did another search, hoping to find a photo of Dorothy so I could make a side-by-side comparison for confirmation, but I couldn't find anything about her online. That didn't really surprise me. A woman who lived in a tiny cabin out in the woods without indoor plumbing and electricity probably wasn't a social media maven.

Still, I wanted confirmation that I wasn't making up connections in my head where none really existed. I downloaded the old photo of the couple and the picture of Victor Clyde to my phone and jumped up from the table. Flossie and Fancy had been snoozing on the kitchen floor, but they woke up in a flash and scrambled to get to the door before me. They burst out onto the back porch as soon as the door was open and somehow anticipated my next move, racing off toward the carriage house before I'd even made it down the steps.

We found Aunt Olivia on the back patio, lounging on the outdoor loveseat with her boot-encased foot propped up. She had a book open on her lap and her reading glasses on, but she set the book aside and removed her glasses when the dogs and I joined her.

'A visit from my favorite human and my favorite dogs,' Aunt Olivia said, patting the spaniels, who'd run right up to her. 'How did I get so lucky?'

Flossie and Fancy wagged their tails and sat as close to my aunt as they could.

'How's the writing going?' Aunt Olivia asked as I sat on a free chair.

'I got some done this morning, but I'm too distracted to write at the moment.'

She looked up from fussing over the dogs. 'I hope nothing's wrong.'

'I'd just like to get your opinion on something.' I woke up my phone so I could find the photos I'd downloaded. 'And I know about Callum now, so you don't have to worry about keeping his secrets from me.'

'You know everything?'

'I know he's watching the farm next door – his farm – and I know he was a successful baseball player. Is there more?'

'That's all.' She sounded relieved. 'I'm sorry for not telling you. I wanted to, but I promised Callum I'd keep quiet.'

'I get it,' I assured her. 'It's fine. I just didn't want you to go on thinking you needed to tiptoe around the subject of him anymore.'

She looked pleased. 'I'm glad the two of you have grown close enough for him to share that with you.'

'We're getting to be friends, I think, but that's all,' I clarified, 'so don't be getting any matchmaking ideas.'

She put on her most innocent smile. 'Would I try to interfere in that aspect of your life?'

'I wouldn't put it past you,' I said. 'Especially when spurred on by your Gins and Needles ladies.'

'They're a hoot, and utterly incorrigible, but I doubt you need any interference from us.' She had a twinkle in her eye as she patted my knee. 'You'll do just fine on your own.'

'Really, Auntie O. Don't go thinking along those lines. I'm not Callum's type.'

She seemed puzzled by that statement. 'I don't think he's gay, darling. I googled him.'

'So did I.' I held up a finger before she could say anything. 'Simply out of interest in his baseball career.'

'Mmm-hmm.' The twinkle was back in her eyes.

'Anyway,' I continued, 'that's not what I meant by not being his type. You should know from your googling that he's into glamorous, leggy blondes.'

'You're a leggy brunette with gorgeous hazel eyes, a killer smile, a creative and smart head on your shoulders, and a heart of gold,' my aunt countered. 'Plus, you do glamorous too, honey. I saw those pictures of you at that film festival last year.'

I got up and kissed her on the cheek. 'Thank you, Auntie O. But I'm actually here to talk to you about something other than Callum.' I sat next to her on the loveseat and Flossie rested her head on my knee.

'We can always come back to the subject of Callum,' Aunt Olivia teased.

'It's not just the other Gins and Needles ladies who can be incorrigible,' I said with a shake of my head.

My aunt smiled, her eyes still twinkling.

I brought up the photo of Jeffrey and Ellen on my phone and passed the device to Olivia. 'Do you recognize either of these people?'

She slipped her reading glasses on and studied the picture. She started to say something, but then stopped, her forehead furrowed.

'What is it?' I asked.

She shook her head. 'For a second I thought maybe the young man looked familiar, but . . . no, perhaps not.'

'How about the girl?' I prodded.

My aunt stared hard at the photo. 'Is that . . .?' She zoomed in on the picture so Ellen's face filled the screen. 'Is that Dorothy as a young woman?'

I stroked Flossie's silky head. 'That's what I'm thinking.'

'Where did you get this photo?' Olivia asked.

I'd figured that question would come up. On my way over to the carriage house, I thought about how much I should tell her. In the end, I decided to go with almost the whole truth.

'I got that picture from the Internet, but I've seen a picture of that couple before.' I told her that I'd caught a glimpse of an old photo at Victor's mansion, but I left out the part about Flossie opening the safe. I didn't like keeping secrets from my aunt, but I wasn't quite ready to share what I knew about the spaniels. I also didn't want to distract her from the current thread of the conversation.

I recounted how I'd followed Byron to his house and had seen Roxy breaking in. When I got to the part where the dogs and I went into the house after Roxy, Olivia interrupted.

'Both of you could have been arrested!' she exclaimed.

'That's exactly what I didn't want to happen to Roxy,' I said. 'I know it was risky, but I really didn't want her getting in trouble.'

'But if Byron is the killer, and he'd found you in his house . . .'

Seeing how pale she'd become at the mere thought, I decided to leave out the part about Byron coming home while we were still in the house. Instead, I made it sound like we'd taken a quick look around his study and then left without incident.

I tapped the screen of my phone, which Auntie O had handed back to me. 'I found this photo of Jeffrey and Ellen when I looked up the unsolved bank robbery reported on in an article on Byron's wall. They're the suspected robber and getaway driver.'

'And there was a picture of the same couple in Victor Clyde's home?' my aunt asked.

I nodded and zoomed in on Jeffrey. 'If you look carefully, do you think this guy could be a younger Victor Clyde? Possibly before having some plastic surgery?'

Aunt Olivia peered at the photo. 'There's a vague resemblance. Maybe that's why he struck me as familiar.' She took her glasses off. 'So, you think that Victor and Dorothy were once a couple and they robbed this bank back in the Seventies?'

'Doesn't everything point in that direction?' I asked with a frisson of excitement running through me. 'I feel like we're onto something.'

'How much money did they steal?'

I consulted one of the articles on my phone. 'More than a hundred thousand.'

Aunt Olivia stared off into the distance as she thought aloud. 'Victor Clyde was rich, and the stolen money wasn't nearly enough to make him that wealthy.'

I tapped away at my phone, conducting another Internet search. 'Let's see if we can find out if he was born rich, or how he got his start in business.'

Aunt Olivia leaned closer so she could see the screen of my phone. The dogs grew bored and lay down on the patio for a snooze.

Several minutes later, I looked up from my phone, thinking over what I'd just learned. 'There's not much about Victor Clyde in his early years. He got into real estate in his twenties and made some fortuitous deals that sent him on the path to success and riches.'

'What about Jeffrey Herring?' Aunt Olivia asked.

I did another quick search. 'There aren't many details about him online. One article about the robbery mentions that he and Ellen came from families of very modest means. Ellen's sister thought they might have committed the robbery so they'd have money to run away together and get married.'

'So, Victor could have used the stolen money to buy his first piece of real estate, setting himself on a path to wealth,' Olivia surmised.

'It fits.'

'But Ellen perished in a car accident,' my aunt pointed out.

'Supposedly,' I said. 'There aren't many details about the accident, but it seems like her body was never found. Everyone assumed she was swept away by the raging river when her car went in the water. They found one of her shoes washed up on the bank.'

Aunt Olivia looked thoughtful. 'So her death could have been staged.'

I picked up that thread. 'Allowing her and Jeffrey to start new lives under new names.'

'And yet they weren't a couple in recent years.' She frowned. 'At least, not as far as we know.'

'Maybe things didn't work out,' I suggested. 'But Avery said she didn't know why Victor had chosen to move to Twilight Cove.'

'It could be because he knew that Dorothy – Ellen – was living here.'

'Exactly,' I said. 'But Dorothy didn't live like she had any money.'

'Split between the two of them, the money they stole wouldn't have gone all that far. Maybe that's what Dorothy used to buy her plot of land when she eventually moved here to Twilight Cove.'

'That could be,' I agreed. I clapped a hand to my forehead. 'Byron!'

'What about him?' Olivia asked.

'I bet he figured out that Dorothy and Ellen are one and the same. He's been digging out in the woods.'

Understanding dawned in my aunt's eyes. 'You think he's looking for a stash of stolen money? There's probably nothing left of it.'

'Maybe he's just hoping that Dorothy still had some.'

'Perhaps,' Aunt Olivia said.

A memory came back to me. 'Dorothy told me she thought someone had been in her cabin recently. She assumed it was Ed Grimshaw, but maybe it was Byron, starting his search inside before he moved on to looking in the woods.'

'That's certainly a possibility,' my aunt agreed. 'We need to pass this information on to Chief Stratton.'

'I can't tell him about Roxy and me being in Byron's house.'

I also didn't want to tell the police about seeing the photo at Victor's mansion. If they spoke to Avery about that, and realized that the photo had been locked in Victor's safe, that would lead to more questions. Questions I wouldn't be able to answer. Not that they would believe the truth even if I shared it with them.

'How can I explain why I looked into the robbery without getting into serious trouble?' I shook my head. 'I can't tell the police. Not yet.'

'But Byron might have killed Dorothy,' Olivia reminded me. 'He might have tried to get her to tell him the location of the stash, if there is one.'

'The police are already looking at Byron because of what happened in the woods, and because of last night's prowler incident.'

I'd given my aunt a brief rundown of the previous night's events by text message that morning. Now, I filled her in on more of the details.

'I don't like this one bit,' she said when I finished. 'A possible killer has his sights set on you. I don't want you taking any risks.'

'I'll be fine,' I said in an attempt to reassure her.

She shook her head, adamant. 'I mean it, Georgie. You need to be careful. If you want to go into town, go in broad daylight. If you want to walk the dogs, take Callum with you.'

'All right,' I relented, knowing that would be the only way to give her peace of mind. 'I was thinking of going into town. I need some groceries and I've been craving an apple fritter, so I plan to drop in at the bakery.' I realized it was Sunday. 'Is the bakery open today?'

'For another couple of hours. It's closed on Mondays.'

'I'll stick with that plan then,' I said. 'Do you want to come with me?'

Regret showed on her face. 'I do, because I don't want you to go alone, but Vera is coming to pick me up in half an hour. We're going out for tea.'

'At the teahouse in that cute Victorian just off of Main Street?'

'That's the one. Why don't you join us?'

'I shouldn't stay in town long,' I said with some regret of my own. 'I need to do more work on my script before I send it to the producer in a couple of days.'

'You'll be going to town in broad daylight. I guess that will be OK,' Aunt Olivia said, as if trying to convince herself.

I squeezed her hand. 'I'll be careful.'

With that promise, I left the patio with the dogs and jogged over to the farmhouse to grab my wallet. I would make a quick trip into town and then I'd get down to work on my script edits.

Since Aunt Olivia wouldn't be home much longer herself, I took the spaniels with me. They happily rode in the back seat of my car, tongues lolling out as they watched the world go by outside the windows. I found a parking spot down the street from the bakery and walked the rest of the way, with the dogs accompanying me.

'I'll just be a few minutes,' I told them, glad that I'd be able to keep an eye on the dogs through the bakery's large display window.

I tied their leashes to a bench outside the bakery door and they sat down to wait.

I was reaching for the door when I heard a man's angry voice yell, 'Hey, you!'

Then someone barreled into me and I crashed to the ground.

THIRTY

'Byron! Have you lost your mind?' a woman's voice screamed, almost drowned out by a volley of barking from Flossie and Fancy.

I was so stunned that it took me a second to realize that Byron had tackled me to the ground. His elbow dug into my stomach and he glared down at me, his face hovering just inches above mine.

I reacted without thinking, planting my hands on his chest and giving him the hardest shove I could manage while flat on my back on the sidewalk. The push sent him toppling onto the ground next to me. I jumped to my feet, and he did the same, panting like an angry bull, his face red.

The spaniels strained at the end of their leashes, barking furiously.

I barely had a chance to register the fact that Shanifa was running toward us before I had to duck. Byron's fist came so close to hitting my face that I felt the swoosh of air as it rushed past my cheek.

With a loud screech and flapping wings, Euclid dived from the sky, right at Byron's head. He raised his arms to protect his face and let out a yell. Euclid swooped away, up into the sky and out of sight. By the time Byron lowered his arms, Shanifa had reached us. She grabbed Byron's wrist when he tried to lunge toward me.

'Stop it!' she yelled at him. 'Are you crazy?! You're going to get yourself arrested!'

Astonished faces watched us through the bakery's front window. I recognized Abigail, Victor Clyde's housekeeper, among them.

Shanifa's husband, Mo, was running along the sidewalk toward us.

'Shanifa!' he yelled.

She ignored him, still facing off with Byron. 'What's wrong with you?!'

Byron jabbed a finger at me. 'I know you're after the money and you won't get away with it!'

Shanifa gripped his arm and tried to pull him away from me. 'Shut up, Byron!'

He stood his ground as she tugged on his arm. 'I've been looking for weeks!' he fumed at me. 'It's mine!'

Shanifa stared at him. 'What are you talking about?'

He didn't answer, instead continuing to glare at me.

I crouched between Flossie and Fancy, stroking their fur and trying to calm them down. They'd stopped barking, but they stared hard at Byron, their muscles taut.

'I haven't been looking for the money,' I said calmly.

Byron's eyes almost bulged out of his head. 'You *do* know!'

Shanifa finally dropped his arm. 'What money?'

Mo arrived on the scene and bent over, huffing and puffing as he rested his hands on his knees. 'Shanifa, what's going on?' He straightened up and glared at Byron. 'I told you to stay away from my wife!'

Byron barely spared Mo a glance. 'I can do whatever I want.'

Mo raised his fist and advanced on Byron.

Shanifa jumped between them and put her hands on her husband's chest. 'Stop! Both of you!'

Abigail and the other customers inside the bakery continued to watch out the window as a police car drove up and stopped in the middle of the road. Officer Williams jumped out of the driver's seat. Another cruiser pulled up behind his and two more officers followed Williams as he jogged over our way.

'What's going on here?' Williams asked, all business. 'We got a call about an altercation.'

'Byron tackled me and knocked me to the ground,' I said.

'You're bleeding,' a female officer said as she and her partner joined us.

I glanced down to see blood trickling along my arm. I checked for the source and found a scrape and cut on my elbow. Only once I saw the injury did I register the pain.

Byron, Shanifa and Mo all started talking at once, so the police officers quieted them down and separated us. I sank down onto the bench outside the bakery and Flossie and Fancy jumped up to sit on either side of me. They pressed their bodies in close to mine, panting. I put an arm around each of them and sank my fingers into their fur.

'I'm OK, girls,' I murmured to them.

Officer Williams crouched down in front of me. 'Do you want me to call an ambulance, Georgie?'

I shook my head. 'I'm fine. Just a couple scrapes and bruises, I think.'

The fact that Byron had attacked me truly sank in for the first time and I shivered, even though the sun had broken through the dark clouds to shine its warmth down on us.

I told Williams what had happened and everything Byron had said to me.

'I think he believes that I'm after whatever he's been looking for in the woods.' I wanted to tell Williams about the photograph and the bank robbery, but I still couldn't figure out how to do that without getting myself into trouble.

Shanifa stood near the bakery door. She'd just finished speaking to one of the other officers and had overheard my last words.

'I knew he was up to something in the woods!' she said. 'Why does he think there's money out there?'

'I'm not sure,' I replied. That was mostly true. I had a theory but didn't know for certain. I decided to ask a question of my own. 'Why did Byron want you to follow me the other day?'

Shanifa averted her gaze and shrugged. 'I don't know what you're talking about.'

'I think you do,' I said, not in the mood to beat around the bush.

When she realized that Williams and I were both staring at her, waiting for her to talk, she cracked. 'OK, fine,' she said with a huff. 'Byron and I share a love for true crime podcasts and cold cases, stuff like that. We thought we could put our heads together and solve Dorothy's murder.' She fixed her dark eyes on me. 'You're our prime suspect.'

'I didn't kill Dorothy,' I protested.

She rolled her eyes. 'Of course you'd say that.'

'Byron accused me of being after money, not murder,' I pointed out. 'And it's not just him who's been out in the woods. You've been there too.'

Shanifa let out another huff. 'So what? Like I said, I knew Byron was up to something in the woods, but he was so secretive about it. I was curious, so I followed him one day, or tried to, anyway. I lost him in the woods and then got lost myself.' She glanced her husband's way. He stood talking with the female officer, looking both annoyed and a little confused. 'My husband's already jealous because of how much time I spend with Byron. Please don't tell him that I was alone in the woods with him. He might get the wrong idea.'

'Was that when Dorothy fired her gun at you?' I asked.

Officer Williams's eyes sharpened. 'She shot at you?'

Shanifa's cheeks flushed. 'Not exactly.' She glanced her husband's way again. 'When I got out of the woods, my car wouldn't start. I had to call Mo to come pick me up. I couldn't tell him that I'd been out there following Byron. He wouldn't have believed me. He would have thought I was having an affair. He already thinks that, even though it's not true. So, I told Mo that I'd gone into the woods to buy some natural skincare products from Dorothy, but I didn't have any purchases to show for it. When I was lost, I slipped and fell in a mud puddle. I was a mess. I should have just told Mo that I tripped and turned back before I made it to Dorothy's, but in the moment I kind of panicked and told him that I fell while running away from Dorothy because she shot at me for trespassing.'

'So, she never fired a gun at you?' I asked.

'No.' Shanifa sent another glance Mo's way. He'd finished talking to the police officer and was heading our way. 'Can I go now?'

Williams nodded. 'I'll be in touch if I need anything more from you.'

Shanifa turned and took her husband's arm, leading him briskly along the sidewalk. They appeared to be arguing as they walked away, but I couldn't hear their conversation.

Williams asked me to meet him at the station to provide a formal statement about the incident. Fortunately, nobody seemed to mind when I walked into the building with Flossie and Fancy. Williams even brought them a dish of water once he had us settled in an interview room. The spaniels lapped up the water gratefully before taking a short snooze at my feet.

When I walked out of the station after providing my statement, I let out a sigh of relief. Williams told me that Byron would be charged with assault. At least I didn't have to worry about him creeping around the farmhouse that evening.

The dogs and I set off along the street, heading back toward my car. When we got close to the vehicle, I pulled out my keys, ready to hit the button on the fob to unlock the doors.

'Georgie!' I heard a familiar voice call.

I turned to see Avery hurrying along the street toward me. Today she wore a pale pink leather jacket with tight jeans and high-heeled boots. The dogs sat down next to me as I waited for her to reach us.

'Abigail told me what happened with that reporter outside the bakery!' she said as she approached. 'Are you OK?'

'I'm fine.' The cut on my now-bandaged elbow stung a bit and I had a few other minor aches, but nothing worth mentioning. 'I'm a little embarrassed that there was an audience when it happened.'

'Don't be,' she said. 'That means there were witnesses. Abigail talked to the police after it happened and told them how he attacked you, completely unprovoked!'

'I'm glad there were witnesses,' I said. 'That way it's not my word against his.'

Shanifa had seen what had occurred, but I didn't know if I could have relied on her to tell the truth if no one else had seen the events unfold. Whatever her relationship with Byron, she was definitely far closer with him than she was with me, a near stranger.

'Abigail also said some big bird dived at the reporter,' Avery said. 'It must have been quite a scene.'

The dogs shifted restlessly, but stayed sitting by my feet.

'The bird thing was probably a streak of luck.' I wasn't about to say that it was my owl friend who'd swooped in to help. 'It distracted Byron for a moment.'

'The bird clearly has good judgement of humans.'

I cracked a smile at that and then changed the subject. 'How are things going for you?' I asked, wondering if she knew anything about Victor and Dorothy's relationship and their involvement in the bank robbery, if my theory was in fact correct.

'Moving along now that Mr Greenaway's partner is back in town. As soon as the police release my stepfather's body, I'll arrange to have the funeral in Chicago. For now, I'm trying to organize everything at the house.'

'If you need a hand, let me know.'

Although I meant the offer as sincere, I did have an ulterior motive in addition to wanting to help. If I could get back inside Victor's mansion, maybe I could poke around and see if there was any evidence to suggest that he and Dorothy were indeed involved in the Tennessee bank robbery. If I could take the dogs in with me, Flossie could unlock any doors or drawers that might be hiding helpful clues.

'Thanks,' Avery said. 'I think I've got things under control at the moment, but I appreciate the offer.'

So much for that idea.

It was probably time to stop worrying about the murder investigation.

Now that the police had evidence of Byron's violent nature, they might look at him more closely as a murder suspect. Maybe they'd even search his house. Once they looked into the cold cases adorning the walls of his study, they might make the connection between the old robbery, Victor, and Dorothy as well. Once that happened, hopefully it wouldn't be long before Byron was facing a charge of murder as well as one for assault.

An idea popped into my head. 'I know some people do photo slideshows for funerals and memorial services. Are you going to do something like that with photos from throughout your stepfather's life?'

'I'll probably just set out a few framed photos from the time he married my mom and onward. There aren't many pictures of him from early in his life. They all got destroyed in a house fire years ago.'

'Oh no,' I said. 'Did the fire happen when you and your mom lived with him?'

'No, it was before we knew him.' Avery shrugged. 'I think I'll still be able to put together a nice display with the photos I've got.'

'I'm sure you will,' I said as my thoughts whirred.

Avery and I said our goodbyes, and the dogs and I headed toward the grocery store. My appetite for an apple fritter had disappeared when Byron attacked me, so I'd decided to forget about visiting the bakery. Although Callum had texted me to say he'd bring the food needed for our barbecue that evening, I'd insisted on providing dessert and cold drinks. I still wasn't keen on leaving the dogs outside while I shopped, but I was beginning to accept that they would be fine by the door for a few minutes. This was Twilight Cove, not LA, and I'd be able to keep an eye on them, thanks to the store's large front windows.

After I'd picked up some food, iced tea, and Callum's favorite brand of beer, the dogs and I drove back to Auntie O's farm, with me thinking about my most recent conversation with Avery. Had Victor's photos from his early years really been destroyed by fire or was that just the story he'd concocted to cover the fact that he'd changed his appearance in order to evade the police?

I doubted I'd ever know the answer to that question, but the story seemed too convenient, considering what I'd learned during my recent research.

Now more than ever, I believed Victor and Dorothy were indeed Jeffrey and Ellen.

THIRTY-ONE

B ack at the farm, I dug some berries out of the freezer and whipped up a blueberry pie with a cookie crumb crust. Then I worked on my script until Vera dropped Auntie O off after their visit to the tea house. I met my aunt in the driveway and accompanied her into the carriage house so I could tell her about the incident with Byron before it reached her through the Twilight Cove grapevine. I assured her that I was fine, and that Byron was in police custody, and she finally agreed to let me out of her sight when the time came for me to take care of my share of the evening farm chores.

Although the altercation with Byron had left me more shaken than I'd let on to Olivia, keeping busy helped to stop me from reliving the incident over and over in my head. I saw Callum from a distance while I worked and waved when he raised a hand in greeting, but otherwise I didn't see him before the barbecue. When I'd finished looking after the animals, I jogged back to the farmhouse with Flossie and Fancy racing ahead of me. I fed the dogs and left them chowing down while I ran upstairs for a quick shower. Callum and I might have agreed to stay in the friend zone, but I still didn't want to risk smelling like manure during our dinner together.

When I returned downstairs, Flossie and Fancy were sitting by the back door, waiting patiently. As soon as they saw me, their patience ran out and they jumped to their feet. Fancy let out a long 'a-woo' while Flossie barked, both of them pointing their noses at the door.

'I get the message,' I said with a smile.

I opened the door and the dogs burst out onto the porch. They veered so sharply to the right that they nearly skidded on the boards beneath their paws. I laughed as I tugged the door shut behind me. Flossie and Fancy had found Callum at the barbecue. He crouched down to greet the dogs, ruffling their fur as they wiggled their bodies and wagged their tails with happiness.

'Hey, girls,' Callum said to them. 'Ready for dinner?'

'They've already eaten, but I'm sure they'll be keeping watch for any tasty morsels that might drop to the ground.'

Callum straightened up, while the dogs continued to gaze at him adoringly. 'It's always good to have a cleanup crew on hand.' He hooked a thumb at the barbecue behind him. 'I hope you don't mind that I already fired up the grill.'

'I don't mind at all. How about I grab us some drinks?'

Callum requested a beer, so I grabbed one from the fridge, along with a can of sweet tea for myself. When I returned to the back porch, Callum had salmon burgers cooking on the barbecue.

When I handed him the bottle of beer, he thanked me and did a double take when he got his first good look at the right side of my face. He set the bottle aside and touched his fingers to my cheek.

His forehead furrowed and his green eyes darkened. 'What happened?'

After my shower, I'd seen my face in the bathroom mirror. I must have hit my cheek on the sidewalk when Byron tackled me, because the right side of my face now sported a bright red scrape and a blooming purple bruise.

'Byron Szabo knocked me down in front of the bakery this afternoon,' I replied.

Callum's fingers ghosted along my cheek, just to the side of the injury, as he lowered his hand from my face. The darkness hadn't disappeared from his eyes. 'Please tell me he's been arrested.'

'And charged with assault,' I said. 'There were plenty of witnesses.'

Callum checked on the sizzling salmon burgers while I explained what had happened in greater detail, although I left out the part about Euclid swooping in to help me.

'He and the woman from the food truck – Shanifa, was it?' When I nodded, he continued, 'They thought you had killed Dorothy?'

'It seems I was their top suspect, anyway. It's kind of funny. They suspected me and I suspected them.'

Callum flipped the burgers. 'Does that mean neither of them is the killer?'

'I don't think it really rules them out. One of them might still have murdered Dorothy. They could have come up with the plan to investigate the murder, or decided to go along with the other's idea to do so to keep up the appearance of innocence.'

'If it was one of them, it was probably the reporter,' Callum said. 'He clearly has anger issues.'

'True, but Dorothy's murder was premeditated and carefully

executed. The killer took the time to sit down to tea with her and drug her before suffocating her.'

'Byron could be just as capable of that as he is of lashing out in the heat of the moment.'

I couldn't argue with that.

We turned our conversation to the sanctuary's animals until we sat down to eat on the padded wicker chairs on the porch. Flossie and Fancy lay at our feet, watching our every move as we started in on our burgers.

'These are delicious,' I said after I'd enjoyed my first bite. 'And grilled to perfection. You can bake and grill. You're good with animals and great at playing baseball. Are you one of those people who is annoyingly good at everything?'

Callum laughed. 'Just at the most important things.' He took a sip of his beer. 'How about you? I know you're good with animals too. And you're a brilliant writer. What else?'

'I don't know about brilliant, but I do all right.'

'And you're modest,' he added.

'Honest,' I countered. Then I shrugged. 'That's pretty much it.'

'I very much doubt that.' Callum regarded me closely, a hint of a smile on his face. 'You don't watch sports, but do you play any?'

'Not recently, though it would be nice to get back into something,' I said. 'I joined the swim team at a couple of my schools, and I dabbled in track and field. I played one season of T-ball when I was really little. I didn't like it, but I think that was because I was playing on a mixed team and some of the boys teased me relentlessly.'

Callum's smile faded. 'They should have been told off.'

'Maybe they were but it didn't work.' I thought back but couldn't dredge up any other T-ball memories. 'I don't remember.'

Now he was watching me thoughtfully. 'So, maybe you've got untapped talent as a baseball player.'

I managed to hold back a snort of laughter. 'Not likely.'

'Maybe we'll have to find out.'

I met his gaze, but the buzz of electricity that charged across my skin became too much and I had to look away.

'Maybe,' I managed to say, though I doubted we'd ever have the chance since we'd be going our separate ways before long.

I probably shouldn't have done it, but I fed a tiny morsel of my burger to Flossie. Callum then did the same for Fancy. The dogs inhaled the offerings and then sat up, hoping for more, their eyes tracking our every movement.

'How are things going with the asparagus farm?' I asked, changing the subject.

Callum set his empty plate on the small table that sat between our chairs. He stretched out his long legs and crossed them at the ankles. 'Done and dusted.'

'You got a confession?'

'With a recording of it. I stopped by earlier today and asked Woodberk for the latest paperwork. Of course, what he showed me didn't jibe with the size of the crop that was picked. He denied the discrepancies, but when I showed him the footage I recorded with the night vision camera, of him sending out shipments on the sly, he cracked. He admitted to selling part of the crop on the sly and fudging the paperwork, but he blamed me for not paying him enough, even though he was getting a generous salary. I terminated him on the spot.'

'Do you think he'll put up a fight?' I asked, worried that might not be the end of the problem.

'Not likely,' Callum said. 'He knows I could press charges. I think he'll slink away and disappear under a rock.'

'Sounds like that's where he belongs.'

Callum nodded his agreement before taking a long drink of his beer.

'Who's going to look after the asparagus farm now?' I asked, wondering if he'd want to leave the sanctuary sooner than anticipated so he could take care of his own place.

'I've found someone who's willing to step in and manage the place, for now at least. Once Woodberk is off the premises, we'll hash out the details.'

I was relieved to know he wouldn't be leaving the sanctuary in a lurch. Not yet, anyway. But I couldn't forget what Aunt Olivia had told me on my first day in Twilight Cove: Callum was here temporarily.

THIRTY-TWO

After I'd taken our empty plates inside and set them in the sink, I topped the blueberry pie with whipped cream and carried generous slices of it outside. By then, the dogs had given up on getting any further treats and were lying on their sides, snoozing.

'Baking,' Callum said, pointing his fork at me after taking a bite of pie. 'That's another talent of yours. This is amazing.'

'It's not something I do a lot of, but I enjoy it,' I said before taking a bite of my own slice.

The blueberries exploded on my tongue and mingled perfectly with the cream and the cookie crumb crust. Auntie O had given me the recipe years ago and it was one of my favorites.

We didn't talk much as we enjoyed our dessert, and soon all that remained on our plates were a few crumbs and smears of cream and blueberry juice. After we carried our plates into the kitchen, Callum insisted on helping me load all the dishes into the dishwasher. Then I grabbed two more bottles of beer from the fridge, one for each of us, and we settled on the porch steps, side by side, while the dogs lay down on the lawn.

The sun had sunk behind the trees, taking its warmth with it. I wished I'd thought to grab a hoodie before coming back outside. I didn't want to go get one now, because I was afraid Callum would take that as his cue to leave. I'd enjoyed spending time with him, and I wasn't yet ready for the evening to end, so I stayed put, despite the goosebumps on my arms.

Callum took a drink of his beer and set the bottle aside. He leaned his elbows on the step behind us as we watched the sky grow darker and the first stars appeared overhead.

'So,' he said after we'd sat in companionable silence for a minute or two, 'the next time we have dinner together, do you still want it to be as friends?'

'As opposed to enemies?' I quipped, even as my heart skipped at the words 'next time'. His question made me too nervous to answer directly.

He laughed, sending a pleasant swirl through my stomach. I really shouldn't have let the sound affect me so much, but I probably couldn't have stopped my reaction even if I'd wanted to.

'I was thinking of something a little more romantic,' he said.

The butterflies fluttering in my chest must have been in my head as well, because I responded with the first words that popped into my mind. 'Enemies to lovers is an incredibly popular romance trope.' I realized what I'd said and my cheeks burned. 'Not that I'm suggesting we should be . . . I just . . .' I sighed and tried again. 'Friends are safe.'

'True,' he agreed, looking out at the darkening landscape before us. 'And I like friends. Friends are good.' He turned his full attention to me. 'But I'd like to take a chance on moving beyond friendship with you, Georgie.'

I scrutinized his face, wanting to make sure he hadn't spoken in jest. After seeing the photos of his ex-wife and former dates, my first instinct was to doubt that he could be serious, even though I'd felt the unmistakable sparks between us.

I didn't find even a hint of facetiousness on his face.

'Why are you looking at me like I've lost my mind?' he asked.

I answered before giving myself a chance to think about what to say. 'I'm so ordinary.'

His forehead furrowed. 'More like extraordinary. Georgie, you're beautiful, creative, intelligent, and you share my love of animals. Why wouldn't I be interested?'

Despite the cool night air, heat spread over my skin at his words.

'I googled you,' I confessed in a rush.

Understanding dawned on his face. 'And read about my past relationships?'

'I saw photos. An actress. A pop star.' Inwardly I cringed at my lack of confidence.

'I'm not looking for a celebrity girlfriend, Georgie,' Callum said without a hint of impatience. 'I wasn't looking for a girlfriend at all. But then I met you.'

His sincerity slipped around my doubts, getting dangerously close to my heart. I stared at the unopened bottle in my hands, needing a moment to steady myself and sort out my thoughts.

'Are you already in a relationship?' he asked, and I knew he was trying to interpret my silence.

'No!' I said quickly. 'Definitely not. It's just . . .' I struggled to listen to my head when my heart was singing. I finally managed to voice my last remaining concern. 'Even if I stay in Twilight Cove, you'll probably be leaving soon.'

After all, he'd taken the job at the sanctuary so he could keep an eye on his farm. Now he no longer needed to do that. And from what he'd said in previous conversations, he wasn't interested in farming vegetables.

'About that,' he said, sitting up. 'I had a chat with Olivia earlier today. I asked her if I could keep this job and she wants me to stay on as the farm's manager.'

'You want to keep working here at the sanctuary?' I asked with surprise.

'Of course. I love it here, and this sanctuary feels like the right place for me. Unless you'd rather I didn't stay.'

'No!' I definitely didn't want him thinking that. I mustered up my courage and spoke the plain, unvarnished truth. 'I want you to stay.'

His eyes, even in the deepening darkness, seemed to burn into mine. 'And what about you?' he asked, holding my gaze.

'I definitely want to stay. It's just . . .' I glanced down at my beer bottle again, but then set it down beside me. I clasped my hands before meeting Callum's eyes once more. 'When I moved to Los Angeles, I told myself I was done jumping from place to place, that I would finally put down some roots, but . . .' I struggled to find the right words. Writing was so much easier for me than speaking.

'Maybe you weren't in the right place for your roots to thrive?' he guessed.

I nodded. I couldn't have put it better myself.

Callum touched a hand to my knee so briefly that it was little more than a ghost of a touch. 'There's nothing wrong with changing your plans when things don't work out as you thought they would.'

He was right about that. It would be silly of me to stay in Los Angeles simply because that was part of a plan I'd made years ago. I hadn't been unhappy in Los Angeles, but I was happier in Twilight Cove. I could breathe more easily here. I felt calmer, more myself. Now that I'd spent time in this town again, I suspected I'd find it more difficult to live in LA.

It was time to make a decision. Deep in my heart, I'd known all along what that decision would be.

'I don't know if I'll be living here on the farm with Aunt Olivia, or somewhere else in town,' I said, 'but I'm moving to Twilight Cove as soon as I can manage it.'

The slow smile that appeared on Callum's face gave me more goosebumps than the night air ever could.

'I'm very happy to hear that.'

We smiled at each other until a wave of shyness overcame me and I averted my gaze.

Callum got to his feet and the dogs jumped up from the grass. Fancy chased after a moth that was fluttering through the air while Flossie sat at the base of the steps, watching us.

Leaving the beer bottles behind, I stood up too, knowing – with reluctance – that it was time to say good night. I followed Callum down to the lawn, where Fancy still cavorted about and Flossie investigated a scent in a nearby flower bed.

Callum stopped on the grass and faced me. The breeze ruffled my hair and he reached up to touch one of my dancing curls. His hand moved from my hair to my uninjured cheek. His eyes met mine and I swore the starlight twinkled in his irises.

His fingers brushed down my arm, leaving a trail of tingles in its wake. He closed his hand over mine and he took my other hand as well. I entwined my fingers with his as he stepped closer.

'You never did answer my question,' he said, his voice low.

'Question?' I couldn't think straight when he was so close. Those green eyes were way too distracting.

'About whether you want to stay as friends or go in a different direction.'

'Oh. That question.'

Before I had a chance to say anything else, Fancy bounded up behind me and crashed into my legs. My knees buckled and I stumbled forward, right into Callum's arms.

'Fancy!' I exclaimed as I regained my balance. I didn't, however, make any move to step away from Callum, and he slid his arms around my waist.

Fancy, for her part, didn't look the least bit contrite. In fact, she gave the back of my leg an insistent nudge.

'I like how she thinks,' Callum said, grinning.

Flossie barked her agreement.

I smiled and wrapped my arms around Callum's neck, looking him right in the eye. 'I do too.'

As his lips touched mine, I thought I heard an owl hoot off in the distance. Then I lost awareness of anything but our kiss. It was slow and deep and all-consuming.

When it finally ended, I had one hand on his chest and the fingers of the other anchored in the hair at the back of his head. Callum kept his hands on my hips as he rested his forehead against mine. The warmth radiating from his body chased the chill of the night away from my skin.

'Does that answer your question?' I asked.

One side of his mouth turned up in a grin. 'I wouldn't say no to further confirmation.'

I smiled at that. This time, I initiated the kiss.

I didn't know how much time had passed while I was completely lost in Callum. Eventually, with my mind hazy and my body feeling light and floaty, I pulled back and sighed.

'I guess it's time to say good night,' I said with reluctance, both hands now resting on his chest.

'Unfortunately.' He kissed me again, far too briefly, and then stepped back, keeping hold of one of my hands. 'Georgie,' he said in all seriousness, 'I really like you.'

I smiled. 'I got that impression.' I squeezed his hand. 'I hope you got the same one from me.'

He grinned and kissed my knuckles before letting go of my hand, his fingers slowly sliding along mine until they parted.

'See you in the morning?' he asked.

'In the morning,' I agreed.

I turned away before calling to the dogs so Callum wouldn't see the big, goofy smile that stretched across my face. Before closing the back door of the house behind us, I peeked out. Callum stood waiting out on the lawn, watching. I waved, and he raised a hand in response. I shut and locked the door, and then looked out the kitchen window. Callum turned and walked off across the farm with easy strides.

I fell asleep incredibly happy that night, and woke up feeling the same way. Although a small voice in the back of my head warned me to be careful about rushing headlong into a relationship, my happiness managed to drown it out. There was nothing wrong with seeing where things with Callum would go.

After a quick breakfast, I set out toward the barn with Flossie and Fancy, eager to see the animals and even more eager to see Callum. The dark clouds from the day before had thickened overhead. A chilly breeze rustled the green leaves of the nearby maple trees.

I was halfway across the lawn when Aunt Olivia emerged from the back door of the carriage house, hobbling along on her crutches.

'Georgie!' she called out as she paused on the patio.

The note of urgency in her voice set off firecrackers of worry in my chest.

I jogged over to her, the dogs racing ahead of me. They bounced around my aunt for a moment and then sat down, tails wagging as they looked up at her expectantly. She gave them each a pat on the head, but her mind was clearly elsewhere.

'What's wrong, Auntie O?' I asked with concern.

'It's Byron Szabo,' she said, her blue eyes wide. 'He's dead.'

THIRTY-THREE

'**D**ead?' I echoed, shocked. 'But how? I thought Byron was in police custody.'

'They released him last night,' Aunt Olivia explained. 'Early this morning, his housekeeper found him dead in his bed.'

'But how did he die?' Recent events prompted another rapid question from me. 'Was he murdered?'

'Apparently, it looks like suicide,' my aunt said.

'That's what the police are saying?'

'That's what Dolores's sister-in-law, Fiona, is saying.' When she saw my look of confusion, she added, 'Fiona is Byron's housekeeper. He won a year's worth of housekeeping in a recent contest. That's just one of so many things he no longer has the chance to enjoy.'

I stared off into the distance, my eyes unfocused, as I tried to take in the news.

Aunt Olivia leaned on her crutches and patted my arm. 'You'd better sit down, darling. You're looking rather pale.'

I sank down onto one of the patio chairs, barely remembering the steps I'd taken to get there. The cushion I sat on was still cool from the night air. It sent a chill through me, one that seeped into my bones.

'Why would Byron kill himself?' I asked, still having trouble digesting what Auntie O had told me. 'Out of guilt?'

My aunt settled on the loveseat across from me. 'Fiona probably shouldn't have said anything at all, but she's a real snoop and has loose lips. I don't think the police will be pleased that she's been talking about what she saw, but Byron left a note, and Fiona read it.'

I shook off some of my shock, allowing curiosity to take its place. 'What did it say?'

'That he'd killed Dorothy and was worried he'd get caught. He couldn't stand the thought of going to jail.'

I absorbed that information. 'So, Byron really was the killer.'

That didn't surprise me, but what didn't sit right with me was the fact that Byron had taken his own life. Maybe he was concerned about going to jail, but when I thought back to the day before, it seemed the only thing on his mind was finding Dorothy's stash of stolen money – if it existed – and keeping it for himself. Of course, the police had then arrested him for assaulting me. Maybe that encounter with the cops had scared him.

That made some sense, I supposed, but I still had some lingering doubts.

'The police are sure it was suicide?' I checked.

Aunt Olivia shrugged. 'I don't know what the police think. The only news I've heard is what came from Fiona, through Dolores.' She studied my face. 'You think Byron could have been another murder victim?'

I shook my head. 'I don't know. According to Shanifa, the two of them were investigating Dorothy's death. Maybe Byron got too close to the truth and the killer silenced him.' I shook my head again. 'On the other hand, maybe Byron really was the killer.'

'That's the simplest explanation and probably the accurate one.' Olivia sighed. 'I'm not glad he's dead, but I am relieved that he can't hurt you or anyone else now.'

I nodded, still thinking. It was true that I wouldn't have to worry about him anymore, and with Dorothy's killer off the streets, the whole town would feel safer.

'I guess it's over now,' I said.

I didn't feel quite as relieved as I thought I should. Maybe that had to do with my lingering remnants of shock. In time, hopefully relief would take over.

I was about to get up, but stopped myself. 'Auntie O, there's something I've been wanting to talk to you about.'

My aunt set her crutches aside and got more comfortable on the loveseat. 'I'm all ears.'

I got right to the point. 'I want to move to Twilight Cove.'

It took a split second for my words to register with Aunt Olivia. Then her eyes lit up and she beamed at me. 'I was hoping you'd say that.'

'You were?' I asked. I'd expected her to be more surprised by my statement.

'I would love to have you close, Georgie,' she said. 'And being here, even just a short time, has already done you good. I can see it in your face.'

'I'm so much more relaxed here,' I agreed.

'I couldn't be happier.' Her smile lost some of its brightness. 'The move will be OK for your career?'

'It'll be fine,' I assured her. 'I'll probably go back to LA now and then, but for the most part, I can work from anywhere.'

'I'm so pleased, Georgie.' Unshed tears shone in her eyes. 'For both of us.'

I smiled. 'I love being closer to you. I know it's the right decision. I have to take care of a few things in Los Angeles before I can settle here permanently, but I don't think that will take too long. Before I leave Twilight Cove, I'll start looking for a place to live. Unless . . . would you consider renting this carriage house to me once you've moved back into the farmhouse?'

Aunt Olivia's smile was so bright it probably could have been seen from space. 'I absolutely want you to stay here on the farm. Not so you can work at the sanctuary – I know you'll want to focus on your writing – but this is where you belong.'

That's exactly what I felt in my heart. 'I wouldn't mind helping with the animals,' I said. 'I enjoy it.'

'You're always welcome to be involved with them if you want,' she said, 'but once I'm back on my feet, Callum and I can handle the bulk of the work ourselves. And speaking of Callum . . .'

'He told me he's staying on permanently.' I tried to contain my smile, not wanting to advertise my feelings with a big goofy grin.

It was too soon to share how things had evolved between me and Callum, although the twinkle in my aunt's eyes made me wonder if she already suspected.

I jumped to my feet. 'I should get on with my chores.'

Aunt Olivia caught my hand in hers. 'One little adjustment to your suggested living arrangements. I want you to have the farmhouse.'

'I can't take over your whole house on a long-term basis,' I protested.

'Ever since your Uncle Howard died, I've felt like I've been rattling around in there on my own.'

A pang of sympathy pierced my heart. I knew my aunt still missed her late husband, despite the passage of nearly two decades since his death. 'I'm just one person too,' I pointed out. 'If you want, we could share the house.'

She shook her head. 'I quite like it here in the carriage house, and I want you to have your own space. Besides, it won't just be you. It'll be you and the two dogs, with room to grow in the future.'

I sat down next to her. 'Please don't set your heart on me having a family, Auntie O. I'm not good with relationships.'

Aunt Olivia patted my hand. 'I don't believe that, but there's no pressure. You're absolutely perfect on your own.'

Fancy let out an 'a-woo'.

'And even more perfect with Flossie and Fancy,' Aunt Olivia said, smiling at the dogs.

Flossie gave a happy bark and thumped her tail against the patio's flagstones.

I laughed and stood up again. 'I will be paying rent.'

Olivia waved off my statement. 'We'll talk about that later.'

'It's a condition of me moving here,' I said, trying to sound firm.

'We'll negotiate. But that can wait.'

I kissed my aunt on the cheek. 'Thank you, Auntie O. For giving me a home now and back in my teens.'

She clasped my hand and gave it a squeeze. 'You're like a daughter to me, Georgie. Wherever you might roam in the future, you will always have a home here.'

I smiled my thanks, because I didn't trust my voice in that moment. When I patted my hand against my leg, the dogs jumped up to follow me away from the carriage house. I waved to my aunt as we set off across the lawn. Flossie and Fancy veered off to go visit the goats, leaving me on my own.

The tightness in my throat loosened by the time I reached the barn, but when I walked inside and saw Callum standing outside of Sundance's stall, stroking the Quarter Horse's neck and talking softly to her, my chest ached from a rush of strong emotions and a wave of shyness hit me. I stopped just inside the barn, unsure of what to do or say.

Flossie and Fancy trotted up from behind me and made a beeline for Callum, drawing his attention. The grin that appeared on his face when he saw me set butterflies dancing in my stomach.

'Morning.' He crouched down to greet the dogs and then straightened up, his green eyes on me again.

I forced my legs to move and joined him by the stall. I stroked Sundance's nose and she snuffled at the pockets of my jeans, looking for treats. Finding none, she backed up in her stall and turned her attention to her hay net. Suddenly I felt incredibly awkward standing there in front of Callum. I became overly aware of my arms hanging at my sides, not knowing what to do with my hands.

Callum solved that problem by taking one of my hands in his. He searched my eyes with his own. 'Hey. You OK?'

'Byron Szabo is dead,' I said, even though that had nothing to do with my attack of shyness, which I knew was what he was really asking about.

The news clearly startled him. I quickly filled him in on the details – the few I had, anyway. He kept hold of my hand the entire time, his thumb drifting back and forth across my knuckles.

'At least he can't hurt you or anyone else anymore,' he said when I'd finished.

'In that sense it's a relief,' I agreed.

'And what about us?' he asked. 'Are you still OK with the new direction we've taken?'

I smiled, glad that my shyness was slowing ebbing away. 'Definitely.'

He stepped closer. I took a small step back.

He eyed me with a mixture of amusement and confusion. 'Then what's with keeping your distance?'

'I'm making sure we actually get the farm work done.'

He laughed and gave my fingers a gentle squeeze. 'Probably a good move. I've got a good work ethic, but you, Georgie Johansen, are one heck of a distraction.'

'It goes both ways,' I said, doing my best to maintain the foot of distance between us. It wasn't easy when all I wanted to do was step into his arms.

'Now that I don't need to keep a low profile, how about I take you to that restaurant you wanted to try?' he suggested.

'How about I take you?' I countered. 'It was my idea.'

'Fair enough,' he said with a grin. He gave my hand another squeeze before releasing it. 'When do you want to go?'

'How about tomorrow evening?' I suggested.

'I'm already looking forward to it.'

I took a reluctant step back, widening the distance between us. 'I'd better get busy.'

'Me too,' he said, pulling his work gloves from the back pocket of his jeans. 'I've got a few more things to take care of and then I'll head into town to the farm supply store. Life's easier now that I don't have to drive two towns away to keep my presence here a secret.'

'I bet.' I took yet another step back, but those green eyes of his were like magnets, holding my gaze.

I finally managed to turn away, but then I threw caution to the wind. I whirled back around, stepped right up to Callum and kissed him. He pressed a hand to the small of my back, holding me close as the kiss deepened. It took every ounce of my self-control, but I managed to pull away.

Not trusting myself to maintain that control, I turned on my heel and resolutely walked away. The warm rumble of laughter that followed me sent pleasant tingles over my skin.

Maybe I was getting in over my head with Callum, but in that moment I didn't care.

THIRTY-FOUR

I was grooming the donkeys out in the paddock – my last task of the morning – when Callum climbed into his truck and drove off with a wave at me through the open window. As I ran a brush along Charlie's back, I glanced up to see Roxy watching from a distance. I waved and gestured for her to come and join me in the paddock.

She greeted the dogs and then climbed the fence and came over to pat Charlie on the nose.

'Is it still OK for me to volunteer here?' she asked.

'Of course,' I said with a smile. 'Have you ever worked with animals before?'

She shook her head. 'Does that matter?' Although there was a hint of defiance in her voice, her eyes told me that she was more worried than anything else.

'No. We can teach you everything you need to know. I'm still learning myself.' After a final stroke with the brush, I gave Charlie a pat and he wandered off to join his friends in the middle of the paddock. 'I'll introduce you to Callum sometime. He's the farm manager.'

'Is that the guy in the cowboy hat?' Roxy asked as she climbed the fence to perch on the top rail. 'The one I've seen around here?'

'That's him,' I confirmed. 'Callum McQuade.'

'But not *the* Callum McQuade, right?'

'As in the baseball player?'

She nodded, watching me closely.

'Then, yes, that's the one,' I said.

Roxy's eyes widened. 'For real?' Before I had a chance to say anything, her eyes narrowed and she asked, 'What's Callum McQuade doing working on your aunt's farm?'

I leaned my back against the fence and glanced up at the sky, noting that the roiling clouds had grown even darker since I'd last looked upward. 'He's the sanctuary's manager.'

'But he's an MLB player,' Roxy said.

'Retired MLB player,' I amended. 'And he loves animals, so he works here now. You're a baseball fan?'

Roxy shrugged. 'Sort of.' She tried to sound aloof, but I could tell from the light in her eyes that she had far more enthusiasm for the sport than she was willing to admit.

I held back a smile. 'Don't you need to get to school?'

Roxy kicked one heel against the fence. 'I guess.'

'You'd better get going then,' I said, not wanting her to miss more classes than she probably already had that morning. 'Just one week left until summer vacation.'

That reminder seemed to cheer her up.

It occurred to me that she might need express consent from a parent before she started volunteering. I decided to raise that question with Auntie O before the end of the day.

'Can you come by on Saturday morning?' I asked. 'I'll introduce you to Callum and we can get you started on helping with the animals.'

'What time?' Roxy asked.

'I'll text you after I've checked with Callum.'

She swung her legs over the fence and hopped down to the ground on the other side.

She hadn't brought up Byron's death, so she probably hadn't heard the news yet. I decided not to mention it. She'd hear soon enough, and I didn't want to dwell on the subject when I needed to be thinking about the script rewrites I had to get done within the next few days.

'See you on the weekend,' I said as she walked away from the paddock.

She waved and then broke into a run. Soon, she disappeared into the woods.

A shudder of anxiety ran through me at the thought of her going that way by herself, but then I remembered that Dorothy's killer was supposedly dead now. Hopefully that was true, and the woods were safe again.

Flossie and Fancy wandered off as I headed to the barn to put away the grooming tools. I dusted dirt and bits of hay off my jeans and washed up at the sink in the tack room before going back outside. My plan was to return to the house, pour myself a cold drink, and get to work on my screenplay.

The dogs were nowhere to be seen when I emerged from the barn, but I'd barely had a chance to start looking around when I heard a volley of muffled barking.

'Flossie? Fancy?' I called out.

The barking paused and then started up again, this time sounding frantic.

I jogged toward the sound, worry gnawing at my insides. The only other time I'd heard the dogs sound so agitated was when Byron attacked me in front of the bakery.

The barking drew me toward the old shed where I'd taken my tumble from the rotten ladder. Callum had fixed the roof a couple of days ago and had carted the old ladder away. A pitchfork now leaned against the shed door, which rattled in its frame as frenzied scratching joined the sound of barking.

Both dogs were shut inside. How they'd managed to get trapped in the shed with a pitchfork against the door, I had no idea, but all that mattered at the moment was getting them out and calming them down.

'It's OK, girls! I'm coming!' I called as I ran.

The barking only grew more frantic.

I careened to a stop by the shed door and stared at the pitchfork. Someone had jammed the tines into the ground and the handle beneath the doorknob so the door wouldn't open.

'It's OK. I'm here,' I said to the dogs, even as I wondered who would have done such a thing.

The barking stopped, but then Fancy let out a long, distressed howl. The sound sent a shiver through my bones.

As I reached for the pitchfork, something flickered in my peripheral vision.

I whipped my head around.

When I saw the gun pointed at me, I froze.

THIRTY-FIVE

'Don't even think about it,' Avery said as my gaze flicked from the gun to the pitchfork.

I returned my focus to the weapon in her hand, my skin suddenly cold and my thoughts in a panicked whirl.

'Turn around and start walking,' Avery ordered.

'But—'

'Do it!' The ice in her voice hit me like a hard slap to my face.

Flossie and Fancy whined and scratched at the shed door as I did as I was told. My feet felt like lead, every step a struggle. At least Avery had locked the dogs away instead of doing something worse to them. I hoped they were unharmed.

As I walked across the farmyard, the dogs began barking again. I stared straight ahead and forced myself to quicken my pace. The last thing I wanted was for Avery to decide to go back and silence the spaniels.

My heart lurched when Avery grabbed my arm and yanked me to the right. 'This way.'

She marched me along the side of the barn rather than across the front of it. I tried to get my brain to work as we walked. Its frantic spinning wasn't doing me any good. I needed help, but Callum might not be back for ages, and Aunt Olivia was in the carriage house with a broken ankle. If she could see us, and realized what was happening, she could call the police. But first the shed and now the barn hid us from view of the carriage house.

If I couldn't count on anyone else to help me, I needed to save myself and then free Flossie and Fancy. Thinking of the sweet dogs strengthened my resolve and chased away the panic clouding my thoughts.

Maybe I could distract Avery and escape long enough to free the dogs and run for help. I slowed my pace, but when she nudged my back with the butt of the gun, I walked faster again. We passed the westernmost paddock and began crossing the big open field at the back of the farm, heading for the woods.

I didn't want to think about what would happen once we disappeared among the trees. I cast around for something – anything – that I might be able to use as a weapon, but there was nothing but the grass underfoot.

'Why are you doing this, Avery?' I asked, hoping that as long as I could keep her talking, she wouldn't pull the trigger.

'Because you've been asking too many questions, sticking your nose where it doesn't belong.'

'I don't know what you mean.'

She let out a short, harsh burst of laughter. 'Please. Drop the act. If you didn't know what this was about, you wouldn't have asked about my stepfather's photographs.'

I hadn't been as subtle with my questions about the pictures as I'd thought. Clearly, I also hadn't focused my attention on the right suspect.

'Why did you kill Dorothy?' I asked, deciding to get right to the heart of the matter.

She nudged me with the butt of the gun when I stumbled on the uneven ground. 'I thought you had that all figured out,' she said.

'Did you think she had money stashed away in the woods too?'

'After all these years?' she asked with disdain. 'Only a fool would think that.'

'Then why kill her?'

'Because if I didn't, she was going to inherit Victor's estate.'

'You said he was leaving most things to charity,' I reminded her as the wind swirled around us, throwing the occasional drop of rain into my face.

'That was a fib,' Avery said. 'He left some money to charities, but there was a lot left over.'

'And he left it to Dorothy?' I guessed.

'Under her real name.'

I slowed my pace slightly, hoping she wouldn't notice. The woods loomed ominously ahead of us, and I wanted to stay out in the open as long as possible.

'They stayed in touch all these years? After changing their identities?'

'No, but Victor must have held a torch for her. After my mom died, he hired a private investigator to find Ellen. The guy tracked her to Twilight Cove, figured out she was living under a different name.'

'Victor told you all this?' I asked, surprised.

'Of course not! I found his correspondence with the private investigator after his stroke and I saw a copy of the will.'

'So you did have the combination to the safe.'

'No, but Victor had another copy in a filing cabinet in his study. He betrayed me and my mom's memory.'

'By leaving the bulk of his estate to Dorothy?'

'And leaving me hardly anything! Unless Dorothy died before him.' She let out a huff of disgust. 'I was his only remaining family and I was his *alternate* beneficiary. Alternate! He should have left everything to me!'

'I thought you didn't need his money,' I said, the wild anger in her voice chilling my blood. 'You have a successful business in Chicago.'

'It *was* successful, for a year or two. Now it's almost dead in the water and my husband and I are up to our eyeballs in debt. We could lose our penthouse apartment, our sportscars. I couldn't let that happen.'

She took someone's life to keep a penthouse and cars?

Her selfishness and callousness sent my fear seeping deep into my bones. I wanted to cry, but instead I kept talking.

'Did you kill Victor as well?' I asked.

'There was no need,' she said, her voice full of scorn. 'I knew he was dying. I just had to bide my time.'

She gave me a shove, sending me stumbling. I managed to stay on my feet, but dismay passed over me like a dark shadow.

We'd reached the woods.

Avery nudged me onward and I had no choice but to step in among the trees.

'I've been scoping out this farm all morning, trying to figure out what to do with you,' she said as we crunched and crashed our way through the undergrowth. 'I couldn't believe my luck when I came across this place.'

Before I had a chance to ask her what she was talking about, Avery gave me a hard shove.

I stumbled forward, and the ground disappeared beneath my feet.

THIRTY-SIX

My left arm smashed against something hard as I fell. I slithered down, scrambling to find a way to stop my descent. I dug my fingers into the dirt and hung on tight. My arm had hit a brick, I realized. There were a few of them strewn about near the edge of the hole I'd half fallen into. Toppled timbers also lay nearby, an old rope tied to one of them. The dirt crumbled beneath my fingers and I slid farther into the hole.

'Avery!' I cried out.

She stood and watched, her eyes cold, as my hands slipped over the edge and I fell down toward the darkness below.

I flailed and my hand brushed against the old rope. I grabbed on to it.

The rope burned my hands as it slithered through my grip, but it slowed my descent as I fell. Then the rope ran out and I tumbled another short distance before landing in shallow water with a splashing crash. Pain radiated through my body, and my stunned brain tried to figure out what had happened. I heard a groan as I tried to untangle my limbs, and I realized the sound had come from me. Everything hurt, but nothing so much as my hands and my left arm.

I blinked grit out of my eyes and took in my surroundings. I was sitting in chilly, murky water up to my shoulders at the bottom of a deep, circular hole. The walls of the hole were made of old bricks, with weeds poking out through the cracks in the mortar.

It was an old well, I realized.

Shivering, I looked up to find Avery standing near the edge of the hole, peering down. Panic shot through me as I realized how helpless I was, stuck at the bottom of the well with nowhere to hide.

'Please don't shoot me,' I beseeched, raising my voice so Avery could hear me.

She held up the gun. 'What? With this?' She lowered the weapon. 'It's not even loaded. I found it in Victor's desk, but he didn't have any bullets. That doesn't matter. It could be years before anyone finds your remains down there. And even when they do, it'll look like you simply had a tragic accident. If only I'd known about this old well before I killed Dorothy, nobody ever would have known it was murder. I thought I had a foolproof plan, but the old witch struggled, even after I drugged her. I don't have to worry about that with you.'

My shivering intensified. I cradled my throbbing left arm against me and scrambled to my feet. My sodden, dripping clothes clung to my skin, but at least the water barely reached above my knees now that I was standing.

Avery grabbed the rope that had likely saved my life – for the moment, anyway – and hauled it up. I tried to grab the end but it was already out of reach. I watched the last of the rope disappear out of the well with a heavy stone of dread sinking in my stomach. Then Avery moved out of sight.

'Avery!'

I don't know why I bothered calling out to her. She wasn't going to have a change of heart and help me out of my predicament.

I heard Avery crashing through the underbrush, moving away from my position. Soon the sounds faded away and all I could hear was the pattering of raindrops. The skies opened up and the pattering intensified to a thunderous drumming.

'Help!' I yelled.

The pouring rain drowned out my voice. Not that it mattered. There wasn't anyone out there to hear me.

My teeth chattered and I knew that time was now my enemy. Even though it was June, with spring giving way to summer, the nights were cool and hypothermia was still a danger. I knew I couldn't count on someone saving me, so I had to get myself out of the well.

I felt along the rough bricks until I slipped my fingers into holes in the mortar. Then I found a crevice to lodge my right foot in and pulled myself up. I bit back a whimper as my left arm ached in protest. I lost my grip on the brick wall and slid back to the bottom of the well with a splash.

I leaned against the rough wall and closed my eyes, trying to regroup. Somehow, I had to fight through the pain and climb out of the well. Otherwise, I would die from hypothermia and Avery would get away with murder. Multiple murders. And who knew who else she might hurt in the future if she wasn't caught now.

She'd already killed Dorothy, and most likely Victor's lawyer, Simon. I was also now certain that she'd killed Byron Szabo. Probably by drugging and smothering him, just like she'd done to Dorothy.

The rain pelted my head and shoulders. Still shivering, I opened my eyes and looked up. The hole was too deep for me to climb out of on my own. I was well and truly trapped.

Despair settled over me, a heavy weight on my shoulders.

In the dim light at the bottom of the well, a shadow passed over me. I looked up again. Euclid perched at the edge of the hole.

My heart lifted at the sight of him.

'Euclid!' I blinked raindrops out of my eyes. 'Can you help me?'

Maybe it was crazy of me to ask an owl for help, but I didn't exactly have anything to lose by doing so. Euclid's head swiveled like he was looking for something, or maybe listening. He hopped out of sight and my heart sank.

Then I heard a rustling sound. Euclid reappeared at the edge of the hole with the end of the rope clutched in his beak. He peered into the well and then dropped the rope. It slithered down to slap the brick wall in front of me.

I could hardly believe what had happened.

'Thank you, Euclid!' I called up to him. 'You're the smartest, most wonderful owl in the world!'

If he thought anything about my praise, he didn't let it show. With a flap of his wings, he lifted up into the air and disappeared from sight.

I grabbed the rope with my sore hands and tested it with my weight, hoping it wasn't ready to snap. When it held, I gritted my teeth against the pain in my hands and arm and lodged the toe of my right shoe into a crevice in the brick wall. Then, slowly, I began my ascent.

I made it only a few feet before I slipped and splashed back down into the cold, murky water. I wanted to cry with frustration and fear and misery, but instead, I channeled all that emotion into a renewed effort at climbing. About three-quarters of the way up, I lost my footing but managed to keep clutching my lifeline. My body bumped against the brick wall as the timber the rope was tied to creaked ominously above me.

Worried that the line might break, I felt about until I found another foothold. It took all the strength I could muster, but I managed to shimmy up another few inches. I was so close to the top now that I could almost see over the edge of the hole.

Just a little farther, I told myself. *You're almost there.*

I tried to keep going, but my body refused to cooperate. My hands wouldn't unclench from around the rope and I was shivering so hard that I lost my footholds and bumped my shoulder against the bricks.

I slipped down an inch.

You can do it, I told myself as I tightened my grip on the rope. *Just keep going.*

Despite my internal pep talk, my hands and feet still didn't move. I hung there, my face slick with rain and probably a few tears too. I slipped another few inches and cried out as the rope cut into my already sore hands.

I couldn't do it. I couldn't hold on any longer.

I scrunched my eyes shut.

They flew open when I heard barking in the distance.

The sound was getting closer, second by second.

That knowledge gave me the strength to tighten my grip on the rope.

I heard more barking, definitely closer now. Then came a voice through the wind and rain.

'Georgie?' Callum called.

Hope welled up inside of me.

'Callum!' I yelled. 'Help!'

The barking stopped, but I could hear Callum and the dogs crashing through the woods.

I called Flossie's and Fancy's names, then Callum's again.

The crashing noises became louder. Then the spaniels appeared at the edge of the hole, panting, their fur wet from the rain.

Raindrops and tears rolled down my cheeks. 'I'm so happy to see you.'

Pounding footsteps sounded close by and Callum appeared next to the dogs.

He swore at the sight of me and dropped down to lie flat on his stomach. He reached into the hole, grabbed the waistband of my jeans, and hauled me up to safety. I crawled away from the edge of the well and then sat in the mud, shivering. Flossie and Fancy climbed onto my lap and licked me all over my face.

I laughed and cried at the same time. When the dogs backed off,

Callum took my hand and pulled me to my feet and then right into his arms.

'What the hell happened, Georgie?' he asked as he held me close.

I could feel his body heat through his wet and muddy clothes. I tried to soak it in, but continued to shiver.

'Avery,' I said through chattering teeth. 'She killed Dorothy. She pushed me into the well because she thought I knew too much.'

'Who's Avery?' he asked, confused.

'Avery Hembridge. Victor Clyde's stepdaughter.'

He kept one arm around me while he pulled his phone out of the pocket of his jeans. 'I don't know who that is either, but I'm calling the police.'

I released him and crouched down to hug Flossie and Fancy. They licked my face and whined.

'It's OK, girls,' I soothed. 'Everything's going to be OK.'

I hoped that was the truth.

THIRTY-SEVEN

Rosie, Daisy, and Violet grazed peacefully in the pasture with the other alpacas. I rested my arms on the fence, watching the animals as I breathed in the fresh air. The sun shone down on me, warming my skin.

Flossie nudged my leg with her nose and I pushed away from the fence, crouching down to pet her and her sister. Flossie rested a paw on my knee and Fancy let out a quiet whine.

'I know, girls,' I said as I stroked their fur. 'I'm going to miss you too. But I'll be back soon. I promise.'

I'd planned to return to Los Angeles once Aunt Olivia was back on her feet and then sublet my studio apartment until the end of my lease so I could move back to Twilight Cove. That plan had changed when I found a fellow screenwriter who wanted my apartment and needed to move in three weeks from now, not six.

After my tumble down the well, Auntie O's friends and neighbors had rallied around, insisting that I rest for a few days while they all pitched in to help Callum look after the animals. Now they had a roster ready and would continue helping out while I was in LA packing up my old life.

I was glad my aunt lived in such a tightly knit community, one that banded together to help their neighbors. Knowing that I would soon be a permanent part of that same community brought me a sense of comfort and security that had so often been missing in my life.

I kissed the dogs on the head and stood up. 'Come on. I need to pack up the car.'

Flossie and Fancy stuck close to me as we walked back to the farmhouse. Only a few days had passed since my terrifying encounter with Avery, and I still had aches and pains that had yet to fade completely. Thankfully, I had no broken bones, but my left arm was black and blue and tender. My raw, red hands had started to heal, but I knew I wouldn't be able to grip my car's steering wheel too tightly as I drove back to California.

Approaching the farmhouse, I spotted Aunt Olivia and Tessa

sitting on the back porch. Flossie and Fancy ran up the steps, tails wagging, to greet both women.

'Can you sit for a few minutes before you leave?' Tessa asked as I climbed the stairs to the porch. 'If I'm not going to see you for nearly three weeks, I need to get my fill now.'

I smiled at that. It was nice to know that I'd be missed while I was gone. I'd certainly be doing my share of missing people and animals while away from Twilight Cove.

As I got comfortable on the porch swing next to Tessa, a police cruiser pulled into the driveway. A knot of apprehension formed in my chest. I hoped we weren't about to receive bad news. Surely there was no way that Avery had been released from custody.

The police had caught up with her at Victor's mansion, where she was packing her suitcase into the trunk of her rental car, preparing to hightail it to the airport. She'd tried to flee on foot when she saw the cops coming for her, but she hadn't made it far before a police dog took her down.

Brody Williams climbed out of the cruiser and came over to stand at the base of the steps. 'Ladies,' he greeted. 'Sorry to interrupt.'

'Come and take a seat,' Aunt Olivia invited. 'Do you have news?'

'Of a sort,' he said. 'The chief and I thought there were some things Georgie should hear from us rather than through the grapevine.'

'You haven't released Avery, have you?' I asked, voicing my greatest concern.

'No,' he said, sending relief rushing through me. 'You don't have to worry about that. The judge denied her bail.'

The tension eased out of my muscles.

'Chief Stratton wanted to fill in some blanks for you,' Brody continued. 'He's tied up today, so I'm here instead. I can't share everything we've learned, but I'll tell you as much as I can.'

'I appreciate that,' I said.

Brody sat down in a wicker chair and stroked the dogs' fur when they rested their chins on his knees. 'Avery told us that she figured out Victor's true identity after she saw his correspondence with the private investigator he hired to find Dorothy. She took that information, did some looking online, and put the pieces together. She told Dorothy what she knew and pretended she wanted to know more about her stepfather's past.'

'So that's how she got herself invited into the cabin for tea?' I guessed.

Brody nodded and glanced at the spaniels as they lay down near his feet. 'The dogs weren't there at the time.'

'Lucky for Avery, but not for Dorothy,' Aunt Olivia said.

Fancy whined quietly. I leaned over to pat her head and Flossie's too. That seemed to settle Fancy, though she and her sister continued to watch us all with their brown eyes.

'We know now that Avery killed Byron Szabo,' Brody continued. 'She drugged and smothered him, just like she did with Dorothy.'

Next to me, Tessa shuddered. 'But why?' she asked.

'Byron approached Avery,' Brody explained, 'asking to interview her for a memorial piece he was supposedly writing about Victor. When he started asking probing questions about Victor's early years, wanting to see photographs, Avery realized he knew Victor's true identity. Then he brought Dorothy into the conversation, suggesting that he knew about her shared history with Victor, and that's when Avery decided she needed to put an end to his questions. Permanently. She told him she'd bring some photographs to his house later that day. During that second meeting, she drugged his coffee, killed him, and wrote a fake suicide note.'

'Has she admitted to all that?' my aunt asked.

'Fortunately, yes,' Brody said. 'She also admitted to killing Victor's lawyer, Simon Greenaway.'

'Because Simon knew Dorothy's true identity?' I guessed.

Brody nodded. 'Simon knew that she was Ellen Dudek, Victor's primary beneficiary, but we don't think he knew about the bank robbery.'

I rubbed my bare arms. My skin felt chilled despite the warmth of the day. 'I guess Avery believed that with Victor, Dorothy, Byron and Simon all gone, there'd be no one left to challenge the widely accepted belief that Ellen Dudek had died decades ago.'

'So no one would stand in the way of Avery inheriting the bulk of Victor's estate,' Aunt Olivia added. 'Someone might have questioned why Victor had included a deceased woman in his most recent will, but it probably would have been attributed to the faint hope that she was still alive or some mild confusion in his old age.'

'Most likely,' Brody agreed.

'The word on the street is that Dorothy made a lot of donations to local charities over the years,' Tessa said. 'Whatever the reason she got involved in the bank robbery, she seemed to live a decent life afterward, or at least once she settled here in Twilight Cove.'

Maybe she was trying to make up for what she'd done in the past through her generosity in her later years. I guess we'd never know for certain.

'What about the stolen money?' I asked, thinking about Byron. 'Was there any stashed away in Dorothy's cabin?'

'We found very little cash,' Brody replied. 'And she didn't have much money in her bank account either. Somehow I doubt she buried any in the woods.'

That was my feeling too. Byron had likely been on a wild-goose chase.

'We've been looking into Victor Clyde's history,' Brody continued. 'The medical examiner found scars on his face from plastic surgery. It seems he used his share of the stolen money to get on the real estate ladder. Victor's housekeeper, Abigail, once saw Victor and Dorothy together at the mansion and got the impression that Victor had a one-sided interest in starting a romantic relationship with Dorothy. Abigail heard Dorothy say that she'd never stopped feeling guilty. About what, Abigail didn't know, but she believed that Victor stayed in Twilight Cove in the hope that Dorothy would one day change her mind and want to be with him.'

'It's sad, all of it,' I said, the weight of recent events sitting heavily on my shoulders.

'At least Avery can't hurt anyone else.' Brody got to his feet. 'I'm glad you're OK, Georgie.'

I managed a small smile. 'Thanks. And thank you for filling us in.'

He paused before heading down the porch steps. 'I heard at the coffee shop that Ed Grimshaw bought some land closer to Portland where he plans to build his beachfront condos. It seems he's given up on Twilight Cove.'

'Thank goodness for that,' Auntie O said, and the rest of us agreed with her.

Tessa walked Brody back to his cruiser and returned to the porch once he'd driven away. She sat down beside me on the porch swing and it swayed back and forth.

Flossie and Fancy raised their heads where they lay near our feet. I followed their line of sight and saw Callum walking at a leisurely pace toward the farmhouse, his cowboy hat on his head and a plastic container in one hand.

Tessa nudged my aunt's arm and got to her feet. 'Olivia, could you get me that recipe I was hoping to copy?'

Understanding dawned on Auntie O's face. She stood up and grabbed her crutches. 'Of course. It's at the carriage house.'

'What recipe?' I asked.

Tessa grabbed one of my aunt's crutches and Olivia used the railing and one crutch to get down the steps.

'Don't leave without saying goodbye,' my aunt warned over her shoulder as she and Tessa started across the lawn.

'What recipe?' I asked again.

'For chocolate chip cookies,' Auntie O replied at the same time as Tessa said, 'Cheesecake.'

They exchanged a conspiratorial smile.

'Subtle,' I called as they continued across the lawn, giggling.

Really, I didn't mind their obvious attempt to give me time alone with Callum. Alone except for Flossie and Fancy. The dogs bounced down the steps and Callum received them warmly, ruffling their fur and patting their heads. Then he took the porch steps two at a time with easy strides and offered me the plastic container as I got to my feet.

'Brownies,' he explained. 'For the road.'

I accepted the container with a smile. 'I'm sure they'll all be gone before I cross the state line.'

He held my gaze. 'Then you'll just have to hurry back for more.'

'I intend to,' I assured him.

I set the brownies on the porch railing and Callum took my hands. His green eyes looked deep into mine. 'You're really OK, Georgie?'

'Thanks to you and the dogs.' And Euclid, I added silently.

I hadn't shared that part of the story with anyone yet. I'd simply said that the rope had slipped back down into the well, letting everyone think that had been pure luck.

When Callum had arrived back at the farm, the dogs' frantic barking had drawn him to the shed. The pitchfork against the door immediately alerted him to the fact that something was seriously wrong. As soon as he released Flossie and Fancy from the shed, they'd led him straight to the well.

I knew I owed my life to the three animals, and I couldn't wait to come back to Twilight Cove and start my new life with them.

Of course, living on the farm had other perks as well. Like the one standing right in front of me.

As I stepped closer to Callum, I saw a curtain twitch over at the carriage house.

'I think we have an audience,' I said.

Callum grinned, unconcerned. 'Then let's give them a show worth watching.'

As soon as his lips touched mine, I forgot about everyone – and everything – else.

I sighed as the kiss ended, far too soon for my liking.

Even though it was the middle of the morning, a great horned owl hooted somewhere nearby. Flossie barked and Fancy bayed.

I laughed, my heart light.

'I'd better hit the road,' I said, not because I was eager to leave, but because I was eager to get back.

Back to Twilight Cove.

Back home.

Acknowledgements

It has taken a team of dedicated individuals to bring *Murder Most Owl* to life, and I'm truly grateful to each and every one. Special thanks to my agent, Jessica Faust, and my editor, Victoria Britton, for believing in this series and helping me to shape this story into the book it has become. Thanks also to Jody Holford for always being willing to read my early drafts and for being such a fan of Georgie and Callum. Thank you to the entire Severn House team, my review crew, and everyone in the online book community who helps to spread the word about cozy mysteries.